The Magician's Children

Artemis Greenleaf

To Sam & Samantha

Artemis Greenleaf

Other Books by Artemis Greenleaf:

Marti Keller Mysteries series:
The Hanged Man's Wife (Book 1)
Dragon by Knight (by "Coda Sterling")

Earthbound
Cheval Bayard
Confessions of a Troll

Acknowledgements

As always, thank you to my wonderful family. This endeavor would not be possible without your love and support. I also appreciate the invaluable editorial and structural help of my critique groups and beta readers. You know who you are, and I couldn't do this without you. I would also like to give a big shout out to the great folks who organize No Refusals nights for MADD, and the kind and patient HPD officers who graciously answer my questions when they are trapped in the car with me during a ride-along.

PUBLISHED BY:
Black Mare Books
Houston, Texas
www.blackmarebooks.com

ISBN: 978-0-9888070-5-1
The Magician's Children
Copyright © 2014 by Artemis Greenleaf

Cast of Characters

Aleksei – a Lesovik, member of Quinn's Mundane Intervention Team
Alpha & Betty – Marti's pet rats
Baba – Old woman saved by Quinn
Bojangles – Emily & Nick's cat
Bruce – The dog form of Quinn, Marti's Labrador Retriever
Cornelia – a minor Norn, bar maid at the Three Sisters Inn
Crammwell, Stanford & Malloy – Law firm representing Benjamin
Fayllor pro bono
Cu – Cassie's puppy
Daphne & Isabella - dryads in Marti's yard
Delilah – Marti's spirit guide
Ellen – terminally ill client at the Tenth Sphere
Eoin – an Urisk, member of Quinn's Mundane Intervention Team
Feliks – resident at Cherngelanov Children's Foundation group home
Fenrir – Giant wolf, Loki's son
Graham – Quinn's younger brother
Halle – Valkyrie, Quinn's ex-girlfriend
Huginn and Muninn – Odin's ravens (Thought and Memory)
Jingle – Marti's dad's deceased Labrador retriever
Jörmungandr – Fenrir's brother, giant serpent that circles the world
Loki – Norse trickster god
Malik – a Djinn, member of Quinn's Mundane Intervention Team
Marilyn – client at the Tenth Sphere
Melissa - client at the Tenth Sphere
Odin – Chief Norse god
Penny – CODIS tech
Quinn – Shapeshifter, kelpie, Mundane Intervention Team leader
Rädsla – Halle's flying, androphagic horse (Fear)
Savannah - client at the Tenth Sphere
Seigfried – Halle's pet raven
Thor – Norse warrior god
Vitali – Russian arms dealer
Urd, Verdandi, and Skuld – the three major Norns (Past, Present, and
Future)
Emily Benson – Marti's sister
Kyle & Aiden Benson – Nick & Emily's twin sons
McKenzi Benson – Nick & Emily's daughter

Nick Benson – Marti's brother-in-law, police officer

Matt Bienski – intern at Greene-Childe Foundation

Boris Cherngelanov – Prominent real estate magnate and philanthropist

Irina Cherngelanov – Boris' wife

Benjamin Fayllor – Lulu's nephew

Hadrian Galanti/Hunter Greene –FBI Special Agent, works for Multiagency Gang Task Force

Sabina Galanti – Hadrian's twin sister

Sara Grace "Gracie" Jackson – Marti's old school friend, dating Hadrian, works for Greene-Childe Foundation

Cassie Keller – Marti's daughter

Marti Keller – Police widow, single mom, former ER nurse

Ryan Keller – Marti's deceased husband

Bertram Kounis – Owner of Kounis Securities LLC , murder victim

Lilian Kounis – Bertram's wife

Sergei "Sveklá" Medved –Boris' right-hand man

Lulu Miranda - Part owner of The Tenth Sphere metaphysical shop

Dr. Grigori Pavlov – psychiatrist who specializes in RAD

Dame Ashleigh Rowan – Quinn's boss at MAMIC

Adele Schmidt – Marti's Mother

Drew Schmidt – Marti's Father

Kai Seelie – leader of a Mundane Intervention Team, Quinn's friend

Belinda Tate – Part owner of The Tenth Sphere metaphysical shop

Table of Contents

Fate is like a strange, unpopular restaurant, filled with odd waiters who bring you things you never asked for and don't always like.
Lemony Snicket

Chapter 1
Five Rubles

Sveklá wiped the blood off his face with the back of his hand. Bertram Kounis wasn't dead. Yet. But it wouldn't take much longer. Sveklá frowned at the gasping man on the ground, blood spurting from his throat with each heartbeat. He'd gotten sloppy and only severed the jugular and carotid on one side of Kounis' neck. He blamed it on the arthritis settling into his shoulder. This was a physical job, and he wasn't as young as he used to be. Sveklá took no joy in killing. But sometimes it was part his job, and he did it as he would any other.

"*Do svidaniya*, Kounis," Sveklá said, taking a five ruble coin from his pocket. "You should have paid." He dropped the silver coin at the other man's feet. "Now, you must be example to others."

A sharp pain pricked him, and Sveklá dropped the edger and shook out his hand, thinking an insect had stung him – he'd always been terrified of wasps. A large splinter was jammed into his palm, and droplets of blood were oozing out of it. He pulled the sliver out and cursed the wooden handle of the garden tool he'd just used to dispatch his victim.

Men like Kounis disgusted him. Greedy, grasping men who thought the world owed them whatever they desired. Kounis had made an agreement with Sveklá's boss to pay $5,000 every other week, a pittance for such a man, really. And in return, the boss would refrain from providing proof to the Securities Exchange Commission that Kounis' investment firm, Kounis Securities LLC, had devolved into nothing more than a Ponzi scheme.

Kounis had gone from investor to the well-connected captains of Houston's thriving industry to shell-game con artist when he'd compounded a spectacularly bad real estate investment with an expensive mistress.

The first time Kounis couldn't pay, the boss had gone easy on him, letting him off with the addition of a 100% interest payment. When Sveklá had come to collect the $15,000, Kounis had gotten angry and refused to pay.

If Kounis didn't pay one way, he'd pay another. Making an example of someone from time to time, kept the others in line.

A noise from the street caught the enforcer's attention. Someone was coming. *Damn.* A glance at Kounis confirmed that he was beyond help. Sveklá fled.

"No. As far as I know, my husband has never been to Russia," Lilian Kounis said.

Her face was pale and her eyes were glassy and red. Head lowered and body slouched, she sat like a beaten dog in the interrogation room. Her voice was barely above a whisper when she answered questions.

FBI Special Agent Hadrian Galanti watched her from behind the one-way glass. He felt sorry for her. Not only had her husband just been murdered, but his death had caused the implosion of the carefully constructed upper middle class façade he had created. His struggle was over, but she was still being wounded by the shrapnel from her shattered life.

Lilian was the second wife, the trophy wife, barely older than Kounis' son, a senior at Princeton. Her job was to look good. And look good she did, her designer sportswear perfectly matched to her pale complexion. Her handbag alone probably cost more than the monthly rent on Hadrian's apartment. As far as personal image went, she was a master. On the other hand, business acumen, or cognitive skills in general, were not required of her. Whether her ignorance was willful or honest was difficult for Hadrian to determine. But she appeared to be just as shocked and surprised as anyone else when Bertram's house of cards came crashing down.

He didn't believe for a moment that she knew anything about her husband's business. What troubled him was the Russian coin found near the dead man's feet. In fact, it was the only reason he'd gotten involved in the case. He felt it was unlikely that it was there by accident. The same type of coin had been found at six other homicides in the past year and a half. The forensics team had recovered a partial print, and was waiting for results from the AFIS database search. If it came up empty, he'd check with Interpol. He doubted he'd get much help from Russia's FSB if the Interpol query failed.

Lilian had reported that she heard a noise, and when she came out of the garage, there was some poor schmuck named Benjamin Fayllor holding the murder weapon and standing over her husband's body. The two men had some heated words earlier in the day, and they were bitter rivals in the upcoming homeowner's association election. It was true that Fayllor had motive, means and opportunity, but Hadrian doubted that he killed Kounis. For one thing, all of the blood was on the bottoms of his shoes. There was none on the tops. There was also no evidence of any blood on his clothes. Several of his coworkers confirmed that he was wearing the same clothes he'd worn to work earlier. For another thing, there were traces of blood on the handle of the edger. The DNA results hadn't come back yet, but both Kounis and Fayllor were blood type O+. The blood on the handle was AB-. Unless Hadrian was very wrong, Fayllor hadn't killed anybody.

That's why it pained him to keep Fayllor in jail. If the five ruble coin meant what he thought it meant, it would be better for the real killer to think that he had gotten away with it. He'd relax, and be off guard. Hadrian would not.

When he'd joined the Multi Agency Gang Task Force three years ago, he'd expected to see mostly narcos from south of the border, and some Asian triads. That was still true, but European gangs, like the Chechens and the Russians, were on the rise. Being a transportation hub made Houston irresistible to them. A breakaway faction of New York City's Odessa Group had set up shop in the warehouse district, and they were just like any other invasive exotic – unappealing to the local predators, but out-competing the native organisms for resources. The Russians didn't have the strength to challenge the more robust, well-established organizations head-on yet, but Hadrian knew the day was coming. There would no bloodless coup, and a lot of innocent civilians would get slaughtered in the crossfire. If he had to hold Fayllor in order to catch some really bad guys, he would do it. Even if he hated it.

Chapter 2
Edging out the Competition

My husband, Ryan, was still dead.

But at least I had finally gotten to say goodbye.

I talk to ghosts. I didn't use to. Not until one of them insisted I help solve his own murder. And that journey led me to discover whole other aspects of good and evil, in ways I'd never imagined. But I digress.

I babysat while my sister, Emily, and her husband, Nick, went to Ian Chambers' funeral. Nick had recently tried fixing me up with Chambers, and that was an epic disaster. But that's a whole other story. As it stood, I wasn't glad he was dead, but I wasn't exactly sorry about it, either.

My daughter, Cassie, and her brand new cousin, McKenzi, were having their morning naps. The late June heat was already fierce, so McKenzi's brothers, Kyle and Aiden, wrestled on the floor with my Labrador retriever, Bruce. Or at least that's what they thought he was. As far as my family knew, he was a stray dog I found and adopted.

They were wrong, but it was just easier to let them keep believing that.

I was very grateful to Bruce for keeping the boys occupied. I had just started working Tuesday and Thursday afternoons at the Tenth Sphere metaphysical shop, and this was one of my days off. It was harder to get back into the routine than I thought it would be.

I felt a little guilty about wishing Nick and Em would hurry up and get back. I adore my family, and I'd do anything for them – but I really needed some space. After narrowly surviving what was quite possibly both the most horrible and most wonderful weekend of my entire life, I've had one or more them in my house nearly 24/7 this week.

Quinn, Cassie and I, had only just gotten home on Monday afternoon. Mom had a scrapbook club meeting, so Dad came for an early dinner and spent the night. Most of the time he's fine, but he sometimes has seizures, so Mom doesn't like to leave him alone for too long. Also, his artificial leg occasionally gives him trouble. On Tuesday and Wednesday nights, McKenzi was colicky, so Nick and the boys camped out in my living room. Last night, Emily slept over because she was on the verge of sleep deprivation psychosis. Mom and Dad stayed at my house with Cassie while I was working. Poor Bruce. He hadn't been able to shift out of dog form the whole time. I hoped it wasn't uncomfortable for him. Actually, Bruce is only his name when he's a dog. That's what I called him before I knew what he was. Otherwise, he's known as Quinn. But he's really a kelpie, sort of like the Loch Ness Monster. He's also a little like an undercover agent, and his job is primarily hunting demons and undoing the damage they cause to this world.

And I desperately needed to talk to him. It was torture having him curled up next to me on the couch (or bed), knowing who he is, what we'd just been through together, and unable to talk about it.

The head, and only the head, of Delilah, my Creole spirit guide, popped up inches away from my face. "Heads up, girlfriend!" she said. Before I could say anything, she was gone. She did that a lot, and it was the most annoying habit that ghosts had.

This did cause me to glance out the window, where I could see my brother-in-law coming up the sidewalk. They only lived six doors down, so it was easier to park the car at their house and walk the kids home. Delilah stopped in to let me know Nick was outside? Must be a slow guide day.

"Guys? Your dad's coming. Go get your stuff together, okay?" I said to the boys.

"Awww. But Aunt Marti…" Aiden complained.

"Bruce will still be here later. I'm sure your dad needs a hug. He's probably feeling very sad."

No, at that moment, I was not above using guilt to manipulate the six year-old twins. I went and unlocked the side door for Nick.

My cell rang. *Uh-oh.* Caller ID said it was The Tenth Sphere. Had I forgotten to do something at work?

"Lulu?" I asked.

"Oh, gods! Marti I don't know what to do." It wasn't Lulu. It was her partner. And she was crying.

"Belinda, what's wrong?" I was concerned. She was not the sort of person to fall apart easily. It had to be something bad.

"Lulu." It was all she can say before her voice dissolved into sobs.

"What's happened to Lulu?"

"In jail."

"What? That's crazy. Why?"

The screen door slapped against the frame as Nick came in. "How were —"

I held up my hand to silence him.

"Accessory to murder," Belinda whispered.

"Murder!" I echoed, too loudly. McKenzi woke up and started crying. Nick went to get her, giving me a quizzical look on the way.

Belinda answered, but all I could hear was "nephew" and "homeowner's," because Cassie also started crying. "Hold on a sec, Belinda. I'm going to have to put the phone down. Do *not* hang up."

I put the phone on the kitchen table and rushed to sweep Cassie out of her crib. I gave her diaper a squeeze. Excellent. She was dry. I plopped her in the high chair and poured some Cheerios on the tray. She knocked them to the floor.

"Come on, Cassie. Please cooperate. I really need to talk to Auntie Belinda."

"Ning!" she shouted.

I took her out of the chair and set her on the floor next to some toys.

"I'll just let you get back to your call," Nick said. I could tell he was curious about why I was having a phone conversation about murder. He had already gotten the kids packed up and the dog slobber washed off boys' hands and lower arms.

"Thanks. Talk to you later," I said.

Cassie found a large plastic ring from a stacking toy and started using it to whack the other toys in the basket. Bruce lay on the floor nearby.

I hurried back to the phone. Belinda, of course had hung up. I called her back.

"Okay, now tell me what's going on," I said as soon as she picked up.

Belinda sucked in a few deep, shuddering breaths. "Last night, we were coming back from dinner. Our elderly neighbor, Mrs. Thompson, was standing on the sidewalk, crying. We stopped and asked her what was wrong. She said that she was taking Cranberry – that's her Standard Poodle – for a walk. He started to chase a cat and got away from her, running across the street. He got hit by a car, and she couldn't lift him. So Lulu walked across the street and picked that dog up. He wasn't dead, like Mrs. Thompson thought, so Lulu wrapped him up in a jacket she found in her trunk, and we all went to the emergency clinic. I took Mrs. Thompson and Cranberry inside, while Lulu stayed in the car and called Mrs. Thompson's son to come get her. He said he was on the way, so we left her at the clinic while Cranberry was in surgery. When we got home, Lulu realized she had blood all over her clothes and the jacket, so she changed and went to the Laundromat, where she could get the stuff washed before the stains set. Probably ten minutes after she left, a couple of police detectives came to the door. Said they needed to ask Lulu some questions about her nephew. I didn't think much of it –" Belinda fell apart again. It took a few moments for her to stop crying. "And I told them where she was." More sobbing. "When they got to the washateria, they found her with a pile of bloody clothes, waiting for a washer, and arrested her."

"For what? Being a Good Samaritan?"

"No. Her nephew was seen fleeing from a crime scene…it was a murder…and they thought that she was destroying the evidence."

"I can't believe that. Surely the people at the emergency clinic can verify she was there. When they do the DNA testing on the blood, they'll see it isn't human."

"She never actually came inside the clinic, and DNA tests could take weeks. They haven't actually charged her yet, but I don't have money for a lawyer. Everything's tied up in the shop. I don't even know if I'm going to have enough to bail her out." Belinda began to sob again.

"Belinda, it's going to be okay. My sister's a public defender. She'll know exactly what to do." I paused for a moment. I hadn't realized that Lulu had a nephew. "Who did Lulu's nephew kill?"

"Benjamin didn't kill anybody! He'd never hurt a soul. He was running for president of the Homeowner's Association. The man that got killed was the current president. His wife said that she went outside and found Benjamin standing over her dead husband, holding a bloody Japanese edger. I don't care what she thinks she saw, Ben would never kill anybody."

"Okay, then. Let me talk to my sister, and I'll get back to you."

I dialed Emily's cell, and was worried that it would roll to voice mail. When she finally answered, her voice was soft and a little gravelly. She said she was very tired and sore from going to the funeral – she'd only had a c-section two weeks ago, after all. Still, she humored me and listened to my problem. That was Emily, always taking care of me.

"Ok. There's nothing I can do about it. I can't even drive yet," she said.

"But—"

"Let me finish. Have your friend call Crammwell, Stanford & Malloy."

"They sound expensive."

"Stop interrupting. Call Crammwell, ask for Leonard Peltier. They'll take care of it. Now, I really need to go lie down. Good luck."

Cassie had changed her mind about eating lunch. She'd pulled herself up on the coffee table and staggered into the kitchen. "Mama! Ma ma ma!"

Yesterday was her eleven month-iversary. I still had some cupcakes left, so I put one on the high chair tray with the few remaining Cheerios. Once I strapped her in, she tried to smash the whole cake into her mouth. I took it away from her, although most of the frosting stayed on her cheeks, and broke it into little bits. I got her a sippy cup of water, and paced around the kitchen, looking for my cell phone. Bruce came in and sat down near Cassie's high chair. She stopped stuffing herself with cake long enough to throw him some cereal.

I called Belinda back, but she didn't answer. I left a message on her voice mail, telling her what Emily had said.

Then I got up, closed the blinds and double-checked that I'd re-locked the door after Nick left. Bruce was no longer in the room. A few minutes later, Quinn came in, dressed in a pair of shorts and tee-shirt I'd managed to pick up for him during the week. That's the slight drawback of being a shapeshifter – clothes don't shift with you.

I wanted to run to him and throw my arms around his neck, partly because I had missed him – missed his human form – and partly because I wanted him to convince me that everything would be fine, and Lulu would be home in time for dinner.

Instead, I stood by the high chair. "Lulu's in trouble."
"I heard."

Someone banged the knocker on the front door.

Even though I knew it couldn't possibly be Belinda, I still hoped it was, as Quinn and I hurried into the entryway.

I thought I must be on some TV hidden camera show.

A woman stood on my front porch wearing painted-on jeans tucked into fur-lined boots and a low-cut, too-tight white shirt. A beaded leather pouch was slung around her hips. Two long blonde braids fell to her waist, and her eyes were ice blue. A glossy black raven perched on her shoulder.

"Halle?" Quinn asked. "It's been...a very long time."

Chapter 3
No Reservations

I bit my lip. Hard. *Who was this hussy showing up at my doorstep at exactly the wrong time?* "So, you two know each other?" I asked.

Halle ignored me and walked right into my house.

"We've been looking everywhere for you," she said to Quinn.

"My team knows where I am. Halle, this is Marti. Marti, Halle."

She looked down at me, which is a rare thing, since I'm 5'9", and flashed something halfway between a smile and a sneer.

"The jötnar are moving again. I think they are looking for Fenrir."

Quinn's eyes darkened, the blackness floating over them like spilled ink for a moment. That was always a bad sign.

"I doubt they'll come here," he growled, his eyes still locked on Halle's.

What did they know that I didn't?

The raven ruffled its feathers and shifted its weight.

Something clattered to the floor in the kitchen. "I'd better go check on Cassie." *I'm sure you can let yourself out.*

My daughter had thrown her sippy cup on the floor, along with about half of her cupcake.

"Booce!" she shouted as I walked in.

"Bruce will be back later," I grumped at her. None of this was her fault, of course. It wasn't her fault that Lulu had been arrested, or that the moment I finally had a chance to talk to Quinn, some leggy blonde chick from his past showed up. So why was I annoyed with Cassie?

She had lost interest in the few bits of cereal left on her tray, so I took her out of the high chair and carried her into the living room.

Quinn and Halle were talking in low voices, and stopped when I came in. Halle's lip curled up as if she'd stepped in something.

"That's not yours, is it?" she asked.

"It?!" I shot back.

Quinn shook his head and moved between us. "Halle. Please?" He reached out and tickled Cassie's foot. She giggled, and he smiled at her. "No. I'm not Cassie's father," he said to Halle. Then he looked at me, his eyes tired and worried. "I need to talk to you."

There was no way I was leaving my baby alone with that woman, if that's what she was, so I picked up Cassie, her stuffed blue rabbit, Mr. Buns, and her nearby busy box, and brought them along with us to my bedroom. I closed the door, and put Cassie down on the floor with the toys. She immediately grabbed Mr. Buns in one hand, and started babbling to the box and pushing the buttons with her other hand.

Quinn sighed heavily. "Halle wants me to go with her." His face was troubled. "Do you know what jötnar – Frost Giants – are?"

"Kind of. Aren't they Scandinavian, and throw boulders at people in the mountains?"

"Close enough. They are older than you can imagine, and they detest the Valhalla crowd, but they like humans even less. There is a group of them who are actively trying to bring on Ragnarök."

"That's like the Norse version of Armageddon, right?"

"Exactly. It means 'Destruction of the Gods,' and most of the best known will die. Odin gets swallowed by a giant wolf, Thor gets poisoned by a giant snake, and Loki and Heimdallr kill each other. Then the whole planet floods. Halle's job is to keep an eye on the Frost Giants, because they will begin to gather for war prior to the start of Ragnarök. It was thought that they were content to wait until Loki and the great wolf Fenrir freed themselves and set events in motion. But with the current weather, well, the jötnar blame humans for the melting ice, and they don't mind destroying the world to get rid of them. Even if it means sacrificing themselves in the process."

"Well, that seems entirely appropriate – an Amazon watching Frost Giants, who are pissed off about global warming."

"Amazon?" Quinn shook his head, puzzled. "No, Halle's a Valkyrie."

At the sound of that word, music started to play in my head. First, frantic violins, then booming brass. Wagner's *Ride of the Valkyrie* would probably be stuck in my head for a while, now.

Quinn stretched out his hand and raised my chin, so that I had nowhere to look but into his eyes. "I don't want to go with her," he said. "But I have to."

"Are you coming back?"

"Do you want me to?"

Here was an opportunity to easily uncomplicate my life. Dangerous folk tended to show up where fae were involved. It might be easier to keep both Cassie and myself safe if he wasn't around. Here was a quick, but not painless, way out. All I had to do was say no.

"Yes." I responded.

When I died last Sunday, my dead husband, Ryan, had told me it wasn't my time to go; but Quinn was the one who made sure my broken body got put back together. He'd also shown me fantastic creatures I would never have believed really existed, if I hadn't seen them with my own eyes. Now that I was aware of such things, I couldn't go back to the ordinary. That, and I was finding it difficult to imagine my life without him, now.

Quinn smiled softly at me. "I don't know how long this will take."

"I understand," I said. I never said I liked it.

Quinn stepped closer. He tilted his head. He was going to kiss me.

My body was greedy for his touch. Yet my mind was both fascinated and terrified. Lulu had warned me that fae have a kind of glamour – enthrallment – that draws humans like moths to a bug zapper. I knew he had used it the first time we met, but since then, it was impossible for me to tell whether it was a natural attraction, or fae magick.

Suddenly, his head jerked away from me. "Nick's coming."

He shimmered like a hot sidewalk and shifted into Bruce. The shorts he'd been wearing fell off of him, but I was still helping disentangle him from the shirt when Nick knocked on the side door.

Bruce barked, for show I suppose, as he trotted into the kitchen. I grabbed Cassie, caught up with Bruce, and let my brother-in-law in.

He was dressed in his police uniform. "Hey, Marti," he said. "I have to go to work, but would you mind looking in on Em a little later? I'm afraid going to the funeral was probably too much, too soon for her."

"Sure, no problem," I said.

"Thanks." He smiled at me, then his jaw dropped open. "Who's your friend?"

I turned to see Halle standing in the doorway between the kitchen and the living room.

I looked at Bruce. He jumped up on Nick and started trying to lick him.

"Bruce! Get down, you nut." I grabbed him by the scruff of his neck and pulled him off of Nick. Bruce seemed to wink at me.

I glanced back at Halle. "Her?" I cleared my throat. *How was I going to explain a Valkyrie in my house?* A perfect idea popped into my mind, so perfect I wondered if it was my own. "She's the dog trainer. She's going to take Bruce for a little bit for obedience training."

Nick nodded. "I see. Gotta go." He nodded again, this time to Halle, and left.

"Okay, you've wasted enough time. We've really got to leave," Halle said to Bruce.

He didn't shift. I knew he wouldn't. He only left my house in human form under cover of darkness. The neighbors would definitely notice a handsome man leaving my house. They wouldn't care if a dog was going in and out.

"Just a minute," I said.

I took an extra-large plastic Ziploc storage bag from the pantry, with Cassie's generous "help," and went to my bedroom. I set her on the floor and gathered up the clothes Quinn had been wearing earlier and put them in the bag, along with his shoes. I heard my baby giggling, so I turned to see her using Bruce to pull up and balance herself. He walked along beside her as she toddled towards the kitchen. I followed them, dreading what was going to happen next.

"He's going to need some clothes." I handed the bag to Halle.

Her bird squawked at me.

"Perhaps." She grinned wickedly at me.

I refused to take the bait.

Cassie had grabbed on to a chair, and Bruce was licking her face. She squealed with delight. "Booce! Booce!" she said.

Then he came to me. I leaned over to stroke his broad back, and he licked my hand.

"Be safe," I whispered to him. Worry twisted my insides. What if he got hurt or killed?

I walked them to the front door, then stood there watching as the kelpie, the Valkyrie, and the raven moved down the sidewalk and faded into the distance.

I sat on the floor and read Cassie a book. It was one of her favorites, with little touchy-feely patches on every page. Afterwards, she crawled off to play with Mr. Buns. I looked in the rat habitat, and noticed that Alpha and Betty's water bottle was almost empty, so I got them some more.

I tried calling Belinda again. No answer. I wondered if Lulu had been charged. I mostly trusted the justice system, but, on the other hand, innocent people did go to jail sometimes. Especially if they couldn't afford a lawyer. I frowned.

"Mama!" Cassie called. I looked up.

Delilah was standing near her, and Cassie was looking right at my ghostly guide.

I rushed to pick my baby up. "She can see you?" I asked.

"Course she can, girlfriend. Most babies do see us, until grownups tell them there's no such thing as ghosts so many times they learn to block us out. Listen, you need to go have a check on your sister. Understand?"

Delilah's usually sassy face was grave.

Cassie protested loudly, as I rushed out of the house and left without bothering to lock the door. I ran the six houses down to Emily and Nick's, and pounded on their door. "Em? Emily?" I called.

I heard footsteps, then Kyle's voice, "Aunt Marti? Mommy's sleeping now."

"Okay. Would you let me in to take care of McKenzi for her?"

There was a metallic click as the lock turned.

Trying hard not to frighten my nephew, I asked, "Where are Mommy and the baby?"

He led me to the living room, where Aiden was playing a video game on the TV. McKenzi was squirming on a quilt in the middle of the floor.

Emily lay on the couch, way too pale.

"Em?" I asked, gently shaking her shoulder.

Nothing happened. I tried again.

Her eyes opened half way. "Hey," she said, her voice dull with sleep.

"Are you okay?" I asked.

She shifted her body, arching her back and stretching out her neck. "Can't seem to get enough air. Making me sleepy. Sure it'll be fine."

She coughed, and droplets of blood spattered on her white blouse.

"I'm calling an ambulance. You need to get to the ER."

I called 911 from Emily's cell. The operator asked me to stay on the line, so I did, telling her Emily's symptoms. There are advantages to living just around the corner from the fire station. The ambulance arrived in less than five minutes.

"I think she's got a pulmonary embolism," I told them as I opened the door. "She recently had a c-section, now she's coughing blood and fainting." A blood clot in the lung was nothing to fool around with.

The paramedics took Emily's vitals and strapped an oxygen mask over her face.

Radio chatter. An IV. Injections. More chatter. More vitals.

I gave the boys little tasks to do, like go give Bojangles – their cat – fresh water, so they would feel useful instead of helpless. The noise and commotion made McKenzi cry, so I cradled her in my arms. This, of course, made Cassie extremely jealous, so I ended up with a tiny baby in the crook of my right arm and an irritable toddler on my left hip. I felt like…my mother, when Em and I were little.

"Are you going to the hospital?" one of the paramedics asked me as the other buckled my sister onto the gurney.

I looked around at Kyle, Aiden, McKenzi and Cassie. What was I going to do with four little kids in the ER waiting room, even if I could figure out how to get them all there? I'd been in a minor accident last week, and my car was still in the shop. And I'm sure McKenzi would need feeding soon. Newborns always needed feeding soon.

"I've got to take care of the kids. I'll call her husband, our mom, and her doctor, though. Which hospital?"

"Methodist West has availability."

"Okay. I'll send them there."

I locked the door as soon as they left. "Don't worry," I told the boys. "They'll take very good care of your mom. She'll be fine. I'm going to call your dad and tell him to go over there, okay?"

Aiden started to cry.

"Shut up!" Kyle said.

"Kyle! No, sir. Do not talk to your brother that way. You need to apologize."

"I'm not sorry. You shouldn't be a baby." Kyle snapped. He was angry with Aiden for crying, but there were tears in his own eyes that he was struggling to hold back.

What I needed were two more arms. "Kyle, you're right that people shouldn't cry over every little thing. But sometimes, if you're very sad, crying can make you feel better. Everybody cries at least once in a while."

"Not my dad."

I had seen Nick cry before, and it was awful. He had come to break the news that Ryan was dead. We'd cried together.

"Even very tough, strong men can cry, if something makes them very sad. And it's okay. You know how when you run water in a glass, and the glass gets too full, and all the water runs over the side? If your body gets too full of emotion, it overflows as tears, just like the water running over the side of the glass."

I carefully put McKenzi on the couch – she couldn't roll over yet, so she should be okay – and Cassie on the floor. My nephews really, really needed a hug.

I held one in each arm. Aiden sobbed, while Kyle cried silently. The girls gave me a few minutes to comfort the boys before they started fussing. I wanted to cry myself, and being surrounded by crying children didn't help. But in spite of the example I'd just given Kyle, I couldn't allow myself to. I had to make phone calls. That would help my sister. Crying wouldn't.

"The doctors are going to do everything they possibly can for your mom. I need to call your dad, now, okay?"

Silently, Kyle and Aiden dragged out a large plastic bin of Lego, and started building. It hurt my heart. I've never seen these two – brothers who put the boy in 'boisterous' – so quiet. Emily was not going to die. I forbade it.

I moved the baby quilt over near me and transferred McKenzi from the couch to it. I needed to use my hands, so I sat cross-legged on the floor with the girls, one on either side. Cassie held onto my shoulder for balance, as she stood watch, protecting me from any mischief McKenzi might get up to. Her little cousin flapped her arms in the air in front of herself.

First, I called Nick. Then I called our mother.

After I hung up, I started searching through Emily's contacts for her doctor. *Why hadn't I thought to ask Nick when I had him on the phone?* I didn't dare call him back. Either he wouldn't answer, or he would answer while he was driving like a maniac to the hospital. Neither option was useful.

I knew Dr. Aziza was a pediatrician because she was also our pedi. The next possibility was a Dr. Carruthers. I tapped the dial option.

"Carruthers Family Dental," chirped the receptionist.

"Oh. I'm so sorry. I misdialed," I said, then hung up quickly.

Dr. Fredricks was her OB/GYN. *Wonder if I should call him, too? If I can't find her GP, I will.*

I kept going down the list. "Dr. Pavlov?" *That name rings a bell.* I pressed the dial button.

"*Zdravstvuĭte!*" a man answered.

"Yes. Hello? My name is Marti Keller. My sister is Emily Benson, and I'm looking for her doctor. She just went to the emergency room."

"*Prosti menya.* Sorry to hear that news. I wish her well, but I am not that kind of doctor."

"Sorry to bother you." I hung up quickly. *Well, that was embarrassing.*

Next up was Dr. Robinson. Jackpot! She was just finishing up her last outpatient surgery of the day, and her office would send her over to Methodist West as soon as she done.

I put my hand out on the carpet. I had half expected to find Bruce there. But my fingers touched only nylon. I wished Quinn was here with me right now, and I hoped he was okay. But I couldn't allow myself to dwell on him. Between Lulu and my sister, I had more than enough to deal with. Imagining him with a six-foot blonde was not going to do anybody any good.

I dug my phone out of my pocket and called Belinda. This time, she answered.

"Thank you, thank you, thank you, Marti," Belinda said. "I called that attorney your sister recommended. He convinced them to run an ABAcard on the bloodstains ASAP — and surprise! The blood wasn't human. He explained how the test works — just like a pregnancy test, except instead of hormones, it finds antigens. Two lines if it's human, one if not." Belinda took a deep breath. "Lulu's being released now. I'm at the jail, waiting to pick her up."

"I'm so glad to hear that."

McKenzi started the cough-cough-cough cry of a hungry newborn. I patted her tummy.

"Belinda, I do want to talk to you some more, but I really, really have to go now. I'll call you later." I hung up without waiting for her answer.

I don't know if it was from being a public defender and dealing with broken people all day, every day, or just out-of-whack brain chemistry, but my sister often struggled with depression. I knew there would be formula in the house. Because of her medication, she wasn't able to breastfeed.

"I'll be right back," I said to McKenzi, giving her tummy a final pat.

I scooped up Cassie and took her with me. McKenzi fussed a little louder. I returned to the living room with Cassie in one hand and the bottle in the other. Needless to say, it was not easy feeding McKenzi with a jealous Cassie in the room, but I got it done, and McKenzi was just drowsing off when my phone rang.

It was my mother calling to say that Emily hadn't needed surgery — the heparin the paramedics gave her had done the trick. She might even be discharged tomorrow. *Hallelujah!*

"Hey boys? That was Nana calling. Your mom is going to be just fine. She's spending the night at the hospital, but your dad will bring her home tomorrow."

It was like the sun coming out from behind clouds, the difference in those two.

Nick stayed at the hospital, but Mom and Dad came to help me get the kids fed.

After dinner, Mom looked at me and frowned.

"What's wrong?" I asked.

She sighed. "There's a problem. When Emily comes home, she's going to need someone to take care of her for a while. I don't think I can look after her and help with McKenzi and take care of Cassie while you're working. I'm not as young as I used to be."

"I know, Mom. I guess the job will have to go on hold for a while. You'll have your hands full with Em, McKenzi and the boys."

Mom looked at the floor. "Actually, the wife of one of Nick's work colleagues is one of the directors over at Briar Ridge Montessori School. The boys will be going there." She cleared her throat and looked up at me. "They have some space in the one-year olds' group."

"You want me to put Cassie in daycare?" I all but shouted at her.

"Calm down, Marti. It's just two half-days a week. You and Emily went to daycare, and you turned out just fine."

"But this is different!"

"Is it? Besides, it would be good for her to be around other kids."

"She is around other kids."

"If Kyle and Aiden don't play with her, they don't count."

I frowned.

"Come with me Monday morning when I drop the boys off, and at least have a look around."

"Fine."

Given that Cassie, always and without fail, wakes up at 6:30, it wasn't difficult to meet Mom and the boys at the school on time Monday morning. Dad stayed with Emily and McKenzi.

As long as they both didn't have something go haywire at the same time, they'd be fine.

I'd had a chance to study the school building. It was designed to look like an old-fashioned schoolhouse – brick red, with a belfry perched on a steeply pitched roof. But that was where the similarities ended. Instead of a one-room schoolhouse, a wing of classrooms stretched out on either side. Once we went in, I could see that the belfry was really a skylight for the administrative lobby.

"Hello, I'm Maria Benecelli, the principal," said an older woman with a clipboard. "Would these two be Kyle and Aiden?" She smiled at my nephews.

"Yes," said my mother.

She and I each received a quick, but firm, handshake from Ms. Benecelli. I wouldn't describe her as plump, but there was a certain roundness about her figure that made her seem soft and grandmotherly.

Mom checked in Kyle and Aiden, while I examined students' projects stapled to the bulletin board. Cassie managed to grab one. Fortunately, the rip was small, nothing a little Scotch tape wouldn't fix. If Ms. Benecelli noticed, she didn't let on.

After the boys were escorted to their classrooms, Mom hurried home to take over from Dad. Ms. Benecelli gave Cassie and me an exhaustive tour. The school seemed nice enough, I supposed. I didn't want to leave Cassie in any daycare at all. The cost of the mother's day out program would be a little more than half of my paycheck. It was worth it, I suppose, to at least slow the drain on my savings, even if I couldn't stop it all together. I reluctantly filled out an enrollment form.

I had spoken with Lulu on Saturday, but I hadn't seen her. The shop was usually closed on Mondays, so I probably wouldn't see her today, either. The house felt empty without

Quinn, and I didn't relish being there, so Cassie and I went to visit Emily.

As we started down the sidewalk, I noticed a big U-Haul in front of Mrs. Paddington's house, across the street and two doors down. Dressed in one of her many colorful patio dresses, she was standing in the front yard, speaking with a sweaty man in a suit. I crossed the street to speak with her.

"Oh, hello, Marti! I was going to drop by later – I wanted to say goodbye."

"Goodbye?"

"Yes. My older sister has had a stroke. She's home now, but needs someone to help her. Can't drive anymore, you see."

"I'm so sorry to hear that."

She leaned in and gave both Cassie and me a hug. "I'm going to miss you, baby," she said, giving Cassie's cheek a gentle pinch. "You be good for your mama, hear?"

While we were talking, the suited man pounded a "For Sale or Lease" sign into the grass.

"You take care of yourself, Mrs. Paddington. Send me your address so I can put you on my Christmas card list."

"Thanks, sweetie."

Cassie and I waved "bye-bye" and continued down the sizzling sidewalk to Nick and Emily's house.

The back door was unlocked – Nick would have a fit, if he knew – so we just walked in and made ourselves at home.

Mom was on the floor with McKenzi, Dad was resting his eyes in the recliner, and Emily was stretched out on the couch, clicking through the channels.

"Hey, Marts," she said, as we came into the living room.

I sat on the edge of the sofa, near my sister's feet. Cassie squirmed to be free, so I set her on the floor, where she scrambled for a large plastic truck in the middle of the room.

"So, how are you feeling?" I asked, giving Emily's ankle a little squeeze.

"Much better. It's a good thing you came over when you did."

Thanks, Delilah. I owe you big time. "Well," I said out loud. "Nick did ask me to check on you."

Emily smiled. "Perhaps. But what I'm most amazed about is that you knew my doctor's name. I didn't think I'd ever talked about Dr. Robertson with you."

"Oh, you hadn't." I shifted on the couch a little so I didn't fall off. "I just went down your contacts list and called the ones labeled 'doctor.'"

"You went through all my contacts?"

"Just the doctors. I didn't need to call Aziza, though."

"All the doctors? Did you call Dr. Pavlov?"

"Yes."

"From my phone?"

"Yes. I also called your dentist. What's the big deal?" *Jeez Louise! I was only trying to help.*

"I need to go make some phone calls."

Emily eased herself up and left the room. I looked at Mom. She only shrugged.

My nose wrinkled involuntarily. *Ewww.* That smell was as unpleasant as it was familiar.

I pretended that I didn't have any clean diapers with me. Truth was, I didn't understand why Emily was mad at me, and it felt awkward to hang around her house.

"Mom, I'm going to have to take Cassie home to change her. Talk to you later."

"Bye, sweetie."

Cassie wanted to walk the whole way home, and I didn't object to not carrying her. She wasn't quite a good enough walker to do it without help. By the time we got home, my back muscles were starting to ache from leaning over to hold her hands, while she toddled like a marionette below.

I didn't notice the young woman sitting on my side steps until we were almost on top of her, and when I did, I took a big step back and scooped Cassie up into my arms. Her unkempt hair reminded me of a thunderstorm at night, and too much black eyeliner besieged her dark eyes. Ripped fishnets covered her legs, overexposed by too little skirt. But the oddest thing, the only thing that stopped me from thinking she wasn't a profoundly lost Goth teen, was her robin's egg blue skin.

"I have news," she said.

Chapter 4
Wing and a Prayer

"Seriously, Quinn? Why are you still a dog? Shift already," Halle said, shaking her head at Bruce as he trudged along beside her.

The raven croaked and stretched its wings.

Bruce continued as if he hadn't heard her. He was already starting to pant. Thick fur was a liability in the Houston summer.

Halle's eye's narrowed. "Well," she said with a malefic smile, "you won't be needing these, then."

She threw the bag of Quinn's clothes, the one that Marti had given her, over her shoulder and into someone's azalea bushes.

Bruce grunted and trotted into the yard to get his belongings. The bag was wedged in between two branches, and he had to use his paws, as well as his jaws, to get it out. While he was working at retrieving his clothing, a curtain moved in the front window.

An elderly man opened the front door and waved his cane at Bruce. "Get out of my yard, you rotten mutt!"

He stopped dead when he his eyes fell on Halle. He tried to stand a little straighter. "Is that your dog, Miss? He sure looks like a purebred."

Halle batted her eyelashes and beamed back at him. "I'm walking him for a friend," she replied.

Bruce's bag came free, and he loped across the grass and down the sidewalk with the clothes in his mouth.

"Bye," Halle waved to the man, and ran after the dog.

He galloped ahead of her, and disappeared behind an open gate. By the time Halle caught up to him, Quinn was slipping on his shoes.

"Was that really necessary?" he snapped at her.

"Worked, didn't it?" Halle was smug.

"Do you have a car?" Quinn asked.

Halle rolled her eyes. "Seriously? Please."

She whistled, two sharp blasts, and searched the sky, using her hand as a visor.

Far above them, something circled on wide black wings. At first Quinn thought it was a black vulture. As it spiraled down to meet them, he could see it was a great black horse. Given the unobstructed view of the horse's underside, it was obviously a mare. She settled down on the sidewalk, eyes glaring yellow, and folded her wings. Halle's raven flew off her shoulder and perched in a nearby tree. The horse wore no bridle or saddle, and she whipped her huge head around to snap at Quinn with wolf-like fangs.

Halle swatted the beast good-naturedly. "Rädsla, stop it. He's with us." She grabbed a handful of coarse mane and leaped onto the animal. "Well don't just stand there – get on!" she said, as the weird horse danced underneath her.

Quinn surveyed the horse. She was quite tall. He took a few steps back to attempt a running start, but still floundered onto the creature's back, struggling to get his right leg swung over her wide rump. Rädsla didn't wait for him to get settled as she half-reared and leaped into the air, huge wings besting gravity, lifting them quickly into the sky. He had to grab onto Halle to keep from falling off. Quinn sometimes shifted into the form of a horse, but he rarely rode one. It had probably been a hundred years since the last time he was astride an equine.

Halle snickered. "Hold on!"

Thick, corded muscles rippled along Rädsla's strong back as she rose easily into the sky. The air cooled with each flap. Quinn shivered. Ordinarily, he liked the feel of deep, cold water against his kelpie skin, but he'd already started getting acclimated to the Gulf Coast heat, at least, when he was in human form. Siegfried fluttered near Halle's head like a petulant bat.

She threw what appeared to be flower petals into the air. As they fluttered around, dancing like red, orange and yellow butterflies, the scene below changed.

Instead of sprawling subdivisions, pristine, snow-capped peaks stretched up towards them. The ozone smell of the Houston summer was replaced by the crisp scent of ice and evergreens. The blazing sun was gone, and angry grey clouds loomed above them like a bad omen. Lightning crackled across the grey backdrop and thunder boomed. Ice crystals stuck to Quinn's hair and melted on his cheeks. He shivered again, wishing he had a coat. A boulder split off the side of a mountain and rolled into the valley.

"Really, Halle? The jötnar don't seem to be doing anything unusual."

"Perhaps. Give it time. You'll see." She leaned back against him. "You're shaking. I know a way to warm you up," she said. "It's been a long time."

"There's a reason for that." Quinn tried to pull away from her, but there was only so much room on Rädsla's back.

"Oh, you're not still mad about that minotaur, are you?" Halle looked over her shoulder at Quinn. "You know," she purred, "his head and horns weren't the only things he got from a bu –"

"Halle! I don't want to hear about it."

"Look, I can't help the way I am. If I want a male, I have him. Doesn't mean I care for you any less." Halle reached behind her and ran the back of her hand up Quinn's thigh.

He grabbed her wrist. "Stop. Not interested."

Halle snorted. "You're mooning after that human, aren't you? I hate it when monsters get sentimental."

"I'm not a monster."

"Oh, aren't you?" Halle snickered. "Besides, what's the point? You'd probably kill her, anyway. And if you didn't do it accidentally, your mother would most likely do it on purpose. Besides, that human will be dead of old age before you look even a day older."

"Don't you think I know that?" Quinn snapped.

Then he narrowed his eyes. "What do you know about my mother?" He asked. When Halle didn't answer, he said, "You've been talking to my brother, haven't you?"

"Graham has only your best interests at heart.

A moving shape, red against the stark snow, caught Quinn's attention.

"What's that?" he asked.

"That is what we came to see."

Rädsla dropped behind an outcropping of rock. As the shape got closer, Quinn could hear the snow hissing with each step the figure took. Large footprints trailed yeti-like behind it, melted deep into the white surface. The figure was bipedal, but beyond that, Quinn couldn't tell what it was. Snow pants covered its lower half, and the upper was obscured by a dark red anorak. Since it was wearing human clothes, Quinn assumed it was human-sized – there was nothing in the bleak white landscape to compare it with. He turned his attention to the figure's trajectory. It was headed toward a gaping crevasse.

Something moved inside the crack in the snow. A jötnar stepped out of the darkness and into the murky light of the stormy plateau. The wind picked up, and limp, wet snowflakes swirled around the giant like dead fairies. When their paths intersected, Quinn saw it was nearly twice the height of the humanoid figure. The two plodded into the crevasse, and out of sight.

Quinn had lost all feeling in his feet and hands. By the time the jötnar and the parka-clad figure disappeared into the ice cleft, he was shivering so hard he could barely stay on Rädsla's back.

"You're cold," Halle remarked.

"Somewhat. Yes," he replied.

She clucked to Rädsla, and the mare wheeled sharply, heading away from the desolate peaks. The snow gave way to bare rocks, then dark trees. It was hardly any time at all before Quinn saw white smoke rising through tall evergreens. Rädsla landed softly, and Quinn slipped off, falling to his knees in the forest litter.

The Valkyrie helped him up. Rädsla trotted off into the forest. Seigfried croaked and re-installed himself on Halle's shoulder. Before them stood a thick-timbered mead hall, its chimney the source of the white smoke. Carved wooden dragon heads adorned both ends of the steep roof. A battered wooden sign hung over the door, and as they approached, Quinn could read *Three Sisters Inn* carved into it in runic letters.

Halle pushed the heavy oak and iron door open, and they stepped into the dim great room. Quinn's stomach growled as the aromas of strong beer and baking bread rushed at them. A barmaid with black hair and brown eyes looked up at them, smiled, and nodded. A sprinkling of cinnamon freckles on her cheeks made her look younger than she probably was. The hall was less than half filled, the patrons like piles of damp laundry, as melted snow gradually evaporated from their clothes.

The ancient spruce floor groaned and sighed as Quinn made his way to the far wall, where chunky logs snapped and sparked in the yawning fireplace. He rubbed his hands and stomped his feet in front of the eager fire. The smell of wood smoke was like a well-worn jacket, slipping around his shoulders and whispering old memories in his ear. He would a thousand times rather have been in hot, steamy Houston with Marti than here in the frozen north with Halle.

Quinn noticed Halle had gotten a flagon of hot mead and two steins from the barmaid, and she sat at one of the heavy oak tables, watching Quinn shake his feet and flail his hands against the pins-and-needles sensation brought by the receding numbness. Siegfried perched on the back of her chair.

"Sorry," she said, when he finally sat down. "I didn't think about you needing a coat."

"I'll live." Quinn took a sip of his mead. "Who was that? The person in the red parka?"

"Not sure. Even Siegfried has had trouble following him. Or her," she added as an afterthought. "I don't think it's human, though."

"Why not?"

"The jötnar haven't killed it."

Quinn nodded. His shivering had lessened considerably, but he was still feeling chilled. He wondered, briefly, what Marti and Cassie were up to, then reluctantly wrenched his attention back to the Frost Giant's visitor. He also noted that an older man with an eye patch and a thick blue cloak briefly made eye contact with Halle. It was probably nothing – lots of men tried making eye contact with Halle.

The barmaid arrived at their table, carrying a tray loaded with steaming food.

"Thanks, Cornelia," Halle said.

Cornelia nodded, but said nothing, turning with her now-empty tray and padding back across the room, silent as a spring breeze.

Although Quinn left the blood sausages to Halle, he still managed to find enough potato pancakes and lingonberry jam to stuff himself with. He hadn't eaten since early in the day, and flying around the frozen mountains had used up all his reserves. He was finally warm and full, and couldn't think of anything he wanted to do now more than sleep. Perhaps, if he was lucky, he'd dream of Marti.

Quinn's mind was too tired to focus; random fragments of ideas and slivers of pictures danced in his head. He had lost track of Halle's small talk, but a frigid blast of air snapped him back from his thoughts. Instantly alert, he looked up to see the front door standing open, framing a figure in a dark red anorak, stamping its feet on the doormat.

"Without being obvious, look at what just walked in," Quinn said.

Halle knocked her knife to the floor, and carefully scrutinized the newcomer as she leaned over to pick it up.

"The jötnar's friend." Halle's full lips curved into lurid smile. A green glow flickered across her eyes.

Quinn involuntarily leaned back in his chair. Valkyries were dangerous, and he didn't want to become collateral damage by getting in between Halle and her prey. He was also wary of traps, as he'd seemed to do nothing but fall into them lately. "Seems a bit convenient, him coming in here."

"Not really. It's the only place within fifteen leagues of the jötnar's lair."

The mead hall's door thumped shut, and the latest guest unzipped his anorak and shook the snow out of the fur-lined hood. Firelight flickered off his reptilian scales, both brightening the pale bronze hue and casting deeper shadows under his flat features. The vertical pupils in his golden eyes widened and contracted, adjusting to the change in light.

Quinn sucked in a deep breath.

"You know him?" Halle asked.

"Our paths have crossed," Quinn said with a deep scowl. "His name is Balcones."

The demon must have felt his furious glare, because he scanned the room until his tawny eyes rested full on Quinn.

"You!" Balcones snarled. His vertical pupils narrowed, and his thin lips pulled back, exposing sharp, jagged teeth. He took something from his pocket and hurled it at the floor. A loud bang shattered the quiet and a brilliant red flash slashed the dim light to ribbons.

By the time Quinn could see again, Balcones was gone, leaving behind a few wisps of smoke and the stink of sulfur.

A rotund dwarf sitting at the bar shook his head. "I hates when they does that," he said, as if it happened every day.

Quinn exhaled heavily. "Percussion portal. Wish I knew how they got their claws on those. We've been seeing them more and more recently." He put his elbows on the table and rested his head in his hands. He was loath to admit it, but exhaustion was catching up to him.

"A room is kept upstairs for me. You look tired and there is nothing more to be done here in the hall," Halle said, her fingers brushing Quinn's shoulder. "We have plenty of time to talk later."

Wearily, Quinn stood and followed the Valkyrie. He had wanted to ask the dwarf a question or two on the way out. But he would be disappointed. The creature was no longer at the bar, and Quinn didn't think he had the energy to hunt for it. He smiled at the barmaid.

"Cornelia? If you don't mind my asking, does that demon, the one in the red anorak, come here often?"

She only shrugged and held out her hand, palm down, and wobbled it from side to side.

"Don't ask her questions. She can't answer them," Halle said.

"Oh?" Quinn glanced at Cornelia, hoping he hadn't offended her.

Halle's face darkened. "A customer propositioned her. She dared to say no. He took her anyway, and then cut out her tongue." She paused, as if to gauge Quinn's reaction. "But I did him one better. I cut out his heart."

"I'm so sorry," Quinn said to the barmaid. "I didn't know."

She nodded, and a wistful smile drifted across her lips.

"Come," said Halle, her fingers again fluttering over his shoulder.

He trudged up the stairs after her. There weren't many rooms above the great room below, but Halle's was, of course, the furthest from the stairs. She pulled a brass key from the pouch slung around her hips and opened the door.

Quinn was suddenly grateful for the extra walk. Halle's room was on the same side as the fireplace downstairs, allowing her to have a fireplace upstairs. He knew why he was so tired and cold. It wasn't about cavorting around near the Arctic Circle on a flying horse. He had been holding his human and dog shapes for too long. He needed to shift into his natural kelpie form and swim. But it wasn't going to happen tonight. Sleep was going to be the best he could do. He sat down in the oversized chair to take his shoes off, and that was the last thing he remembered until someone shook him awake.

"Wake up, sleepyhead," Halle's voice sounded near his ear.

Quinn stretched and opened his eyes. The fire had died down substantially, but it was still strong enough to send gold and orange light shimmering along Halle's bare skin as she stood naked in front of him.

"Don't tell me you're not interested," she said, looking down his body.

Parts of him were very interested. But not the most important ones. It wasn't easy, but Quinn forced himself to look only into her eyes.

"I need to get to water. Preferably fresh, but seawater will do if it's closer."

He was surprised that she didn't argue. Instead, she took a step back and studied his face.

"Your eyes," was all she said before she turned away and started getting dressed.

A glance into the mirror above the wash stand showed Quinn what he already knew. His eyes had ceased to look human. Instead, they were glistening obsidian spheres – kelpie eyes. He ran his tongue over his teeth, just to confirm that the flat, human molars had given way to the sharp teeth of a predator. Even his skin had taken on a greyish cast.

"I can't hold this shape much longer," he said.

Halle pulled on her boots. "Let's go, then," she replied.

Kelpies are not land animals. Like whales, they are large and need support from the water to keep them from slowly suffocating under their own weight. They can survive out of the water for brief periods, but if Quinn shifted into kelpie form, and didn't' have the strength to shift back to a size that could fit through the door, he would die, trapped in Halle's room.

Outside the *Three Sisters*, Halle whistled for her horse. The black mare seemed to solidify out of the dark between the trees, and stretched her wings. Halle gave Quinn a leg up, onto the horse's back, then vaulted up lightly behind him. Rädsla's great wings beat the air, and she quickly rose high above the chilly spruces.

"Where's your bird?" Quinn asked.

"On business," Halle replied.

The mare flew on as her two riders fell silent.

Before long, a slender strip of blue twisted through the valley up ahead of them. Quinn could smell the water in the alpine lake, and it called to him like a siren song.

His left shoe creaked as the seams ripped apart. A clawed flipper stretched out of his pants leg, growing longer and wider.

"Hurry, Halle!" Quinn tried to shout, but his vocal cords were already changing. It came out as a throaty growl.

Rädsla spooked at the noise and nearly sent Halle and Quinn tumbling.

"Easy," Halle said, stroking the mare's neck.

Quinn's other shoe tore away and fell off, and another flipper emerged. Then the stitches of his jeans began to pop loudly, as one by one, the threads snapped. Rädsla struggled to maintain her altitude, but failed, flapping nearer to the rocky ground with each stroke of her wings.

The roaring of water cascading out of the lake and into the river below intensified. The side seams split on Quinn's shirt. Rädsla struggled to keep aloft. She snorted with the effort and her hooves dangled barely twenty feet above the ground.

The instant he felt the spray from the waterfall on his skin, Quinn pushed himself off Rädsla's back and tumbled into the flowing water. As soon as his weight was gone, Rädsla sprung into the air as if she'd been released from a slingshot.

"Quinn!" Halle called.

Rädsla regained control of herself, and swooped down above the frothing waterfall basin, but there was no sign of Quinn.

Halle clucked to the horse, and flew downstream for half a mile or so. Quinn wasn't there, either. When they came back to the falls, Halle smiled. A large dark grey hump protruded from the water. Slowly, a long neck that even a giraffe would envy curled out of the water, followed by a head that was neither horse nor crocodile, but a bizarre mixture of both. Halle waved and turned Rädsla back towards the *Three Sisters Inn*.

Chapter 5
Defense Tactics

FBI Agent Hadrian's vision was blurry from staring at a computer screen all day. There was an odd connection between Benjamin Fayllor's aunt and Ian Chambers, a disgraced investigator from the District Attorney's office. Chambers was the former college roommate of a cop named Nick Benson, and Benson's sister-in-law, Marti Keller, worked for Lulu Miranda, Fayllor's aunt. The gangster that Chambers had worked for had an extensive business relationship with the Odessa Group. It could be just coincidence – he'd seen odder things – but perhaps Fayllor wasn't as innocent as he'd originally supposed. What he really needed to do was get a closer look at the coin, to pick it up and hold it. He'd make a point of going down to the Homicide Division first thing in the morning. He also wanted to talk to Fayllor again. But not before he dropped by the aunt's shop and tried to get a feel for the legitimacy of the business.

The clock in the bottom right of his computer screen read 6:50. Time had gotten away from him, and he was going to be late. Again. He quickly shut down the laptop and locked it in his drawer. *On the way*, he texted his girlfriend.

He made it to the Museum of Natural Science in record time, and managed to tag along at the tail-end of the group. The company Sara worked for, the Greene-Childe Foundation, was having a retirement dinner for the current chairwoman. The catered buffet dinner was set up in the Paleontology Hall, and Sara was already there, small plate of appetizers in one hand and a glass of red wine in the other.

Hadrian knew that she'd given up waiting on him ages ago, and accepted that he'd show up when he could. He didn't know why she put up with that. He wasn't sure that he would, if the roles were reversed. Perhaps it was because she was a commitment-phobe, and she liked the benefit of having him as a pleasant accessory at parties without the tiresome details of running a household together. For his part, he was very fond of her – she was highly intelligent, funny, very dedicated to her work as a child welfare advocate, and an excellent lover – but he wasn't sure that he loved her. Still, their relationship worked well for him, because she didn't seem to mind that he sometimes disappeared for weeks at a time, or was always late to social engagements because of his work. Perhaps someday, he'd change to an office job with mostly regular hours, get married and have kids, but that would not be any time in the foreseeable future.

She smiled as soon as she saw Hadrian, and excused herself from the young man who was chatting her up to go and greet him with a kiss on the cheek.

"Hey Blackbird," she said.

She called him that because he had a tattoo of a raven that spanned his chest, arm and shoulder blade. He'd been shot once, in the hollow of his chest where the collarbone joined the shoulder. The ugly scar reminded him daily of how he'd screwed up and not done a good enough job searching for weapons on the suspect. So he had it covered with a tattoo. Now, when he got out of the shower, instead of a mark of failure, he saw a guardian and reminder that he had cheated death.

"Hey, babe," Hadrian said as his arm slipped around her slim waist for a brief hug. "Sorry I'm late."

Sara nodded. "Better late than never."

Hadrian followed her to the hors d'oeuvres table.

It was a pleasant enough evening, talking to Sara's coworkers. He knew most of them from various parties and functions that he'd attended with her. However, he was not disappointed when the evening was over. Sara did not live far away, and had taken a taxi to the event, partly because she was planning on having wine, and partly because she was expecting Hadrian to take her home. He never drank. His father had been an alcoholic, and he was only too aware of the potential for devastation that swirled in every ounce of liquor.

As they were saying their goodbyes, Hadrian noticed the young man that had been talking to Sara earlier watching them. She hadn't bothered introducing them, and he wondered if it was more than an oversight.

"Your friend over there seems a little disappointed that the party's over," Hadrian said, cutting his eyes toward the observer.

Sara followed his glance. "Oh, that's Matt. He's a summer intern. Works in my department. I expect he and Becky will go on a pub crawl after this. He's probably looking for her."

The drive to Sara's townhouse was short, and as Hadrian pulled into the visitor parking area, he considered going home and doing some more research. But when Sara leaned towards him so she could reach down to fish for her shoe that had slid under the seat, she kissed him softly, just under the jaw. He decided that the research could wait.

Dressed in a thickly padded Red Man suit, short, bulky Sveklá looked like a refugee from a low budget superhero comic book.

"World is dangerous place. Is important you know how to defend yourself," he said to the children sitting on the mats in front of him. "Feliks, come," he said to an older teen, the largest boy in the room.

Feliks stood up. He was much taller than Sveklá, but his body had not quite made the transition from boy to man.

"Attack me, any way you wish," the older man said.

This was not Feliks' first session with Sveklá, and he took a few moments to consider his strategy. He lunged at the teacher, his forearm up and parallel to the ground, going for a clothesline maneuver to the throat. Sveklá stepped into his path, grabbed Feliks' arm and twisted around, using the boy's own momentum to roll him across the trainer's back and onto the mat. Then he demonstrated the hip toss with Feliks in slow motion, several times.

The students paired up to practice, and Sveklá walked around correcting techniques and offering advice. Sometimes, he challenged his pupils to test their capabilities against him. Teaching martial arts was one of his favorite things in life. The skills he gave his students made their bodies strong, taught their minds focus, and gave them confidence. And these particular children needed all the strength and confidence they could get.

Chapter 6
Identity

"What do you mean you have news?" I asked the young lady with the wild hair and blue skin who was camped on the steps to the side door of my house. My heart skipped a beat. *Please be good news.*

"Expect his return tomorrow night. Or Wednesday morning."

"Quinn? You do mean Quinn? Is he alright?"

"Yes. And yes." The blue-skinned woman removed a bracelet from her wrist and held it out to me. "He sent me with this. Put it on. Do not remove it for any reason."

An unpleasant incident with a dragon-based talisman had taught me to be wary of magical jewelry. "What does it do?"

"Wards off demons."

Demons?! "Okay."

I took the bracelet from her and put it on my left wrist. It was pretty – a gold charm bracelet with tiny silver bells that dangled between alternating lapis lazuli and obsidian stones. I shook my wrist and it jingled softly. Cassie immediately grabbed at it, and I had to shift her to my other hip. She protested loudly, and the blue lady rolled her eyes.

She reached out her hand and twisted her wrist, as if tuning a doorknob. As she pulled her arm back towards herself, an invisible door opened, peeling away from the background of my house and side steps. As she stepped through it, I caught a glimpse of an ancient forest, with huge dark trees and tall bracken ferns on the other side. It snapped shut behind her, leaving nothing but a puff of cool air and the smell of damp trees.

I dug out my keys and took Cassie inside. A few weeks ago, this would have been weird. Now, it was just another Monday.

I'd had a terrible night's sleep. I was more excited about Quinn's return than I wanted to admit. I was also anxious about sending Cassie to Briar Ridge Montessori for the first time tomorrow afternoon. When she started babbling at 6:30, I wasn't really ready to get up. All night I'd had fitful sleep and strange dreams I couldn't quite remember.

My car was ready this morning, so Mom took me to pick it up after she'd dropped off the boys. The mechanics had done a great job. No one would guess it had been sideswiped and run up on the curb. Mom was in a hurry to get back to Emily, McKenzi and Dad, so I took Cassie out for lunch, just for a change of pace. And because I could afford to, now that I had a job.

Once we pulled up into Briar Ridge Montessori's parking lot, I sat in the car for several long minutes. It was a pretty school with leafy gardens and bright flowers in front. I looked for an escape route, but taking Cassie to the Tenth Sphere just wasn't feasible. I picked up her bag of diapers and change of clothes and carried her in.

I had wanted to stay in the classroom for a few minutes, just to make sure she was okay. But the teacher –politely – shooed me out. Cassie started crying when I handed her to the teacher's assistant, and I cried all the way to work.

Lulu hugged me as soon as I walked in the door. "Thanks for your help getting me out of the pokey," she said. She must have noticed my red-rimmed eyes as she pulled away. "Are you okay?" she asked.

"Dropping Cassie off at daycare was harder than I thought, that's all."

Concern creased Lulu's brows. "I thought your mother was watching her."

"She had been, but my sister had some complications, so she's taking care of her and McKenzi."

Lulu nodded and patted my back.

"I'll be okay. And so will Cassie. Glad you're out of jail," I said.

"Well, I'll be in and out of the shop a lot, honey. I'm helping the attorney with Benjamin's case."

"Benjamin? That's your nephew, right?"

Lulu nodded.

I didn't doubt for an instant that Lulu was innocent. But I'd never met her nephew, and the circumstantial evidence – having a violent argument with the victim, then being seen standing over the body, holding the murder weapon – seemed pretty damning. I was a little concerned that Lulu was letting her affection for her nephew cloud her judgment.

The shop was mercifully busy, but I was getting antsy, beyond ready to go pick up my daughter, and wondering if Quinn would be home when we got there. There was still half an hour left in my shift, and I struggled not to be snappy with customers.

It was about then that a man walked into the shop. I noted that he seemed much younger than our average male customer – I'd guess thirty, give or take. He was pleasant looking, but not walk-into-a-signpost gorgeous. His round, wire-framed glasses seemed to belong on his face, but I'm not sure I would have even noted him, except for a thin, white scar that etched a narrow valley as it curved down his right cheek between his eye and his jaw. He smiled at me before he started looking through the figurines near the cash register.

"If there's something I can help you with, please let me know," I said, then glanced over his head at the clock.

He nodded. Then he browsed slowly through the shop. I just wanted him to go so I could go find either Belinda or Lulu and see if I could leave a little early.

At ten minutes to five, Lulu came out of the back room. She smiled at the customer, then looked at me. "Marti, are you coming to circle on Thursday night?"

I hadn't really thought about it. "Maybe. I'm not sure."

"Try to make it. I think you'll like it."

"I'll see what I can do. Is it okay if I scoot out of here a couple of minutes early?"

"No problem, honey. Go."

When I came out of the back room with my handbag, Lulu was talking to the man about the Thursday night mediumship circle that she held in the store.

I didn't speed or run any red lights on the way to pick up Cassie, but I did push the envelope on a few yellow ones. When I arrived, she was playing with foam blocks. I picked her up, expecting her to be happy to see me. She cried. Some days, you just can't win.

"She had a good nap from two 'til just after three," the teacher said. "She's a very good baby. I'm looking forward to seeing her again on Thursday."

I let Cassie roam around the living room while I made us dinner. I wondered if I should make a little extra for Quinn, then chided myself. He wasn't my spouse. He wasn't even my boyfriend, really. But I missed him, anyway.

Dinner came and went. Cassie's bedtime came and went. Still no Quinn. I lay on the couch, trying to read a book, but I couldn't focus on it.

"Girlfriend, you sure you want to do this?"

I jumped at the sound of Delilah's voice.

"Do what?"

"You know. Let that shifter back in your life."

"I thought you said he wasn't so bad, after all."

"Girl, they're all dangerous. Even the not so bad ones. Just sayin'."

"What would you do?" I noticed I was picking at the skin along my thumbnail.

"I can't decide that for you, girlfriend. Ain't nobody but you really knows the answer to that question."

Delilah grew more and more transparent. The last thing to fade away was her smile, hanging for a second like a maternal Cheshire Cat.

A tap on back door window startled me. I got up and turned on the porch light. Quinn squinted in the yellow glow of the bug bulb.

I fumbled with the alarm and got it turned off before I opened the door and he stepped inside. Although I had planned to maintain a certain amount of decorum and proceed with caution, I hurled myself at him and hugged him around the neck. His arms wrapped around my waist, crushing me against the hard warmth of his body. He smelled of rain on a hot day. What I wanted to do more than anything at that moment was to tear his clothes off.

"Ahem," Halle said.

Quinn released me and frowned. Halle stepped into the circle of light by the back door.

"Hello," she said with a little wave.

I suddenly felt like an old balloon, trailing limply on its cheerful ribbon after all the helium has leaked out.

I stepped away from Quinn, and Halle pushed her way inside.

"I'm sorry," Quinn said. "But I needed reinforcements."

"Reinforcements?" *Really? Is that what she is?*

"Just a precaution, to make sure you and Cassie stay safe." He took my left hand in his right, shaking it just enough to make the little charm bracelet jingle. "That's why I sent you this."

"The blue chick said it wards off demons."

"Nothing will really stop a determined demon. But every little bit of discouragement helps. It's probably just me being over-protective."

I didn't think that he was lying exactly, just not telling me everything. But I refused to argue with him in front of Halle.

"You'll need somewhere to sleep, I suppose?" I said to her.

I didn't wait for her answer before turning on my heel and heading to the linen closet to get her a blanket. Unfortunately, I didn't have any scratchy woolen ones. An odd-sized cotton waffle weave was the closest I had, so I scooped it up and dropped it on the couch. "Good night."

I looked in on Cassie on my way to my bedroom. She was snoozing away, arms sprawled above her head, without a care in the world. I almost envied her.

Quinn was already in my bedroom when I arrived. I was more than a little annoyed with him for bringing Halle along to my house. A quick glare, then I cut my eyes away from him and started fiddling with the pictures on my dresser.

He came and stood behind me, a foot or so away. I could see him watching me in the mirror. "I'm sorry," he said. "I know that Halle isn't your favorite." He traced a finger from my shoulder to my elbow, and I shivered.

Well, after all, Halle was in the living room. Alone.

I turned to face him.

"If I didn't care about you and Cassie, I wouldn't have brought her."

I frowned. There was a "but" coming, I could tell.

"Whatever you think of her, she will never lie, and if she says she will do something, it absolutely will happen. She's a fierce fighter, and cannot be killed."

"What is she? *The Terminator?*"

Quinn cocked his head to the side and furrowed his brow.

"Never mind." I shook my head. "What is it that you're so worried about that both you and Halle need to be here?"

"That is kind of the problem." Quinn looked down at the floor.

Realization dawned on me. "You aren't planning to be here, are you?" I took a step back.

"I'll be here as much as I can. This is personal. The jötnar - the Frost Giants – will never come here. They wouldn't survive the heat. But I don't want to take any chances. They've already killed someone else I loved. To make things worse, they're dealing with an extra-slimy demon named Balcones. That scaly bastard ambushed my team and killed my cousin."

His eyes turned black with anger, but only for an instant.

'Someone else I loved' Quinn had said. As I considered what that might mean, he stepped closer to me, ran the backs of his fingers along my jaw. He lowered his head to kiss me, and I closed my eyes.

Bam! Bam! Bam! Halle knocked on the door as she opened it, and stepped into my bedroom. "Excuse me. I would like some water, but I don't know how to work your machine."

Can't be killed, huh? I might have to test that theory.

I stalked out of my room and into the kitchen. "Glasses are in this cabinet," I snapped, jerking open one of the doors. I snatched a plastic cup off the middle shelf and shoved it under the water dispenser. "Put the cup under the spout, then push this button." I filled the glass half way, then shoved it into her hand, slopping some of it on the floor.

As I reached for a towel to clean up the water, Quinn said, "I have to go." He quickly stepped in and his lips brushed mine, sending shockwaves throughout every nerve ending in my body and turning my knees to jelly. He paused and looked back at me for a moment as he left through the back door. I sat down in the nearest chair, leaving the puddle of water where it lay. I was too much of a puddle myself.

"You know that's a really bad idea, right?" Halle asked.

"What are you talking about?" I growled at her.

"Mortals and fae. Never really works out, especially not for the mortal."

I rolled my eyes at her in response.

She shook her head, long blonde plaits shimmering under the kitchen lights. "What fools these mortals be!" she beseeched the ceiling.

"So now you're going to quote Shakespeare at me? Now there's an immortal mortal."

Halle snorted through her nose. "Please. Do you really think *he's* a human?" Halle's head swiveled ever so slightly back and forth, and the sheerest of smiles curled across her lips.

"What has this got to do with anything?" I wanted to shout at her, but I wanted Cassie to remain asleep even more.

"Look, Graham asked me—"

"Who's Graham?" I snapped.

"Quinn's youngest brother. He asked me to come try to talk some sense into Quinn, get him to leave you alone. Graham wants to spare his brother from suffering at your death. Which may come a lot sooner than you expect, if you continue meddling in affairs that are none of your concern."

"Are you threatening me?" I asked, crossing my arms.

"Not a threat. Just a friendly warning."

"Charming," I said.

"What is the life expectancy of a human?" Halle asked.

"Depends. Eighty, give or take."

"What do you suppose the life expectancy for a kelpie is?"

"Don't know."

"Twelve hundred years. Do you see how this could be a problem?"

Maybe she made logical sense. But I didn't care. I wanted him. My nerves were still tingling from his kiss.

"Fine. Whatever. I'm going to bed," I replied.

I didn't give Halle a second look as I strode out of the kitchen. A peek into Cassie's room showed me she was still blissfully asleep. I left my bedroom door ajar, so I could hear any comings or goings, and changed into my nightshirt in the bathroom. I looked at myself in the mirror as I brushed my teeth. *What if Halle was right?*

What if being with me only ended up hurting Quinn? His brother was obviously concerned about it. Well, Quinn was an adult, for Pete's sake, and he was perfectly capable of making his own decisions. After all, he knew before he even met me that his lifespan was more than ten times what mine was. Still, I wondered how long he would stay with me, once the first grey hair sprouted, and the little wrinkles started showing. I was suddenly a whole lot less sure about what I wanted from him. The whole idea of our relationship twisted and squirmed like a boa constrictor in my head, until exhaustion took its toll.

Wednesday was awkward, what with my newfound Valkyrie shadow. I thought it was odd that Mr. Douglas down the street stopped mulching his azaleas to wave at us when we took Cassie for her morning perambulation. He never waved at anyone, just sat behind the screen door, daring anyone to set so much as a toe on his precisely fertilized, perfectly manicured grass. That sort of thing seemed to happen when Halle was around.

On Thursday afternoon, I grabbed Cassie's go-bag and headed for the car. Halle came, too.

"Okay, I'm not trying to be difficult here, but you can't go to work with me," I said. I had been looking forward to having a break from her.

Halle nodded. "I will not enter your place of business. But I am coming with you."

"Suit yourself."

Cassie cried less when I dropped her off today than she had on Tuesday. I cried about the same. When I got back into the car, Halle wrinkled her nose.

"What is this liquid coming from your eyes? Are you injured?"

"Tears, Halle. Surely you've heard of them? I'm just feeling a little sad about leaving Cassie here, that's all."

"Valkyries do not have tears."

"Good for you."

I felt a little bad for being so snappy. "When you were little, did your mother leave you with someone while she went out?"

"I have never been any other way than I am now. Valkyries do not have mothers."

"Really?" It was my turn to be perplexed. "Then where did you come from, if you don't have a mother?"

"Odin All-Father created us. Valkyries are the choosers of the slain. We select the best of the mortal warriors, to fight with the Aesir at Rägnorok. That is our purpose, and why we exist."

"Do you get lonely, having no family?"

The car behind us beeped. I hadn't noticed the light had gone green.

"I have many sisters," Halle said, glancing into the rear view mirror. "And, of course, a father."

"Actually, I meant like a husband and kids," I said.

"Valkyries do not have children. And I have no need for a husband – I can have any man I wish. Quinn, for example is an excellent lover."

I felt heat flash into my cheeks. I wanted to crawl underneath the seat. There was nothing in the world I wanted to talk about less with Halle than Quinn. And especially not about sex with Quinn. I whipped the car into a parking spot.

"Look, here we are at the Tenth Sphere. Don't know what you're going to do, but I'm going to work."

I practically fled from my car before she could say anything else. She got out more slowly, and I clicked the remote to lock the doors as I retreated.

The cowbell on the Tenth Sphere's door jangled as I opened it, and I breathed in the calming sandalwood scent of the store.

"Are you alright?" Belinda asked from behind the counter.

"Fine. Just a little hot."

The hint of a frown wrinkled her lips, as if she didn't quite believe me. "Lulu is out this afternoon. At the lawyer's office again. This whole thing with Benjamin has really knocked her for a loop."

I nodded, then chewed my lip. "Belinda? How certain are you that her nephew didn't kill the guy?"

"Benjamin would never do anything like that. Sure, I've seen him get angry before, maybe shout a little, but never once have I seen him raise his hand to anyone. He just doesn't behave that way."

"Sometimes people can surprise you."

"Perhaps," she replied, her lips pressing and un-pressing as if the word tasted unpleasant. "Lulu wanted me to ask if you were coming to circle tonight."

"Maybe, but I doubt it. Child care."

Belinda nodded.

Business at the shop was painfully slow. I spent more time dusting the shelves than anything else. Once, I thought I saw a reflection of a man's face in one of the highly polished rutilated quartz points, but it was just a combination of glare and the inclusions. There was one customer all afternoon, and she only bought one small piece of moonstone and some incense. I left at the stroke of five.

I scanned the parking lot for Halle, but couldn't find her. But by the time I got to the car and unlocked the door, there she was, as if she'd fallen out of the sky.

She smiled as she got in the car, but I had no idea what to say to her.

"Good day at work?" she asked.

I shrugged. "A little slow."

The silence on the way to Briar Ridge Montessori was discomforting. Halle waited in the car while I ran in to pick up Cassie, who of course, cried and didn't want to leave.

When I pulled into my carport, Cassie squealed. "Booce!"

I looked up. Sure enough, an over-sized black Lab sat on the back porch, tail thumping against the 'Welcome' mat.

I grabbed my baby and hurried inside. I didn't intentionally drop the door on Halle. But accidents happen. I opened the back door and Bruce trotted in. He headed straight down the hall to the bedroom.

It didn't take long for a clothed Quinn to return. "Your brother-in-law was looking for you."

"Nick? Wonder what he wanted."

I smiled weakly at Quinn. When he'd left, I was so sure of what I'd wanted. Now, I wasn't. Yes, he was smokin' hot. And he stirred up feelings that had been comatose since I lost my husband two years ago. But what if our being together was only going to end in suffering? For both of us. Body said, "Yes, please!" Brain said, "Run! Run away!"

"Let me just call Emily's right quick and see what's up."

As it turned out, Nick, Emily, and my parents were getting Chinese takeout, and wondered if Cassie and I wanted to join them. But we were too late. Also, Mom was planning Cassie's birthday party, and even though it was still three weeks away, wanted to know what kind of cake to bake and what color paper plates and napkins to buy.

Quinn held Cassie while I made the phone call. She giggled and flapped her arms. I couldn't help but smile. He was so good with her, and I briefly wondered if he had children. But it did give me an idea, even if it would do nothing more than postpone the inevitable.

Halle, my chaperone, was noisily filling a cup with ice cubes from the water dispenser, so I moved in close to Quinn.

"Could you do me a huge favor?" The heat of his body was giving me goose bumps, and it was hard to speak coherently.

"Such as?"

"I really wanted to go to circle tonight, but Mom can't watch Cassie. She — Cassie, not my mom - adores you, and I was wondering if…" I paused, wondering if he knew the term "babysit."

"If I would look after her?"

He looked almost confused. Perhaps males didn't watch children in his culture.

When his head tilted, his breath fell on my collarbone. I had to step back slightly, or I wasn't going anywhere. "Would you? It's just an hour."

"Da da da!" Cassie interjected.

"If…that's what you want. But only if Halle goes with you."

I wasn't sure which was worse, having Halle come with me, or her staying at home with Quinn. "Fine," I replied.

The man with the scar and glasses that was in the shop on Tuesday somehow ended up next to me when we formed the circle. He introduced himself as Hunter. When we joined hands during the smudging, I noticed his right hand was strong, but not calloused – he had an office job. Halle stuck to my other side like a cocklebur.

The circle was largely uneventful, at least for me. Delilah appeared only for a moment, saying "Remember, girlfriend, there ain't no such thing as an accident."

Marilyn, one of the circle regulars, embarrassingly threw herself at Hunter. He declined. Perhaps he noticed the ropey scars across her wrists, too.

I trusted Quinn with Cassie. He'd already saved her life once. But I missed my baby. If I hurried, I could get back before she fell asleep. Then, who knows? I might even get a private word or two with Quinn. I dragged Halle out of the Tenth Sphere before she could say anything to anybody. We got halfway down the block when I realized I'd left my phone in the shop.

"I have to go back. Left something in the shop," I said as I stopped and turned around.

"Fine," Halle answered.

She waited outside for me while I ran inside. When I came back, I thought it was strange that she had a smudge of dirt across her cheek. I didn't say anything about it, though. I just chalked it up to Halle being her usual odd self.

When we got home, Quinn was sitting in the recliner, reading a book on my tablet. Cassie was fast asleep, sprawled across his body. The afternoon at Briar Ridge must have been a little too much for her.

"I seem to be stuck," Quinn said, pleasantly.

I carefully picked my baby up and carried her to her crib. I was a little disappointed that she was already asleep, but she and Quinn had looked so cute together that it softened the blow a little.

When I got back to the living room, there was no smudge on Halle's face. In fact, I wondered if the dirt I thought I saw nothing more than a trick of the shadows in the poor light.

"I'm starved," she announced.

It was true that provisions were running low. I was waiting for my pay to be EFT'd to the bank tomorrow before I went grocery shopping. But I was sure she could find something if she tried hard enough.

"Are there any inns nearby?" Halle asked.

"Inns aren't the same thing here," Quinn remarked. "You want a restaurant."

"Are there any of those nearby?" she responded.

"There are always restaurants nearby in Houston. What do you want to eat?" I said.

"Meat. Bread. And beer."

"Well, that's specific," I said.

"What food was it that your mother brought over last week?" Quinn asked.

"She made fajitas."

"Yes, I think Halle might like those. Where can you get them?"

He was probably just trying to be nice. But I still felt a twinge of jealousy. "If you want fajitas, it's Guillermo's Cantina. It's 8:30 on a Friday night. It'll be packed – bet there's an hour wait." I wanted to discourage him from taking Halle out to dinner.

"Here." Quinn held out a handful of bills to me. "Is this enough?"

Four twenties. "Should be."

He flapped it at me. "Bring something back for me?"
"What?"

"I don't know. The same as whatever you have."

"No. I meant – I thought you were going."

"I have some calls to make. You take her. Besides, someone's got to stay with Cassie."

Me taking Halle out to dinner was only a slightly different kind of hell than watching Quinn take her out.

"Fine," I said. "You do have my cell number, right?"

"Of course."

I would much rather have gone out to dinner with him, but I didn't trust Halle anywhere near Cassie. But, since I was clearly being kicked out of my own house, I decided to try to make the best of it. Ordinarily, I would have put up more of a fight, but my current ambivalence toward my relationship with Quinn made it seem easier to avoid confrontation.

I looked in on Cassie before I slipped on my shoes. Couldn't believe she was less than a month from being a year old.

"Let's go." I jingled my car keys at Halle.

As luck would have it, the Astros were playing baseball tonight, there was a concert at Cynthia Woods by a major band that I'd never heard of, and the hottest Broadway play on tour was at the Alley. Because of this, the quirky little restaurant row on Houston's western edge of I-10 was merely busy, instead of cheek-to-jowl. I had to give my keys to Guillermo's valet, because there was no more self-parking available. I smiled sheepishly at him, hoping he wouldn't judge me too harshly over my clutch. It had started slipping, just a little, recently, and I was going to have to take it to the shop.

Guillermo's was not exactly deserted, but we did only have to wait twenty minutes for a table. That would have been unheard of, if not for the other events going on. Out of force of habit, I ordered the cheapest thing on the menu – a spinach and mushroom quesadilla. I asked them to bring me a second one to go when they brought the check. Halle was clearly alarmed when the server brought out the sizzling cast iron dish of fajitas –

steaming seasoned meat strips on a bed of sautéed onions and bell peppers. Admittedly, I felt a little bit superior, as I have never been startled by a noisy meal. I had to teach Halle how to wrap her fajitas in the tortillas, and she was not a fan of pico de gallo. And the way she was putting away the Negro Modelo, it was a good thing she didn't drive. I hoped Quinn had sent enough money. There was enough (barely) for the check and a decent tip. *Be careful what you wish for*, I thought when I saw that the waiter had written his name and phone number on the receipt. He'd been flirting with Halle since he'd taken our drink order. We collected Quinn's to go box and headed for the door.

It took the valet almost twenty minutes to return with my car.

"Oh, that's just great," I grumbled.

There was a huge dent in the right fender, part of the grill was missing, and one of the headlights was shattered.

"What happened?" I asked the valet, not as kindly as I probably should have.

"*Prosti menya*. Was like that when I went to get. Another car, perhaps backed into it?"

Prosti menya. Where had I heard that recently? The young man had an odd accent, as if English wasn't his first language, but he had spoken it for longer, diluting, but not conquering the original.

"I'd like to speak to the manager," I said, fighting to stay calm. I'd just gotten my car out of the shop. This was the last thing I needed.

He nodded and disappeared into the restaurant.

The manager came out, alternated between apologizing profusely and disclaiming responsibility, gave me his card and $100 worth of Guillermo's coupons, then scurried back inside. I wasn't sure which I wanted to do more – cry or follow him inside and punch him. But I did neither. It wasn't really his fault. Possibly, the valet wrecked it, but given the array of BMWs, Mercedes, and muscle cars in the parking lot, it seemed unlikely that he'd choose to go for a joy ride in a six year old, four cylinder Corolla.

My hands shook as I sifted through the pile of papers, looking for the current insurance card. I took some pictures and called for an insurance claim number. Two uninsured driver claims in less than thirty days. They are either going to jack up my rate or drop me, I'm sure of it. I took notes on one of the many expired insurance cards in my glove box, then got into the driver's seat.

"Well, I hope we don't get stopped on the way home," I said to Halle.

"Stopped? Who would stop us?"

"The police. For driving with a broken headlight."

She nodded, but I don't think she understood.

We were perhaps four blocks from Guillermo's when not one, not two, but four police cruisers surrounded us, lights flashing.

"Pull over to your left and exit the vehicle. Keep your hands where we can see them," the officer closest to us announced over his PA.

The Valkyrie scowled and shifted in her seat.

"Halle, don't do anything stupid. Just be calm, and let's find out what this is about."

I did as I was instructed. As the first officer approached us, I asked, "Is this about the broken headlight?"

"You could say that," he replied. Two other officers inspected the front end of my car with their flashlights.

"A vehicle matching this description, with your license plate was used in a crime at approximately 9:30 PM."

"We were having dinner at Guillermo's. I paid the check, maybe a quarter of ten. If you will let me get the receipt out of my purse, I can prove it. When the valet brought my car back, the headlight was broken. I spoke with the manager about it. And I'm sure the waiter will remember us." *He'd remember Halle, at any rate.*

Two more cruisers pulled up, and a sergeant got out of one of them. She talked to the two officers who had been examining my vehicle. A dark sedan pulled up and three men got out, wearing black windbreakers with "FBI" in huge yellow letters on their backs.

"Holy moly. What is going on here?"

An officer retrieved my purse from the car and looked in it, checking for weapons I guessed, before he handed it over to me. I opened my wallet and dug out the receipt and the handful of coupons.

"The manager gave me these because of the damage to my car. Here's his card. Please call him." I handed the papers to the cop, who took them to the sergeant.

Halle and I stood in front of the squad car that had blocked my car in. I knew that everything we did and said was being recorded by the dash cam. Halle shifted back and forth, and glowered at the police.

"You're going to get us in trouble. Just relax," I hissed at her.

The FBI agents were now in conference with the sergeant and the two officers with the flashlights. Cell phones came out, calls were made, and more talking was done. I was very tired, my feet hurt, and I was both scared and irritated. Why wouldn't they at least tell us what was going on? When were they going to let us leave?

A seventh cruiser arrived. The officer got out and opened the rear door, then helped an older woman and a youngish man climb out of the car. It was hard to get a more accurate idea of their ages in the red and blue strobe of the light bars.

As they approached us, the man said, "Is that them? Is that who killed Pappa?"

He didn't wait for her answer, but charged at us. An officer tried to block his way, but the man had both a height and weight advantage. Other officers came running, but they were yards away. Something blurred past me, and the man was on the ground, moaning and holding a probably broken nose, blood gushing from between his fingers.

Halle was now on the other side of me. I stared at her with my mouth hanging open. How did that happen?

"What?" she shrugged and held out her hands, palms up. "He tripped."

"Does anybody have any gauze, or at least paper towels?" I asked loudly. "Sir, you're going to have to sit up. There you go. Now lean forward just a little, so you're not swallowing all that blood. It'll just make you vomit," I told the man as I knelt beside him and guided him to a sitting position. "Don't worry – I'm a nurse."

Somebody handed me a few brown paper towels and a pair of disposable gloves. I did the best I could to pack his nostrils and stop the bleeding. "You'll need to have this seen about," I said to him.

When I stood up, I saw that the woman he had arrived with was talking to the FBI and the sergeant, in between sobs. The sergeant said something to one of the officers. He came over and said, "The witness said that one male suspect was driving the car, not two women. Your story checks out; however, there was some blood found on the bumper and a few hairs were caught in the broken light. We're taking the vehicle to the forensics lab to collect evidence. Is there someone you can call to come pick you up?"

"Wait. Blood? Hair? Did someone get run over with my car?"

"I really can't comment on that, ma'am."

I called Nick. He had already gone to bed – it was after 11:00 – but he'd come get us as soon as he got dressed.

An ambulance arrived and carried the man with the broken nose away to the ER.

While we waited for Nick, I gave my contact information and a formal statement to the officer with the clipboard. I asked when he thought I'd get my car back, but he said he had no idea, although it could be quite a while.

When Nick finally showed up, he stopped and chatted with a couple of the officers before he came over to us. He motioned for us to join him to the side of the car, off camera.

In a very low voice, so quietly I could barely understand him, he said, "Seems your car was used in a homicide. Victim was in the federal witness protection program." Nick nodded towards the FBI agents. "You didn't hear that from me, by the way."

I was too stunned to do much talking on the way home. *Somebody stole my car, not only to kill someone, but someone in the witness protection program?* Halle, on the other hand, plied Nick with questions. I was dimly aware of them talking, but didn't pay much attention to what they were saying. When we got back to my house, I carried the sadly congealed quesadilla in for Quinn. I set it on the end table by the door and heard footsteps as he came in from the living room. I opened my mouth to introduce him to Nick.

"What the hell are you doing here?" Nick growled at Quinn.

Chapter 7
Dog Days of Summer

"What do you think you're doing, leaving your baby with a junkie?" Nick said to me.

This was the last thing I'd expected to hear.

"Long time, no see, Officer Benson," Quinn said. "I told you two years ago that I got my act together. Got a job and everything."

Then I remembered. Quinn had known my husband and Nick. But they didn't know who, or what, he really was. This was well beyond awkward. And what did he mean by "junkie?"

"Once a junkie, always a junkie. And I thought you'd left town, McLeod."

"I had." Quinn smiled. "But now I'm back."

Nick's glare shifted to me. "How'd you hook up with this…person, anyway?"

"He works with her," I said, looking at Halle. Well, it was true. Sort of.

"The dog trainer. So where's the dog?" Nick asked.

"Still at the kennel," I said.

I didn't like this game of verbal ping pong. It wasn't high stakes in that someone could die. But damaged relationships were hard to fix. I wished I could just tell Nick everything. But he'd never believe me – he'd just think I'd lost my mind. A few weeks ago, I wouldn't have believed me, either.

"Thanks for picking us up," I said to him. Although I knew I was likely to be disappointed, I hoped he would take it as a hint to go home.

"I really wish you would reconsider your association," he gave Quinn a hard look, "with these people." He crossed his arms over his broad chest.

There would be no persuading him at this point, I knew. "Nick, please don't worry. Everything is okay."

He responded by snatching up my hands and rotating them so that my wrists faced him. Out of the corner of my eye, I saw Quinn take a step closer to me. Nick gave him a warning look, and he stopped.

"You're not doing drugs, are you?" Nick asked me.

"What? Of course not! Why would you even think that?" I answered, somewhat hurt by his accusation.

"You've changed your habits, you're associating with a known drug user, and you would never leave Cassie with a stranger. Not *normally*, anyway."

I yanked my hands out of his and planted my fists firmly on my hips. "So I get a dog and a job, so now I'm a junkie? Really?" I risked a glance at Quinn. "Besides, he —" I stopped myself. I couldn't tell Nick that Quinn wasn't a stranger, because then he'd want to know how I knew him. "He comes highly recommended," I finished lamely.

Halle burst out laughing.

Yes. She had highly recommended Quinn earlier this afternoon. At least both he and Nick were looking at her, and not my flaming cheeks.

"Not to worry," Halle said. "We were leaving, anyway." She smiled at me. "I'll bring your dog back soon."

"Goodnight, then. See you later," I said, following them to the door. "Oh! Don't forget your quesadilla. Sorry. I think it's gotten a little cold." I handed Quinn the takeout bag from Guillermo's, and electricity jolted up my arm as his fingers brushed mine.

Nick lurked on the front porch long enough to watch them disappear down the sidewalk.

"I'm really not comfortable with those people hanging around. McLeod is a known criminal. And a substance abuser. Bad things tend to happen to people who run with *that* crowd."

I took a deep breath to compose my thoughts. I knew that under ordinary circumstances, he would be right. But these weren't ordinary circumstances. And I couldn't tell him that. I had to tread very carefully here.

"Nick, thank you for caring. I really appreciate that. But it isn't like I'm dating the guy. He just sat in the living room and watched TV while Cassie slept. If someone hadn't stolen my car to run somebody over, we would have been out an hour or less. But I'm back now, and everything's fine."

"Are you sure?"

As much as I believed in Quinn, Nick's question sent a shiver up my spine.

"See for yourself," I said.

I headed down the hall to Cassie's room. If I was wrong, I'd never forgive myself.

I opened the door a little and a yellow wedge of light fell across Cassie's face. She groaned and wrinkled her forehead. After I closed the door and waited a moment to make sure I hadn't woken her, I led Nick to my bedroom. I opened the top drawer of my dresser and pulled out a box from the depths, then opened it to reveal my engagement and wedding rings. Along with an emerald tennis bracelet that Ryan had given me for Christmas once, they were the only valuable pieces of jewelry I owned.

"See?" I said.

"Okay. It worked out fine. This time. But promise me you'll be more careful about who you leave your kid with."

"You *know* I would never willingly endanger Cassie."

He nodded. "I have to get back to the house. Something's happened to Emily's sequestered witness and she's all kinds of crazy."

"Isn't she supposed to be on maternity leave?"

"That's what I told her."

It didn't occur to me until after he'd left that the person who had been run over with my car was in the witness protection program. I hoped Emily's person was okay – it seemed like a bad night for witnesses.

When my alarm baby went off at 6:30, I found myself moving slower than normal. Cassie had mostly lost interest in nursing these days – only before bed now, and not always then.

Use it or lose it, kid. I took her into the kitchen and set her up with some munchies. I had half-expected Quinn and Halle to come back after Nick left last night, but they never showed. Just in case, I peeked out the back window. Bruce was curled up on the doormat. He sat up when I opened the door, then yawned, stretched, and moseyed into the house.

After he'd shifted and dressed, he came into the kitchen, poured himself a cup of coffee, and sat down at the table. This was the first time I'd ever seen him drink coffee, and it made me wonder what else was going to be different.

"No Halle today?" I asked, cautiously optimistic. I unloaded the dishwasher as we spoke.

"She's around, just keeping a low profile. Listen. About last night. That episode with Nick."

"Yeah. You told me that you knew him. And Ryan. But you never told me the details."

Dishes clattered as I stacked plates and bowls together.

Quinn propped his elbows on the table, laced his fingers together, and rested his chin on his knuckles. "It's a bit complicated." He paused, as if considering how much he should tell me. "I borrowed the identity of a NED named Marc McLeod. He wasn't exactly what you'd call an upstanding citizen."

"I'm sorry. Did you say a 'ned?'"

"Non-Educated Delinquent. NED for short. Only thing he was good for was he looked a bit like me. McLeod was a junkie, and a thief to boot. It was an accident, really, that I ran into Nick and Ryan at all. I strayed into a crime scene they were working. I had to tell them something. And as Mr. McLeod was done using his identity, I had borrowed it for just such occasions. You can hardly blame Nick for not wanting a piece of shite like that hanging about."

"That explains a lot."

I got that Nick thought McLeod was a lowlife. And I could understand why he wouldn't want him around. But Quinn wasn't McLeod. "This is a real problem. How do we convince Nick that you aren't this McLeod person?"

"We don't."

"What?" I frowned at him.

"For the time being, I think it's best for him not to see me in human form."

"That doesn't seem fair, especially not to you." *Or me.*

"I know. But we have bigger problems right now. This demon, Balcones – the one I told you about the other night - knows that I'm tracking him. He'll try to get me before I get him. Demons like to make their targets suffer, and one of their favorite ways to do that is to go after the friends and families of their intended victims. My mother and brothers are not where demons can get at them. You and Cassie are. No matter how much I might want to, for your safety and my own, I can't afford to…be distracted right now."

I nearly dropped the stack of plates I was loading into the cabinet. I felt a chill in the pit of my stomach that froze all the way through my body to my spine. What had I done? I'd been so stupidly giddy, like a lovesick teenager, that I'd put Cassie and myself in this situation. That wasn't entirely true. There were circumstances well beyond my control that had thrown Quinn and me together. But still, I knew it could be dangerous, keeping company with a shifter, especially one that belonged to a clandestine operations team. But it didn't stop me from wanting him.

"I see. What about Halle? You said she was around somewhere."

"She is. And there are others – my team – as well. But you don't know how cunning demons can be. My plan is to stay in canine form for now. My senses will be sharper, and it won't antagonize your brother-in-law. I don't want to drag him into this as well."

I nodded, hanging up the damp dishtowel and closing the dishwasher door. I didn't like it, but I was unlikely to be able to change his mind. Quinn stood up, gave Cassie a little tickle under her chin, then moved closer to me. He kissed me then. Softly, quickly, his lips just grazing mine, but sending a thousand little thrills through my body.

"It's going to be okay. I promise," he said, then turned and walked out of the room.

I pushed the stroller along the bumpy sidewalk. The three of us, Cassie, Bruce, and I started out on our morning walk. I was amazed to see a moving van parked across the street. Had Mrs. Paddington's house really sold that quickly? That would be the fastest escrow ever. I crossed the road to check out the new neighbors. Burly men in pale blue uniforms carried furniture from the truck to the house. A compact car, hatchback open, sat in the driveway, back filled with smaller moving boxes.

A man walked out through the garage, sweat glistening off his bare chest and soaking the top of his cargo shorts. A tattoo of a black bird, body on his upper left arm, wings wrapped around his chest and back, made me think of Halle's pet. The man saw me gawking at him and came over.

"Hello," I said. Realization struck as he got closer. "You're the guy from the shop. You came to Circle last night. It's Hunter, right?" It was the man with the wire-framed glasses and thin scar on his cheek. And he looked better with his shirt off than I would have expected.

"Guilty as charged." He smiled and wiped his hands on a small towel that stuck out of his front pocket. "I'm indeed Hunter. Hunter Greene, actually." He reached out to shake my hand.

Bruce sat down in between us, and rolled over onto one hip.

I raised an eyebrow. "Hunter Greene?"

I picked up Mr. Buns. Cassie had dropped him over the side of the stroller.

"Yes. My grandmother was an art teacher, and she named my dad Forrest. I have a sister called Kelly. My aunt's named Jade, but she's a Sanders now. Nice dog you've got there. Seems very well trained."

"Yes. He does seem that way. But he can be quite a handful," I replied.

"I'm sorry. I'm terrible with names. I know we were introduced last night. Molly?"

"Marti, and this is Cassie. Welcome to the neighborhood. I'm amazed that you're moving in so quickly – Mrs. Paddington just put her house on the market a few days ago."

"Actually, I'm just leasing it. My company," he wiped his glasses with the towel, "moves me around a lot. Not much point in trying to buy anything. Especially since it's only me."

"Oh."

"I don't have kids or anything, not even a goldfish." he replied.

"Ah. Well, that makes sense, then." He seemed to be going out of his way to let me know he was single. Maybe I should start wearing my wedding ring again.

Cassie started to fuss a little, and Bruce let out a deep sigh. "I've got to get going. I'm sure I'll see you around."

While Cassie had her afternoon nap, I called my insurance agent to tell him what had happened with my car, and he told me he would need a copy of the police report before he could do anything. What was I going to do without a car for who knows how long? Theoretically, Mom could take Cassie to Briar Ridge Montessori when she took the boys, but then she'd be there all day, and that would cost more than I was earning. Maybe Em would let me borrow her car – it wasn't like she could drive right now, anyway. I had a long weekend to think about it – the Fourth of July was Monday, so there really wasn't anything I could do before Tuesday, anyway. I called the Tenth Sphere to let Lulu and Belinda know I might have some trouble getting to work.

"I see," Lulu said, after I explained the situation. "I might have a solution for you, honey. I'll ask Benjamin if it's okay for you to drive his car while all this unpleasantness is being sorted out."

"That would be great." *And a little weird.* "I really appreciate that, although I hope it doesn't take too much longer for his problem to get straightened out."

After I hung up with Lulu, I looked at Bruce. "You know, Nick's at work. There's no way he'll show up anytime soon."

Bruce gave me a sad puppy look and rested his head on his outstretched legs.

"Fine."

Our family tradition for July Fourth was to have a big barbeque for friends and family at Mom and Dad's late in the afternoon, then climb up on the roof to watch fireworks. The top of the screened in porch was flat, and when Kyle and Aiden were little, Nick and Ryan had installed a railing around it. It looked a little odd, until there were people milling around up there. Even after the sun went down, the roof was sizzling hot, so Mom always put down some old blankets so we wouldn't roast our toes.

Nick had rented a huge inflatable water slide and put it up against the edge of the porch so the kids could jump off the roof onto the slide. Looked like a broken arm waiting to happen to me, but the dozen or so kids – most of them neighbors - that were skidding down the rubber incline and splashing into the pool at the end seemed to be having a great time.

This was Cassie's first Fourth of July, and I hoped the firecrackers didn't scare her. People firing guns in the air wasn't a big problem in our neighborhood, but there was always somebody who defied the city's ban and shot off fireworks.

Dad and Nick had dueling barbeque pits going, and the smoke carried hints of brisket, corn, and grilled peaches my way.

As soon as we went through the back gate, Emily waved and motioned me over to the back porch, where she sat with a small knot of women, in the shade and under the ceiling fan, half hidden by the bouncing slide. Bruce followed us silently and slouched into a disorderly heap on the wooden floor.

"Hey, Em. How're you feeling?"

"Okay. As well as can be expected, I guess. But I have to tell you something, an unbelievable coincidence," Emily said.

"What's that?"

"There was a case I was working on right before I went on maternity leave. The trial just started, and one of our star witnesses was sequestered because he was just about to go into the federal witness protection program. Two days before he was supposed to testify, someone ran over him with a car. Would you like to guess whose car they used?"

"Um," was all that would come out of my mouth. It took a couple of seconds for me to wrangle my thoughts into anything remotely sensible. "Mine? That's just crazy. The odds of that have to be similar to winning the Lotto or something."

"Yes. If it's a coincidence."

"If? You think someone deliberately chose my car to kill your witness? Why?"

"I don't know that. It just seems peculiar that you called him on an unsecured line and he ended up in the morgue."

"What do you mean I called him?"

"Dr. Pavlov. Remember?"

I swallowed hard. "I just…I don't know what to say. I had no idea." Was I really at least partly responsible for this man's death? It hardly seemed fair to blame me – I was just trying to save my sister's life.

Cassie started squirming in my arms, desperate to get down and explore.

"Oh, Marti! Let me see that baby, huh?" Miss Polly asked, from the chair next to Emily's.

Miss Polly lived two doors down from me, on the other side of Mom and Dad, and she and my mother had been friends for years. Emily and I had grown up out in the country, but we moved into town when I was a senior in high school, after Dad had his accident. She brought over some home-baked bread the day we moved in, and she and Mom bonded over iced tea. I'm not sure what her last name is — she introduced herself as "Miss Polly," and that's what we always called her.

Cassie did not want to be held. She wanted to go see what the other kids were doing, and she cried when I handed her over.

Miss Polly shook her head. "She's growing so fast! I can't believe how big she's gotten." She winked at me. "This little girl doesn't want to hang out on the porch with the old folks. Get her out there with the kids." She turned back to my mother. "No, Adele. As I was saying, those aren't crows. That's the oddest thing. They're common ravens, I'm sure of it. You see how they have shaggy feathers around their throats and their beaks have a bump on top? They aren't supposed to live anywhere near here."

I glanced up and saw two large, shiny black birds sitting in the branches of the pine tree that grew in my back yard and overhung Mom and Dad's. I wondered if those ravens belonged to Halle. Where was she, anyway? Wouldn't it be just like her to barge in to my family gathering?

Cassie led me off the shady porch and out into the yard. With a grunt, Bruce got up and followed. Most of the kids were much older than Cassie, but there were two her age, playing in the shade with a bubble machine. They giggled and squealed as they lurched around, grabbing at the iridescent spheres that bobbed and danced over the grass. Cassie walked a little better than the other two, and she seemed to enjoy lording it over them.

Bruce's ears pricked up (as much as floppy Lab ears can, anyway) and he snorted. I turned around and noticed a man standing under a tree at the back of the yard. Something seemed odd about him, but I wasn't sure what it could be. Other than he had his back to the crowd of people. And he just stood there, dressed from head to toe in beige. He wasn't someone I recognized, and I thought I knew everybody at the party. I got up, dodged through a game of horseshoes and approached him.

"Excuse me, sir? I don't believe we've met," I said.

He turned around. Now I knew why he seemed strange. His eyes were sunken and dark-ringed. A bloody wound gaped underneath his jaw, and gouts of blood clung to his shirt.

I gasped and took a step back.

He vanished.

A moment later, Delilah appeared. "Girlfriend, do you know who that was?"

No idea.

"That man was Bertram Kounis. The dude Lulu's nephew is accused of killin'? He's been trying to show himself to her since he died, but she's so stressed and obsessed with getting Benjamin out of jail that she can't see him. That's why I suggested he come to you."

You suggested? Why on Earth would he need to come to me?

"Benjamin didn't kill him. He wants you to find out who did."

Chapter 8
Number Five

Water dripped from Quinn's hair and soaked the back of his shirt. He'd only come downstairs into the common room at the Waterhorse Inn a few moments ago, after taking a long swim in the over-sized millpond at the back of the inn. It was good for both his body and mind to shift into his kelpie form and spend time in the water. That's why the extra-large pond had been created when Quinn's mother's great-grandmother had built the inn, back before Blackthorne was any more than a market square and a well. He sat on one side of the bar, playing with a piece of toast that he had intended to eat, but somehow couldn't manage to get into his mouth.

Graham was loading clean beer glasses into the cabinet.

"Halle has come down from the northlands and into the Mundane world. You wouldn't know anything about that, would you?"

"Yes," he said. "I saw Halle in town and asked her to pay you a visit. You know what it was like when Mother killed Gretchen. I was trying to save you – and your paramour – from the same fate."

"I appreciate your concern, but I don't need my youngest brother to protect me," Quinn said.

"We're family. We protect each other."

Quinn sucked in a deep breath and let it out slowly. "You're right. I'm sorry. Halle can be abrasive, and I guess my nerves are a little raw." Quinn discovered long ago that some battles aren't worth the energy it takes to fight them, and it is more efficient to placate than argue.

Graham nodded. "So you're back for a while, then?"

"No. You remember when Tam was murdered last month? I've found the demon that did it. I think I can take him down, and I've got to get my team together."

"You and that Mundane Intervention Team," Graham said with a scowl. "Hasn't it almost got you killed enough times? And I won't even mention those close to you that have died. I don't understand why you don't just give it up. I was sure you would, after the jötnar killed Siobhan."

Her death was still painful to Quinn, even after three years. But he wouldn't rise to the bait. "Sometimes, little brother, I wish I could. But I can't change who I am. If demons are allowed to multiply unchecked in the Mundane world, what do you think is going to happen to Faery? How long do you think the barrier will hold? You think you'll be happy serving them all pints of bitters?"

Graham's nostrils flared slightly. "I understand that. I'm just not sure it's still your fight."

"It has to be somebody's fight," Quinn said as he tore the toast into quarters. "Anyway, I'll be gone for a while longer. Not sure how long this will take."

"And I'm sure your ladylove has nothing to do with your extended stay in the Mundane world."

Quinn shot his brother a warning look. "I'm off then. Cheers."

The overstuffed chair in Dame Ashleigh Rowan's Mundane Activity Monitoring and Intervention Center (MAMIC) office was not comfortable. Quinn squirmed like a small child in a church pew while he waited for her. Thoughts – pleasure, pain, home, danger, risk, reward - churned and whirled in his mind, turning his brain to battered mush. He couldn't decide what to do about Marti. So he decided not to decide, at least for now. He had a demon to capture, and if he failed, Marti and Cassie's futures would likely be decided by Balcones. And that would be a bad day for everybody.

Metal snicked against metal, and the door swung open. Ashleigh Rowan swept into the room. "You have news?" she asked, setting down a folder and pulling out the chair behind her mahogany desk. She was never one for idle chat.

"Yes. Halle took me to the north lands and showed me what she's observed. Balcones, the demon that killed my cousin Tam, has been meeting with the jötnar. "

"Yes. I had spoken with her about this before she went off to the Mundane world. Were you able to determine the purpose of this new alliance?" She tapped a pencil absently on the desk.

"No."

Rowan frowned. "Well, it isn't likely to be good, is it?" Then she cocked her head to one side. "I'm not sure why she took it upon herself to involve you. Are you seeing Halle again? That one always was something of a wildcard."

"No. We're not together. She just wanted to discuss her findings with someone in the field."

"And she chose you."

Quinn shrugged. "It's complicated."

"It always is with her. Just keep that Valkyrie away from the humans. You know how she is. The last thing you need is for this mission to get any more complicated by a rash of human males disappearing. Organize your team, and get Kai if you need help." She reached for the folder she had just set down.

"Yes ma'am." Quinn stood up to leave.

"I've heard of this Balcones before. You're not the first to try catching him."

"The others failed?"

"The others died. Be especially careful with this one."

Anger flashed through him as he remembered the cruel and needless way Balcones had snuffed out his cousin's life, draining his life force like a vampire, for no other reason than to torment Quinn. Trapping him would be difficult, and others had failed. He could not. He would not.

* * *

It had taken until Saturday morning to get his team rounded up and briefed. Partly because Malik and Marti had gotten off on the wrong foot, and partly because, as a djinn, Malik was impervious to heat and cold, Quinn sent him to surveil the jötnar and report any signs of demonic activity. It was a good thing that time in Faery and the Mundane world were only loosely connected. He had to be back there two days ago. It tended to get tricky after three days, but leaving Faery on Saturday morning and arriving in the Mundane world on the previous Thursday would not be very difficult.

He would keep Eoin, the half-goat urisk, and Aleksei, the blue-skinned Lesovik, in place with Halle, near Marti and Cassie, and he wanted to get them situated before Marti got home from work.

Quinn gathered his team and they slipped through the portal and into Marti's back yard. He stationed Eoin there. Hopefully, he would spend more of his time watching for Balcones than flirting with Daphne and Isabella, the dryads from the old oak and pine trees behind the house. Eoin could easily blend into the oakleaf hydrangea and frangipani bushes near the birdbath. If he moved, a human might catch a glimpse of him out of the corner of her eye, but like all fae, he was almost never seen. Unless he wanted to be. Quinn positioned Aleksei across the street, next to the neighbor's elaborately planted waterfall and pond. Any humans that looked at him would see nothing more than a large shrub, and if they even bothered noticing it, the memory would slip quickly from their minds, trickling down to where all forgotten things hide.

Quinn double checked that he was not being observed before he lifted the latch on Marti's gate. The cyclone fence around the back yard didn't offer much privacy, but there was a sheltered patio off of her bedroom that was safe from prying eyes. He took off his clothes, folding each item neatly and stacking it on the bistro table, next to the pot of red zinnias. Through the sliding glass door, he could see the ceiling fan spinning above the bed, making it all the more inviting, as beads of sweat skated down his back. After Balcones was caught.

Then. Then he might allow himself such indulgences. That is, if he could figure out a way to do it without harming Marti. He knew fae who were happy enough to rut with humans, not caring that they left a trail of corpses behind. But he was different. Marti was different. Graham almost certainly knew the secret, but, Quinn suspected, probably wouldn't tell him. But even if he discovered it, then what? Marti and Cassie would be better off with their own kind, not being constantly put in harm's way because of him. Quinn sighed to himself, shimmered, and shifted into his dog form.

His hearing was about the same as his horse form, much better than his human form, but not as good as in his kelpie form. But his sense of smell made up for any deficiencies. Even in human form, it was supernormal; in dog form it was freakishly acute. It wasn't just that he could smell peanuts on the breath of the mama squirrel sitting in the top of Marti's oak tree, he could smell a demon as it started to come through a portal, and if it tried to approach on foot, he could detect it nearly a mile away. Quinn closed his eyes. It was disorienting, going from seeing the wider color spectrum humans saw, to the blue and yellow shades that dogs see. He would adjust – he always did, but it would take a few moments. In the meantime, he trusted his nose, and he realized it was the key to protecting Marti and Cassie.

Keeping track of time is not so easy for a dog. He wasn't sure what time it was when Nick started to come through the gate. Bruce trotted over towards him, barking, hackles raised. Nick backed hastily out of the yard and left. No one else came, not for a long time. Bruce sprawled on the back porch, half dozing, half listening, until he heard Marti's car turn onto the street. He sat up, anticipating her return.

Quinn made the switch from dog to human form. When he told Marti that her brother-in-law had stopped by, she phoned him, just to make sure her sister was still doing well. Cassie giggled in his arms while her mother made the call. Humans, with their short lifespans, concentrated all of their joy and wonder into tiny little bubbles of time. Cassie's escaped from her in short, contagious bursts that made him forget, just for the moment, about Balcones and the jötnar.

Marti finished her call.

"Could you do me a huge favor?" she asked, moving in close to be heard over Halle's noisy use of the refrigerator door ice maker.

"Such as?" Inches away, the smell of her hair was intoxicating, like winter lemon blossoms.

"I really wanted to go to circle tonight, but Mom can't watch Cassie. She – Cassie, not my mom - adores you, and I was wondering if…"

"If I would look after her?" It was a golden opportunity to speak with Kai, without alarming Marti.

"Would you? It's just an hour."

Marti hadn't really expected to take Halle with her. Quinn wanted a chance to talk freely to Kai, with no one to eavesdrop. Well, no one but Cassie, and she wasn't telling. Besides, she was busy with a peg puzzle. He smiled to himself and pulled out his cell.

Kai, however, was busy trying to get his two children ready for bed. His wife, Breena, was away for a few days. He said he'd call back when he got everything sorted.

Quinn closed the tablet's picture book app. Cassie was asleep, her lavender-scented head on his chest, one arm flung across him, and the rest of her snuggled between his arm and ribs. She reminded him so much of another little girl who'd left a bittersweet scar across his heart that sometimes he nearly slipped and called her Virginia instead of Cassie. He didn't dare move – he didn't want to wake her and sour the sweetness of the moment. He wondered what it would be like to stay in this world with this family. Right now, demons seemed far away and almost unreal. Almost.

There is something soporific about a sleeping baby, and he felt his own eyelids getting heavy. He tapped the screen to bring up his own book, *Le Mort D'Arthur*, and started reading.

He'd read it at least a hundred times. He even had a first edition copy, and discovering it on Marti's e-reader was one of the things that made her so endearing to him. With half-open eyes, he scanned the electronic pages, each one more slowly than the last, until the tablet was lying across his stomach. When he heard Marti's key in the front door, he snapped awake, turning on the tablet, which had also gone to sleep.

When Marti and Halle came in, Halle reeked of adrenalin. He noticed a smudge of dirt across her cheek, and his heartbeat quickened. Obviously, she'd handled some problem. But it made him uncomfortable.

Marti lifted Cassie off of Quinn's chest. He suddenly felt cold. As soon as they left the room, he turned to Halle.

"What happened?" he asked.

"What makes you think something happened?"

"I can smell the fight on you. And you have a big smudge of dirt on your cheek."

Halle frowned and used the back of her hand to wipe blindly at her face. "There were two men," she said, switching cheeks. "They followed us after the meeting. I saw them when Marti went back into the shop to get her phone. I disposed of them. They will not be found."

Suspecting that Rädsla was having an unexpected feast somewhere, Quinn shook his head. "You know, you can't just go around killing folk as you please."

Halle's eyes flashed electric green. "Of course I can. That is why I was created." She smiled at him as if she were speaking with someone who was impaired.

Marti returned from Cassie's room.

"I'm starved," Halle announced. "Are there any inns nearby?"

"Inns aren't the same thing here," Quinn said. "You want a restaurant."

"Are there any of those nearby?" she responded.

"There are always restaurants nearby in Houston. What do you want to eat?" Marti said, crossing her arms

"Meat. Bread. And beer," Halle replied.

"Well, that's specific," Marti said.

Quinn noticed that she dug her nails into her bicep as she spoke to Halle, and wondered if she was even aware that she was doing it. While he was not sorry for pressing Halle into service to guard Marti and Cassie, he was well aware that she could be difficult.

"What food was it that your mother brought over last week?" he asked.

"She made fajitas."

"Yes, I think Halle might like those. Where can you get them?"

"If you want fajitas, it's Guillermo's Cantina. It's 8:30 on a Friday night. It'll be packed — bet there's an hour wait." Marti answered, her tone bordering on sullen.

"Here." Quinn held four twenty dollar bills. "Is this enough?" Quinn was never sure how much things were meant to cost in the Mundane world.

"Should be."

"Bring something back for me?" Quinn wished that he was taking Marti out to dinner. But he knew she would never trust Halle to look after Cassie. And he also knew that her mistrust was completely deserved. Halle had neither the faintest idea how to nor the desire to learn about caring for a baby.

Marti was clearly not pleased about chauffeuring Halle, but she did it, leaving Quinn and Cassie to their own devices.

Agitation forced Quinn outside. Kai had not called back, and Quinn found himself too impatient to sit still.

"Eoin?" he called softly.

The urisk appeared among the frangipani leaves. "Yes?"

"Seen anything interesting?"

"Not a thing."

"Thanks."

The moon was behind some thin cirrus clouds, causing them to glow translucent silver against the night sky. Closing his eyes to enhance his hearing and sense of smell, he took a slow, deep breath and listened. A gray tree frog, sounding almost like a bird, chirruped nearby. A toad answered. Cut grass, wet concrete, car exhaust, small animals and night were the only smells he identified.

A stick snapped, and Quinn's eyes flew open.

A large opossum waddled across the back yard, headed for Adele's compost pile next door. Quinn smiled to himself and went back inside.

Given that there was nothing left to do but watch and wait, he found the remote, and turned on the TV. He didn't really know how to work the remote beyond the most basic functions – there seemed to be far too many buttons on the thing. He could, however, use the Channel Up or Channel Down arrow buttons. There seemed to be an endless supply of channels, none of which showed anything he was interested in watching. Finally, he got to the music channels and stopped on the classical one. The concerto was familiar – he'd helped Mozart write that one. He relaxed in the chair, ears and nose on high alert, mind drifting with the music, as one piece blended into another, surfing the crescendos and pianissimos, climbing through arpeggios.

He'd lost track of time when he heard the car doors slam. It was late, and he realized that Marti and Halle should have been home a long time ago. He was startled to hear them coming up the front walkway, not from the side of the house where Marti usually parked her car. Also, there were three sets of footfalls. His nose twitched. Why was Nick with them? Had something happened?

This could be bad. There was always the chance that Nick wouldn't remember him, but that was unlikely. He couldn't shift into Bruce, because then it would seem that Marti had left Cassie home alone. There was no choice but to remain where he was and hope for the best.

"What the hell are you doing here?" Nick said, his eyes narrowing and lips curling into a scowl.

Nick turned on Marti. "What do you think you're doing, leaving your baby with a junkie?" he snapped at her.

It tore at him, the way Nick was going after Marti. And it was almost entirely is fault. "Long time, no see, Officer Benson," Quinn said, trying to redirect Nick's anger toward himself. "I told you two years ago that I got my act together. Got a job and everything."

"Once a junkie, always a junkie. And I thought you'd left town, McLeod."

"I had." Quinn smiled. "But now I'm back."

Nick looked at his sister-in-law. "How'd you hook up with this…person, anyway?"

"He works with her," Marti said, looking at Halle.

"The dog trainer. So where's the dog?" Nick asked.

"Still at the kennel," Marti replied. She sighed. "Thanks for picking us up."

Nick, however, wouldn't drop it. It was bad enough that he accused Marti of using drugs, but when he snatched her arms to look for track marks, Quinn almost went for him. Reflexively, he took a step forward, then stopped himself. He knew that Nick wouldn't hurt Marti. He was just concerned about her welfare. In an assertive way. Quinn stood down and let Marti handle it.

He realized that Nick was going to be a major distraction, as long as he saw Quinn and thought that he was Marc McLeod. He might be able to win Nick over, but now was not the time. It was one more thing to add to the list of things to be done after Balcones was caught. Quinn shook himself. Why was he even thinking that? If he really cared about Marti and Cassie, he should just let them be. But not now. Now they were targets, and he had put them in harm's way. The two men that Halle had neutralized had proven that. Of course Balcones would send humans after her instead of demons. Demons stood out – they could be smelled and felt. Men would just blend into the sensory sea already filled to capacity with humanity. If he had any hope of snaring Balcones, Quinn could not afford to become embroiled in family dramas or emotional complications, and he would need every advantage he could get. There was only one solution, and he knew it would be unpopular.

As they left Marti's house under Nick's watchful eye, Quinn felt Nick's eyes boring into his back, so strongly it seemed like a digging beetle, and he couldn't help reaching over his shoulder to scratch at the itch.

"I like him," Halle said. "He's strong."

"Don't you be getting any ideas about Nick," Quinn said. "He's married to Marti's sister, and they have three children."

"So?"

"Don't, Halle. Just don't." Quinn shook his head.

Halle tossed her long blonde hair as if she were a lion defending its territory, but said nothing.

When they got to the strip center at the edge of Marti's neighborhood, Quinn turned and led Halle behind the buildings.

"I need your eyes," he said. "I have the rest of my team in place, but you have abilities that they don't."

"Yes. I saw Aleksei and Eoin when we returned. That makes three of you. Where are Malik and Siobhan?"

Halle knew all of Quinn's Mundane Intervention Team. They'd gone to MIT training together, and even been a team, briefly. "Malik is watching the jötnar."

"Siobhan? I haven't seen her in ages."

Quinn looked away and shook his head.

"Oh," Halle said. "I'm —"

"Jötnar, Halle. She was killed by jötnar three years ago. Isn't that why Graham chose to send you?"

"You would have to ask him," Halle said, and her eyes narrowed. "Surely, you've found a replacement? Anyone I know?"

"My cousin, Tam. But we lost him as well. He has not…been replaced."

"Tam," Halle said, then chewed her bottom lip. "I think I remember him. Isn't he the one who liked to do cannonballs into the pond and splash all the old ladies?"

"Yes." The tiny word was strangely difficult to say.

"That is unfortunate," Halle said. Then she cocked her head at him. "Are you asking me to be the last member of your team?"

"For this mission. You did bring it to MAMIC's attention, after all. Besides, you're the local frost giant expert."

Halle laughed, then lowered her head and looked up at him through her lashes. "Perhaps. What would you have me do?"

Quinn ignored the flirtation. "You can fly. You can be in places to see what others can't. And maybe," Quinn lowered his voice conspiratorially, "you can get the crows to help."

"They will bargain. What will you give them?"

"Depends on what they want."

Halle shrugged. "We shall see."

With no further ado, her eyes turned to black, followed quickly by her hair and skin. Within seconds, a large raven stood on the pavement before him. Halle shook her feathers, hopped a few steps, and flew away.

Quinn stood behind Aleksei, at the neighbor's across from Marti's house, so he could not be seen from the street. At least, not by humans, anyway.

"Halle will be helping with this mission," Quinn whispered to Aleksei.

"That is good idea?" he answered.

"Probably not. But I don't have a better one."

After the car that had been puttering down the street at sub-pedestrian speed finally pulled into the garage two doors down from Marti's house, Quinn slipped across the street and into the back yard.

Humans would consider it telepathy, but that is only because they could not hear the call that Quinn sent out to Eoin. Aleksei had difficulty hearing it because he was a wood fae, but Eoin, as a fellow water entity, had no trouble.

Quinn's heart skipped a beat when Eoin did not respond.

He called again.

Eoin stepped from behind the pine tree, Daphne's hand quickly pulling away from him and disappearing into the trunk. Eoin's eyes were slightly glazed and his thick lips curved into a crooked smile.

"Bloody fool! Are you mad? What have I told you about keeping your post?" Anger had replaced fear, lowering the pitch of Quinn's message to near-audible levels.

The goofy smile fell off of Eoin's face, and he looked for it on the ground, poking at fallen pine needles with one hoof. "I'm sorry."

"You're meant to be watching for a bloody demon, Eoin. And not just any demon – the demon that killed Tam. And what are you doing instead? That sort of carelessness will get somebody killed."

"It won't happen again."

"See that it doesn't."

Quinn stalked to the secluded patio and ripped off his clothes, piling them haphazardly on the table. He turned himself into Bruce, and used his ultra-keen nose to make a perimeter check. He detected nothing out of the ordinary, then made three more passes for good measure.

As he predicted, Marti did not like his decision to remain exclusively in canine form. He didn't like it much, either. But he was glad that Delilah had told him about the ghost of Bertram Kounis showing up at Marti's family picnic. That would give her something to do, and with any luck, keep her from trying to persuade him to shift back into human form. Because she just might succeed.

Chapter 9
Lingering

Hadrian tapped into the security cameras and spent most of Tuesday watching the parking lot in the strip center where the Tenth Sphere was located. The store was busy, but none of the patrons stood out as being anything other than metaphysical shoppers. If anyone from the Odessa Group used the business as a drop, they didn't do it today. If he wanted to get inside the shop, he'd better get a move on – it wouldn't be open much longer, and he needed to touch things. He'd gone down to Homicide Division this morning on the pretense of examining the evidence from the Kounis crime scene. What he really wanted to do was hold the coin that was dropped at Kounis' feet. Unfortunately, the detectives working the Kounis case were out on another investigation. He could, perhaps, have pressed the issue, but thought better of it.

His sister, Sabina, was the only other person who knew about his special ability. If he held something in the palm of his hand, sometimes he knew things about the person it had belonged to, or at least who had touched it last. He couldn't always interpret what he saw, and sometimes he got nothing. But it had helped him solve more cases than he could easily tally. The Bureau frowned on the woo-woo stuff, so he never told anyone about it, not even Sara. Sometimes, he wondered if he should have become a remote viewer for the CIA. They claimed they'd shut down that program. But he also knew that disinformation was their first line of defense.

He put on the wire frame glasses with the plain lenses. He wanted to look erudite.

When he got to the Tenth Sphere, he recognized Marti Keller from the photo in his files. She was a bit of alright, as his British friend, Trevor would say.

"If there's something I can help you with, please let me know," she said.

She glanced over his head at the clock, and he wondered where she was so anxious to go. A date perhaps?

He looked around the shop, starting with the figurines near the cash register, and picking up random pieces. The problem was that so many people had handled them that there was no clear residual image or vibration, just a muddle of hazy snapshots.

After a while, an older, plumper woman came out of the back room. This must be Lulu Miranda. She smiled at Hadrian, then said, "Marti, are you coming to circle on Thursday night?"

"Maybe. I'm not sure."

"Try to make it. I think you'll like it."

"I'll see what I can do. Is it okay if I scoot out of here a couple of minutes early?"

"Sure. Go."

Lulu turned back to Hadrian. "In case you're interested, we do have a Thursday night Circle. We have a variety of activities. Often, we do mediumship, but sometimes we do table-tipping, aura reading, scrying, and psychometry."

"Really?" Hadrian said. "I might have to check it out." He wondered if that might give him access to objects that were kept from the general public. He would decide then if the Tenth Sphere warranted further surveillance.

Hadrian had set the feed from the security camera in front of the Tenth Sphere to run through the facial recognition software on his computer. It would alert him if it got a hit on any known gang members. Just as he was leaving to go to the Thursday night Circle, he heard a beep, so he checked the screen. Two men walked past the store and around the corner to the back of the building. The computer identified them as two very low-level members of the Odessa Group.

"Well, well, well, Ms. Miranda. You seem to have some interesting visitors."

It took longer than he anticipated trek west to the Energy Corridor from downtown. He'd wanted to get there early enough to evaluate escape routes and potential danger zones. But he would have to settle for a quick scan of the parking lot. If the two Russians were still around, they were laying low.

There were cars in the parking lot, but the Tenth Sphere's door was locked. Hadrian knocked. A few minutes later, the lock turned and a thin woman with salt and pepper hair let him in. He surmised that she was Belinda Tate, Lulu's partner.

"They just went upstairs," she told him, nodding towards the back of the shop.

She locked the door behind him and followed him to the large conference room. Lulu was standing on a chair, pulling the battery out of the smoke detector. He figured it was best not to draw attention to himself by pointing out that it was a fire code violation to do that.

He squeezed in next to Marti, and forced himself not to stare at the knockout blonde with waist-length braids next to her. She looked too amazing to be real, and her outfit should have been illegal. On the other side of him sat a bony peroxide blonde, and he noticed that she seemed dark and desperate even before he spotted the thick scars across her wrists.

It would have been much easier for him to pity Marilyn, the suicide blonde, if she hadn't kept throwing herself at him the entire time. He was still undecided about the surveillance at the end of the Circle. He followed Marti and her friend, whom he'd heard Marti call Halle, out the door. He sat in his car, pretending to be returning text messages on his cell phone. He saw the two Russians step out of the darkness at the edge of the building. Marti turned back, and at first Hadrian thought she intended to speak to them. They ducked back into the shadows as she approached, then she passed them and went into the shop. Halle looked around as if she'd heard a noise and moved to the edge of the building where the thugs were hiding. Hadrian got out of his car, fearing for her safety. He heard the crash of something metallic being knocked over and, inexplicably, the neigh of a horse. Halle emerged from the dark, and Marti came out of the shop.

Hadrian waited until they had disappeared down the block before he went to investigate. He found a metal shopping cart lying on its side, flattened cardboard boxes spilling out of it, and a smear of blood on the wall, but no Russians. He used his cell phone to take a few photos and an evidence swab to collect a sample of the blood, then headed back to his office. The Tenth Sphere surveillance operation was a go.

Naked, Sveklá brushed his teeth and gently probed the port wine stain on the top of his head with the fingers of his other hand. He'd noticed it getting thicker recently. The doctors had said it would do that as he aged. His boss had offered to pay for a laser treatment to remove it, but he'd refused. If it was good enough for Mikhail Gorbachev, it was good enough for him. It had given him is nickname, Sveklá, or beet, and if he no longer had the mark, then who would he be?

He'd had another name once. It was long ago, but he still remembered it. How could he forget, when that is what Irina called him? According to the official records Sergei Medved died in a fire in 1992. The body had never been recovered, but that was because he was looking at it in the mirror.

The story that he had been told by the nurses at Tri Babushkas Orphanage was that his mother was unmarried and could not support him, so she'd left him there, as one would a cast-off toy or an unwanted pet.

Baby Sergei had not thrived. Even though he was quite stout, he grew up much shorter than the other boys at Babushkas. There was one boy who always stood up for him when the other children teased him about his birthmark or made fun of him about his size. He shared his own insufficient food with Sveklá on many a night after other boys had beaten him and taken away what little supper he had. The nurses, and he had believed they were actually nurses until he was about ten, often punished the children for transgressions by locking them in cells in the basement, without dinner, for the night. It was a game, no, not a game, but a survival tactic, to try and get other children in trouble while avoiding blame. The food of those in solitary was distributed among the others. Sveklá had spent far too many shivering nights in solitary, and those miserable nights of utter darkness, with nothing but sounds of rats gnawing on the walls and the eerie cry of foxes for company.

One of the nurses, and perhaps it was because she was young and not yet ground down by the system, would sneak food to Sveklá on nights he was locked down alone. But it wasn't every night, only the ones she could slip away from the supervision of older nurses. When Sveklá and his protector had gotten big enough, they ran away from the orphanage. And after the escape, Sveklá went to work for him.

He looked at his bare chest in the mirror. The eight-pointed stars under each clavicle had faded to a bluish grey. The two stars on his knees were darker. Lenin's face, attached to a hairy cherub's body, leered out at him from over his heart, fluttering over the tops of minarets which stretched almost to his groin. He was proud that he had no spiderwebs – drug addicts were the most pathetic of a pathetic lot. He only had one epaulet with a skull tattooed onto his shoulder. He'd gotten a terrible infection with that one and it had almost killed him. But he'd gotten his ink a long time ago, when tattoos had to be earned. Not bought, like today. He sighed, both nostalgic for the past, and glad it was done.

There had been the most beautiful girl at Babushkas. She had hair like black silk, and her grey eyes were huge and bright. He'd fallen hard for her, but never dared voice his feelings. Such an angel would never accept lowly Sveklá as a lover, much less a husband. But she had run away with them. He saw her nearly every day, as she had married his boss.

Oh, lovely Irina, do you really love him? Sveklá often wondered when he saw them together. He suspected that she knew of the faithlessness of her husband. It made his heart ache whenever the boss man took on new conquest. But Irina, she was part of the business, and she could never leave him. Not with her life.

He rinsed and spat into the sink. If he turned his face at the right angle, the birthmark on his head was nearly invisible. If only Irina could see him that way. He longed to comfort her when she was alone all night, often imagining in exquisite detail the smell of her skin, the softness of her body, and what he would eagerly do if she were to take him into her bed. But he knew such a prize could never be his.

As he did every night, he dropped to the floor and quickly performed fifty pushups. When that was done, he rolled over and did one hundred sit ups. Standing up, he smacked his hard stomach with the flat of his hand and grunted with approval.

Sveklá generally eschewed luxury, but the one thing he did allow himself was expensive Egyptian cotton pajamas. It was the only thing he ever asked for, and Irina always brought a pair or two back for him when she went shopping in New York. The pair he was pulling on had come from her latest excursion.

He slipped into bed, and hoped he didn't have the usual nightmares. It would make a nice change.

Chapter 10
Life in Review

It was Tuesday morning, and I hoped I'd have a way to work. Lulu had said she'd let me know about the car. There wasn't anything I could do about that, so I flipped on the television while I folded laundry, half listening to *AM HTown*. Until they got to the weather forecast.

"There's an area of disturbed weather in the western Caribbean that's moving north-northwest. A high pressure ridge along the East Coast is going to keep pushing it to the west. We may be looking at tropical storm conditions anywhere from southern Mexico to probably Cameron Parish in Louisiana. There's so much moisture being pulled in across the Gulf Coast by an area of low pressure off to our west that I think that any development would likely bring a lot of rain, wherever it makes landfall. Back to you, Ephram and Mary Jo."

Well, it has been dry lately and we could use some moisture. I just hoped we didn't get it all in a couple of hours.

"And speaking of storms, Mary Jo" Ephram said, "few kids have had a rougher time than young Ivan. His name has been changed to protect his privacy, but his story is one hundred percent real. Ivan was abandoned at Tri Babushkas Orphanage in Russia, when he was only three months old. He lived there, under extreme conditions, until he was adopted by the Smith family, who only agreed to speak with us if we concealed their identities. Ivan has been diagnosed with an uncommon condition called Reactive Attachment Disorder, or RAD, that is unfortunately, common among abused and neglected children. These children are unable to form an attachment, or bond, with caretakers. In the worst cases, these children act out violently towards their adoptive parents. Here is the tape of my interview with the Smiths. "

A graphic window flew to the center of the screen and zoomed in to the Smiths. The studio lights went down. On the big screen, a man and woman sat together on a couch, their faces hidden in shadow.

"Mr. and Mrs. Smith, thank you for allowing us to interview you for the AM HTown show. What led you to adopt Ivan from Russia three years ago?"

"My husband and I couldn't have children of our own," replied the digitally blurred voice. "We wanted to make a choice that would do the most good. We thought," her voice broke, and the man next to her rubbed her shoulder. "We thought that adopting from these overcrowded and under-staffed facilities would be the best. Our adoption advisor told us that Tri Babushkas Orphanage was the worst of the worst."

"Ivan looked like a little angel when we first saw him. His white-blond hair was naturally curly and his eyes were so blue and so sad. We just couldn't leave him there," the man said.

"And how old was Ivan when you bright him home?"

"He was eight," the man answered.

"And when did you start to think there was something wrong?"

"Immediately," the woman answered. "He hated being touched. We thought it was just how he'd been raised, and that he'd get over it in time."

"But he only got worse," the man added. "By the time he was ten, we were so afraid of him that we put a lock on the inside of our bedroom door."

"He often told me he was going to cut our throats while we were sleeping, then burn down the house. He got kicked out of every school he attended. He," Mrs. Smith's voice caught in a sob. "he killed our cat, Mittens. We'd had her for ten years. Said he'd do the same to me."

"I tried to take him to tae kwon do class, thought it would help him learn some self-control. He hit me with the board he was supposed to be breaking and broke my jaw," Mr. Smith added.

"We didn't know what to do. Then our adoption advisor told us about the CCF – the Cherngelanov Children's Foundation. He agreed to take custody of Ivan. We thought it was best for everyone. He needs more help than we could give him." The woman sniffled and dabbed at her nose.

The silhouettes in the window stopped moving. The lighting shifted, revealing Mary Jo and Ephram sitting with a well-dressed man. He looked fifty-ish, tall, but wiry rather than muscled. His smooth-shaven head was lumpy, and I wondered if he had suffered a lot of injuries as a child. The wisp of tattoo that peeked out from the cuff of his crisp designer shirt was the only hint that there was more to him than a successful real estate business. The tape of the interview with the "Smiths" faded, to be replaced by a slide show of the new guest. First he appeared in a three piece suit with the backdrop of downtown Houston, next as a sweaty volunteer, passing water down from a truck, bucket-brigade style, and finally, decked out in climbing gear, a coil of rope over his shoulder.

Bruce sat up and whined.

"Do you need to go out?"

He snorted and shook his head.

Ephram said, "We have in our studios today, Mr. Boris Cherngelanov. As many of you know, Mr. Cherngelanov is a prominent Houston businessman and philanthropist. Mr. Cherngelanov, please tell us about your foundation."

"*Zdravstvuĭte*, Ephram and Mary Jo. Is nice to be on television with you this morning. My mother died when I was young child. My father, he was alcoholic, left my sister and I at Tri Babushkas Orphanage."

The chirpy host broke in, "Does your sister also live here in Houston?"

"My sister died at Babushkas."

"I am so sorry. Please, continue."

"Because I know how it was like in Babushkas, and afterward, for those who survive. I can not fix the troubles in that place, but perhaps I help those who got out. I understand them."

"How does your foundation help?" Mary Jo asked.

"I provide home for children, with as you say, RAD. Provide therapists and counselors to teach children life skills. Also, provide job training. Is very difficult, yes. But most of these children can be helped, and not live rest of lives as criminals in prison."

"That is so wonderful," gushed Mary Jo. "And would you tell our audience how Ivan is doing now?"

"Ivan is well. Will be starting sixth grade in technology magnet school in fall. Is very bright young man."

"Thank you so much for being on our show today, Mr. Cherngelanov. We've got to take a commercial break here. When we come back, we'll have a bevy of beauties – that's right, our own Houston Texans cheerleaders – to present the adoptable pet of the day."

I switched off the TV and shuddered. Any type of attachment disorder was a scary thing, but RAD was terrifying. Good thing it wasn't common. I hugged Cassie tightly. As I moved to pick up the laundry basket, the phone rang. Caller ID said it was Lulu.

"Okay, honey, Benjamin said you could drive his car. I got the spare key yesterday, and I'll drop it off on the way to the attorney's."

"How is that going?" I knew I needed to tell her about Bertram Kounis, but it just sounded so weird.

"Well, it's going as well as can be expected, I guess. He asked me not to talk about it, though."

"Okay. Umm..." I said. *Might as well just come out with it.* "I saw Bertram Kounis yesterday."

"What do you mean?"

"Delilah brought him to me at my parents' Fourth of July barbecue. Benjamin didn't kill him."

"Oh, honey! That's great! Did he say who did?"

"Well, that's kind of the problem. He had his throat cut and he doesn't seem to be able to talk."

I swear I could hear Lulu frown over the phone.

"Hmmm. I'll have to think about that," she said. "That isn't anything I can take to the attorney."

"Maybe Delilah can bring him back and translate for him."

"I'm on my way."

I wanted to tell her that now wasn't a good time, but she had already hung up.

It took her less than ten minutes to knock on my front door. She was carrying a brown paper lunch bag.

"Hey, cutie!" she said to Cassie, who grinned back at her. "Living room or kitchen?" she said to me.

"Huh?"

"To set up, honey. To see if we can get Mr. Kounis on line."

"I guess living room."

Bruce had made himself scarce. I could hardly blame him, given that Lulu was always trying to convince me to get rid of him.

She opened her bag and took out a sage smudge stick. "I always keep a couple in my car for emergencies."

The rattle of the bag brought Alpha and Betty climbing to the top of their cage, hoping for a treat.

"Most people keep first aid kits in their cars," I said as I opened the bag of yogurt drops.

Lulu smiled, showing her teeth. "Different kind of first aid."

The rats took their treats and scampered to eat them in the chew log. Lulu pulled out a box of matches and lit the smudge. The ceiling fan scattered the smoke, and threatened to blow out the smudge stick.

"Can we turn that off?"

Once the wind had ceased, the smoke hung in it, slowly curling and twisting in Lulu's wake. Cassie, sitting on the floor by the couch, watched it intently, even pausing her extended gnawing session on Mr. Buns' ear. Lulu sat down near her, holding the burning smudge over a sales circular she'd retrieved from the recycling bin.

"Try and call Delilah," she said, her eyes closed.

Delilah? Are you around? Lulu and I would really like to talk to Bert, if you can manage it.

"Girl, don't call him Bert. He does not like that."

A grey mist formed itself into an oblong cloud in the middle of the living room. It gradually congealed into the form of Bertram Kounis. But he was standing on a closely clipped lawn with a garden hose sprayer in his hand. A man approached him. He was shorter than average, but built like a bull, with thick arms and no neck. There was a purplish growth on one side of his head that spoiled the symmetry of his otherwise perfect flattop. Kounis backed away from the man, pointing the sprayer at him as if it was a weapon. The two seemed to be arguing, but the whole scene took place in eerie silence. The argument got more heated, with the short man waving his arms. Kounis backed up until he ran into the wall. As the other man closed in on him, Kounis sprayed him in the face. The man yanked the sprayer out of Kounis' hand and hit him hard across the bridge of the nose with it. While Kounis was cradling his face in his hands, the shorter man picked up something off the ground. A pole or stick? No. It was a lawn edger, a garden tool that did not look vastly different from a battleax. I suddenly realized where this vision was heading and I lunged for Cassie. I wasn't sure if she could see the murder re-enactment, but I didn't want to risk it. I picked her up and turned her toward me just as the bull-necked man slammed the blade into Kounis' throat with such force that he was lifted off his feet. If the stroke had been dead center, he would probably have been decapitated. As it was, blood welled up and cascaded down Kounis' chest, spurting with each heartbeat. He clutched at his throat as he slid down the wall, leaving a bright red smear behind him. He fell forward, sprawling on the manicured grass, his heart pumping his blood onto the ground. The bull-necked man dropped the edger as if it were on fire and flapped his hand in the air. After he examined it and removed something from his palm, probably a splinter, he calmly reached into his pocket and dropped something small at Kounis' feet. He glanced over his shoulder, as if he heard a noise, and ran in the opposite direction. Another man, and I assume by Lulu's gasp that it was Benjamin, entered the scene. He saw Kounis and grabbed the edger, which had fallen across his body. A woman opened a door and put both hands to her mouth, screaming silently, but vigorously. The scene dissolved into mist and dissipated through the room.

"I knew it!" Lulu said.

"Now you just gotta find out who the short guy is," Delilah remarked.

It was really weird, watching Bertram Kounis act out his own murder. Made me feel like I was watching a snuff film. He certainly didn't airbrush out the blood and gore. I rubbed my own throat, even though I knew I wasn't hurt. Still, it caused a chill to set into my solar plexus.

Cassie squirmed, and I set her down.

I glanced at Delilah and nodded. "So, if Benjamin didn't do it, how do we find the short guy with the nevus?" I asked. "Do you think it might be someone your nephew knows?"

"The man has a what, honey?" Lulu asked.

I patted the top of my head. "The purple blotch on his head – a port wine stain."

"Oh. Why didn't you say so?" Lulu shrugged. "Maybe, he knows him, maybe not. How many of your friends know each other?"

I frowned. She had a point. "Well, it doesn't matter what we know, it's what we can prove that counts."

My eyes fell on the clock. "If I'm going to get Cassie to Briar Ridge on time, I've got to get a move on."

"Oh, right. Here are the keys, honey." Lulu set them on the coffee table.

"Thanks, Cassie and I really appreciate this."

"No problem." Lulu's eyebrows knitted together. "Did you see what that was, honey, that the killer dropped at Kounis' feet? My eyes aren't as good as they used to be."

"I'm not sure. It looked like a coin."

"That's kind of what I thought. Well, I'll see you at the shop."

Lulu gathered her things, and I followed her to the front door to let her out. Bruce came out of hiding, and I gave him a pat on the head.

"See you later," I said to him, wishing he'd shift so I could talk to him about what Bertram Kounis had just shown us. I didn't know if he'd been able to see it or not.

Delilah? I thought, after I'd locked the door behind Lulu. I grabbed my kid and her go-bag and headed for Benjamin's a maroon Crown Victoria in my driveway. I opened the door and the car smelled like older cars often do; perhaps it's the vinyl that's been cooked by the sun too many times, or the carpet that gradually builds up a layer of dirt that can never be removed.

"What's up, girlfriend?" I heard her voice, but couldn't see her. She sounded sleepy.

Who was the short man? Does Bertam know him? It would sure help a lot if he could drop a name, or clue, or something our way.

"Girl, that ain't happenin' anytime soon," Delilah said. "He used his last bit of etheric energy on that drama he just put on for y'all. That shot him straight up into the astral, and he's being cocooned right now."

Fortunately, Emily and Nick had a car seat that I could borrow, so I didn't have to run out and buy a new one while I was waiting to get my car back. Since the police didn't' even have a lead, it might be a while. I grunted as I pulled the lap belt tight against the base of the seat. "Come on, Cassie." I had to coax her across the expanse of vinyl back seat so I could get her strapped in.

Cocooned? What does that mean? How long does it take? "Ow!"

I bumped my head on the door frame as I backed out of the car. I was sure I heard Delilah snickering, but I ignored it.

"Cocooning is 'bout like it sounds. The soul enters an energy cocoon, where it can be healed. Happens a lot when somebody dies real sudden. They get kinda disoriented and need a little help gettin' stabilized."

The car started easily, and I turned the AC on high while I buckled up and adjusted the seat and mirrors.

What are you saying? You can't talk to him?

Crap. I just knocked over Mom's trash can as I backed out of the driveway. I had to jump out and set it back up. Benjamin's car was a lot wider than my little blue Corolla.

Delilah sounded like she was sighing. "No. He'll be out when he's ready to come out, girlfriend. Ain't nothin' I can do about that."

Fine. I'd better focus on my driving, or Cassie and I are going to be up there cocooning, too.

I did not cry this time, after I dropped Cassie off. And I couldn't decide if that was better or worse.

I had the shop on my own for almost an hour. Belinda left when I got there and Lulu was at the attorney appointment. As soon as she came in, I told her what Delilah had said about the cocooning.

Lulu scowled. "That's not what I wanted to hear." She considered the fluffy duster on the glass jewelry case. "I suppose we could try contacting him on Thursday night."

"Maybe."

The cowbell on the door clanged, and a woman wearing a bright green turban came in.

"Hello, Ellen!" Lulu said. She went around the counter to give Ellen a hug. Ellen looked so frail, that I was afraid Lulu would break her.

"How are you feeling?" Lulu asked.

I made an effort to keep smiling. Ellen's skin had taken on a greyish cast. She had recently had chemo for acute myeloid leukemia.

"I'm hanging in there. I'm going to Anderson for some tests on Thursday, and I have to spend the night, so I won't be able to come to Circle. I just wanted to let Belinda know how much I enjoyed her book."

"She'll be so sad she missed you, honey. She went to go run some errands. When will you hear back about your tests?"

"Depends. Sometime next week. Do you know when Belinda's planning on having the next book out?"

Lulu smiled. "She's been working very hard on that. I think she's just about ready to send it to her editor."

Ellen nodded. "I'm looking forward to it. I've got to go, sweetie. My daughter's waiting for me in the car, and she's not very patient with me coming here."

Lulu hugged her again "You just do your best to get yourself well. We'll see you at the next Circle."

"Course you will."

"Bye, Ellen," I said. "Hope your test results come out well."

She smiled and waved good-bye, then ambled out the door.

When Lulu turned around, there were tears in her eyes. She sniffled and wiped her eyes with her fingers.

"Lulu? You okay?"

"I'm sorry. I'm not sad for her. I'm sad for me. I'm really going to miss her."

I rolled my lower lip between my teeth. "You don't think she's going to get a good report?"

"She's starting to separate from her body, I can feel it." Lulu shook her head. "It happens to us all, and Lord knows she's been suffering terribly."

"I'm so sorry, Lulu. But it is possible that you're wrong." I picked up the duster and twirled it over some of the nearby knick-knacks.

"I'd give anything to be wrong. But I'm not."

It was after work time, and customers started to trickle into the shop. It got busy enough that I was a few minutes late leaving to pick up Cassie, and I just barely dodged the late pick up fee. Of course, that meant we got stuck in traffic, and by the time we got home, I was frazzled.

Ordinarily, I think I would have been more alarmed than annoyed when I saw the side gate standing open. This afternoon, it just made me mad.

Lugging Cassie and her accoutrements, I shut the gate and went into the house. It was strangely silent.

"Hello?" I called. "Bruce? You there?"

There was no answer.

The back door was ever so slightly ajar. Fear began to creep up my back like a freezing spider.

"Bruce? Where are you?"

There was no sound but the squeak of the exercise wheel in Alpha and Betty's cage.

I let my purse and Cassie's go bag fall to the floor. I clutched her tightly as I went from room to room, calling.

Bruce was gone.

Chapter 11
Bad Wolf

Contrary to popular belief, most sociopaths are not stone-cold killers. Boris Cherngelanov, however, was.

That's why Quinn was so surprised to see him on the morning TV show, touting his home for damaged children. There must have been a reason for it. That type of "prominent businessman" usually tried to stay under the radar, rather than being on television where people who knew how he really got his money might notice him. Interesting, but it was not his concern just now.

When Lulu showed up to try and conjure the ghost of Bertram Koinis, he hid himself in Cassie's room. Lulu and Quinn were not exactly friends.

"Why you hiding up in here, shifter?" Delilah asked him. "You might want to watch the show."

He hadn't even noticed her materializing in the room. Also, he didn't like the ghostly figure that floated near her. He'd obviously been murdered – blood soaked his beige shirt and a bloody gash stretched from under his left ear to his right jaw. Quinn suspected it was not a random act of violence. The man just had a mean vibe to him.

Quinn padded after Delilah and the man, until he got to the doorway of the living room. He stayed in the shadows, just out of sight.

The ghostly reenactment of Bertram Kounis' murder started to play, and as soon as he saw the short, barrel-chested man attack Delilah's companion, he knew exactly who the attacker was. He went by a single name – Sveklá – and he was Cherngelanov 's right-hand man. Wouldn't be the first time he'd enforced someone to death. He would wait until Marti went to work, then leave her a note. That way he wouldn't be tempted to distraction.

After Marti left, he made a perimeter check. He couldn't really turn the doorknobs with his dog paws, so he looked out the windows, listened, and sniffed. The front and side yards were fine. Nobody but him was inside the house. Then he heard a tapping, as if someone was impatiently drumming his fingers on a table, coming from the back deck. He went to the door and looked out.

A tall man sat there on the deck. He had shoulder-length white hair and a patch over one eye. His blue shirt exactly matched the icy blue of his unobscured eye. The man seemed both ancient and vital, and Quinn knew he was not a human. But he wasn't fae, either. Quinn was sure he'd seen him at the Three Sister's Inn, when he was in the northlands with Halle.

"Are you just going to stand there, or are you going to let me in?" the man asked.

Two ravens swooped out of the oak tree to land on the table near him. Quinn was sure one of them was Halle, but he couldn't tell which one. He saw Eoin peek out from behind the pine tree, and Quinn gave a soft woof. Then he rushed to the guest room, shifted into human form and pulled on his clothes.

By the time he opened the door, two more ravens had joined the others.

"That's better," the man remarked. "I felt a bit odd talking to a dog. Do you always have to do that?"

"Do what, grandfather?" Quinn asked.

The man laughed. "No need to be so formal, fay. Do you always have to go and put on clothes when you shift into human form? Seems very tiresome to me. You may call me Vegtam, by the way." One of the ravens croaked, and he added, "Or Odin, if you prefer. Shall we go inside? It's blistering hot out here."

"Of course. It can't be helped. I am not able to maintain clothing between shifts."

The world was so cluttered with gods and goddesses that Quinn found it impossible to keep up with all of them. He had met Zeus once, but found him somewhat unlikeable. He'd heard of Odin – he was Halle's father, after all – but he didn't know very much about him.

As soon as the door closed behind them, the one raven who wasn't actually a raven, shifted into her human form.

"My father has news of the Frost Giants. It seems they have had another visitor besides Balcones," Halle said.

"Loki has escaped from his bondage," Odin said heavily. "If he succeeds in freeing his son, the wolf Fenrir, it will bring about Ragnarök."

Both Odin and Halle looked dour.

"That sounds bad," Quinn said.

"The end of the world usually is," Halle replied.

"It is not the end of the world," Odin said. "The world will be drowned in the sea, but it will eventually return, refreshed and fertile, ready for new gods and a new population."

"All humans and animals would die?" Quinn asked.

"Almost all of them," Odin said.

"And the gods?"

"Them, too. It is the fate of the world and it cannot be changed. But would you think me an old fool if I wished to delay it a while?" Odin said.

"Who would choose differently? Fate is what you make it," Quinn replied.

He wondered if Faery would be affected by a submerged Mundane world. As their fortunes were linked, he suspected it might, although there were plenty of natural disasters that affected the Mundane that had little or no impact on Faery. It was a discussion to be had with Dame Rowan, perhaps. But at a later date.

Odin's eye sparkled. A man who could smile in the face of his own annihilation was either incredibly brave, or seriously insane. But then again, perhaps being a god gave one more special privileges than he had thought.

"Loki might be a little annoyed about being bound with the intestines of his son and having a serpent hanging over his head, dripping burning venom on him, for the last millennium.

And he's very clever, more so that most people give him credit for," Odin said.

Quinn could understand why Loki would be displeased – what the god had just described sounded like a capricious and cruel punishment. Still, the jötnar weren't the types to go out of their way to help anybody. "Why would he go to the Frost Giants for help?"

"They're his relatives," Halle answered.

Quinn nodded. "So, where is this Fenrir? If we can snatch him, Loki will have to turn up sooner or later. And if we move the wolf to a location that suits us, all the better."

"Fenrir must not be unfettered! He would be the death of us all," Odin said.

Halle shot an alarmed glance at Odin, leading Quinn to believe that this discussion had come up before.

"Fair enough. What's your plan, then?" Quinn asked.

"Loki has many friends amongst the jötnar, fell dwarves and other evil peoples. It was the dwarves that forged Gleipnir, the impossible chain, that binds Fenrir. It cannot be broken or unmade, but it can be unfastened and untied."

"So we find Fenrir and set a trap for Loki?" Quinn asked.

"We must be very cunning to lure him out of hiding. He will be expecting a trap, and will look to turn the tables on us."

Quinn wondered if there was a way to kill two birds with one stone and capture both Loki and Balcones. He hoped so, because he was hard pressed to see a way to stop Loki and Balcones both separately and concurrently. He would leave Eoin, Aleksei, and Halle in place, guarding Marti, while he helped Odin stop Loki. If he wasn't stopped, Balcones wouldn't matter. What were Marti and Cassie's chances of surviving a drowned world? He had no guarantee that there would even be a safe place in Faery to take them to. Besides, he had a score to settle with the jötnar.

"Where do we start?" Quinn asked.

"We must go north, to see what is to be seen there," Odin answered.

"Let me have a word with my people, and I need to leave Marti a note."

Odin nodded.

Quinn told both Eoin and Aleksei what he had learned from Odin, and asked them to get word to MAMIC. Neither of them seemed too upset about missing an opportunity to participate in a surveillance mission in the ice and snow.

He had to hunt around to find a piece of notebook paper, but at last he found one that Cassie had scribbled on one side of in the recycling bin. He smiled to himself – Cassie would be quite a little artist soon. Even though it was all her fingers could do to grasp a crayon, she scribbled on everything she could find. Quinn located a pen and wrote a note to Marti.

Dear Marti,

I have to follow up on a lead. Eoin, Aleksei, and Halle are guarding you, even if you can't see them. Not sure when I'll be back, but I will return as soon as I possibly can.

You and Lulu are looking for a short, bald killer. He's an enforcer for Boris Cherngelanov's organization – goes by the name Sveklá. That's all the info I have on him.

Stay safe, and I'll see you soon,
Quinn

He stuck the note on the fridge with a magnet.

"Don't forget your coat," Halle said with a helpful smile.

"Right," Quinn answered, then trotted off to retrieve the jacket he'd brought back with him from his trip with Halle.

When Quinn returned to the kitchen, dressed for the cold, Halle and the other raven were already gone.

"I'm ready," he said.

He was already starting to sweat in the heavy coat. To save electricity, Marti kept the thermostat for her air conditioning at 80°F, so it was already uncomfortably warm.

"Wait," said Odin. "May I?" he asked, reaching for Quinn's belly.

Quinn didn't resist, but he wasn't enthusiastic as Odin opened Quinn's coat and lifted his shirt. He traced a symbol, something like a diamond with legs, around Quinn's navel.

Odin muttered some words Quinn didn't understand and the outline suddenly felt warm. Then it got uncomfortably hot as it glowed coppery red. Within a minute or two, the heat left the mark, and it turned a dull bronze.

"That should do it. Now you won't have to worry about keeping clothes available. Whatever you were wearing prior to your shift will still be there when you return to human form." He nodded, and tossed a handful of something that looked like leaves over their heads. Quinn coughed as the air entering his lungs went from stifling to freezing.

He found himself standing next to Odin on a snowy hillside, and an icy wind cut through his coat as if it wasn't even there. In front of them lay a narrow, sparkling alpine lake, with a rocky island in the middle of it. The rough beauty of the island was marred by an ugly structure crouching on it. A large white sign with red Cyrillic letters stood on the bank.

Odin huffed in disgust. "Runes I can read. This looks like the scratching of a chicken."

Quinn wished that Aleksei was here. The Ukrainian Lesovik was fluent in Russian. Not only could he read the sign, he'd probably be able to give a history and commentary about the building behind it. Quinn knew how to say, *hello*, *goodbye*, and *thank you*, in Russian. That wouldn't help him much if he tried to ask the locals about the island. On the other hand, the area seemed to be desperately short of locals. There wasn't even a road in sight.

Quinn looked out across the water. Covering most of the island, a low-slung building sprawled behind a razor wire fence, menacing the floating sheets of ice that intermittently drifted across the water. The building itself was not extraordinary – dingy white, one story, few windows. But Quinn felt a sense of foreboding as he looked at it, lurking in the middle of the lake like an ancient beast.

"What is that place?" he asked.

Odin's brow furrowed. "I am not sure. It has been long since I came to this lake, and there never was a building on the island before." Odin closed his eyes and took a few slow, deep breaths. "There is much unhappiness there, much sickness and death." One of the ravens croaked and flapped its wings. The other just sat on Odin's shoulder, feathers puffed out to ward off the cold.

"Muninn, go," Odin said to the bird.

He closed his eye as the bird took off, and Quinn watched a variety of expressions sweep across the old man's face. Then Quinn realized what he was doing. Odin was using the bird's eyes as his own.

"What do you see?" he asked.

"Not much worth looking at. Fences, building, pavement, trash, piles of snow," Odin said.

Quinn silently called for Malik. He knew the djinn was in the northlands watching the Frost Giants, so he would be close enough to hear him. Perhaps he could be of some use.

"Is there something I can help you with?" Malik's voice sounded loudly and suddenly in Quinn's ear.

Both he and Odin jumped.

"You know I hate when you do that," Quinn grouched.

Malik smiled broadly. "There is very little to do here. I must take my entertainment where I can."

Odin raised one eyebrow. But whether he was annoyed or entertained by Malik's sudden appearance was difficult to tell.

"Odin, Malik. Malik, Odin. How are the Frost Giants?"

"They seem to be waiting for something to happen," Malik said.

"Huh. That makes one more mystery for us." Quinn pointed to the island. "Can you find out what that building is?"

"I know what that building is. It is the Kola Correctional Colony, known colloquially as Bright Falcon Prison. It is for the worst of the worst offenders, and has the highest prisoner death rate of any facility in Russia."

"How do you know this?" asked Odin.

"Did I mention there isn't much to do around here?" Malik replied.

"What were you expecting to find here, Odin?" Quinn asked.

"Fenrir."

"So, the Aesir just left him chained to a rock in the middle of an island, and no one's ever thought to check on him now and again?" Quinn asked.

"There was no need. Gleipnir is unbreakable, and Ragnarök cannot be prevented," Odin replied.

"Well, now there's a big building where you left him. Maybe he's inside it," Quinn said.

"If humans had discovered a giant wolf chained to a rock, and put up a building over him, do you not think they would be selling tickets? Would there not be a bridge out to the island? And a flashing marquee?"

Odin had a point.

"Okay. Could they have killed him?" Quinn asked.

"No. It is not the fate of Fenrir to be slain by a mortal man."

"Could he have escaped? Or been set free?" Quinn asked.

"Ragnarök has not come to pass. Fenrir is still bound."

"What if the prophecy is wrong?" Malik asked.

Odin looked as if Malik had slapped him. "The prophecies have never been wrong."

"Then where is he?" Quinn asked.

"More importantly, does Loki know where he is?" Odin asked.

That was the $64,000 question. If Loki was already in custody of Fenrir, then there was little they could do to stave off Ragnarök.

"We must consult the Norns," Odin said.

"The who?" Quinn asked.

"The Three Sisters – they see the past, present and future. If any can tell us the whereabouts of Fenrir, it will be them."

"Before we go running off through the snow, why don't we see if Malik can take a look inside the building?"

Malik took a deep breath, and his eyelids fluttered. Minutes passed, or seemed to.

His breath rushed out in a loud gasp, and he jolted forward, nearly falling on his face.

"There is a wall…dark…heavy magick," he panted.

"Can you breach it?" Odin asked.

"Not without them knowing about it. They have set watchers on it. Evil things. I surmise they are the work of our friend, Balcones. They have a goetic feel to them." He shuddered and brushed his arms as if something was crawling on him.

Quinn turned back to Odin. "So. The Norns. Where do we find them?"

"Their cave is three days' walk from here," Odin said.

"What about those leafy bits you have? Can't you just use those to magick us there?" Quinn asked.

"Are you familiar with the concept of quantum entanglement?" Odin asked.

"The idea that two partner particles can affect each other at a distance," Malik answered.

"Exactly," Odin said. "Now, if you think about sewing two pieces of fabric together, you would put the two pieces so the right sides were facing each other, sew along at a set distance from the edge of the cloth, and then press open that seam allowance, the gap between the edge of the fabric and the stitching. The Mundane world is one piece of fabric, and the Magical world, or Faery, as you call it, is the other. We are standing in the seam allowance, where they overlap, and that is how humans were able to come to this place. The two worlds cast reflections and shadows upon one other, and that is how I am able to use the entangled particles to travel from one world to the other. These "leafy bits" are like a map. They enable the transference of my idea of the place I want to visit to the appropriate partner particles and envelop us in the interaction. But this map only works on particles in the corresponding alternate world."

"So that would be a no, then. I doubt we have three days. Malik, can you zap us there?"

Malik looked skyward and put on a strained smile. "Of course."

The wind swirled around them, picking up snow and pebbles in what humans would call a dust devil. Quinn shut his eyes against the blowing debris, and when the wind stopped a moment later, he found himself outside the mead hall where he had stayed with Halle.

"What is this place?" Malik asked.

"It is the *Three Sisters Inn*. Think of it as a way station owned and operated by the Norns. They keep many treasures and artifacts here. Follow me," Odin said.

He strode off into the forest, and Quinn had difficulty keeping up with him. Fortunately, they did not have to go far into the trees to come to a boulder-strewn cave entrance. Odin stopped just inside the opening. The cavern was large, and calcite glimmered like stone tree roots in the flickering light of a fire.

"Urd? Verdandi? Skuld? Are you about?" Odin called.

A woman in a long dress and red cloak stepped from the utter blackness at the cave's throat. Her face was hidden by a hood, but her eyes glimmered from the shadow with the same green fire as Halle's.

"Greetings, Allfather," she said.

"Greetings to you, Urd," Odin said. "We seek the advice of the wise."

"Then you have come to the right place," said another female voice.

She emerged from the dark and stood by her sister. She wore a green cloak over her dress, with the hood also covering her head.

"Greetings, Verdandi," Odin said. "Will not Skuld join us as well?"

"She will not," Verdandi replied.

"Very well. The two of you know more than enough, I'm sure, to help us."

"Then follow," Urd said.

She turned and headed into the darkness at the back of the cave. Verdandi followed. Quinn and Malik looked at each other, then followed Odin into the gloom.

Wrought iron sconces held the torches that lit their way as they walked carefully down a rough-hewn path that wound into the deep heart of the cave. The air was chilly, and bordered on dank. After a while, the trail flattened out, and they came to an underground river. An arched bridge, made of white stones, curved over the clear water, and Quinn was sure he glimpsed the heavy scaled tale of a dragon resting in the stream.

The path sloped downward again, and now the air began to get drier and warmer. Up ahead of them, an orange glow spilled out of a smaller cavern.

As they entered it, Quinn saw that there were shelves on the walls of the chamber, and a triangular wooden table with three chairs stood to one side. In the middle was a well, built from dry-stacked stones. The orange glow came from the walls - there were no fires, torches, or lights that Quinn could see.

"The Well of Fate," Urd said, nodding to Quinn and Malik.

She turned the crank handle and brought up a bucket, then ladled some of the water into a black onyx bowl. After she emptied the bucket back into the well, she carried the bowl and set it in the middle of the table. She sat in one chair, and Verdandi sat in another. Their eyes glowed green under their hoods as they stared into the water.

At last, Verdandi spoke.

"The eyes of Fenrir see neither sun nor moon. The sword of Tyr has been removed from his jaws; he feasts on the wicked, and he grows more fell and strong, adding their evil to his own. Gleipnir yet binds him to the great rock Gjöll, though sun and snow touch it not."

"He feasts on the wicked," Malik said to Quinn.

"You said Bright Falcon prison had an unusually high death rate," Quinn replied. He shuddered. "I guess we know why."

"That is a cruel punishment, even for humans," Odin said.

"Can they give us a hint on what Loki is planning?" Quinn asked, glancing at the Norns.

"Possibly," Odin replied. " Urd sees all of the past, Verdandi sees all of the present."

"And Skuld sees all of the future?" Malik asked. "Should we be concerned that she declined to participate in this discussion?"

"Skuld has her own reasons for doing as she does," Verdandi said. "Would you know your own fate? Perhaps a defeat brings tools for a future victory, and a victory brings with it the seeds of your own destruction. If you knew, would you try to change that, even if these things must happen for the greater good?"

"Fate is a tricky thing," Quinn said. He was not a strong believer in fate, but he wasn't about to argue with the Norns about it.

Verdandi nodded, and he wondered if she knew his thoughts.

"If you would look for Sigyn, Allfather, you will find her in Asgard, in her old abode," she said to Odin.

"Thank you," he said. Turning to Quinn and Malik, he said, "We must plan. Let us take ourselves to the inn to quench our thirsts while we do so."

Cornelia smiled at Quinn as he, Odin, and Malik came through the heavy wooden door of the Three Sisters Inn.

Because he didn't require food, Malik scanned the sparse crowd while Quinn and Odin ordered at the bar.

"I don't know when we will have the opportunity for another repast. We might as well fill our stomachs while we plan," Odin said, nearly tipping over the wooden bench as he sat down. "I will speak with Sigyn. She may or may not help us."

"Who is Sigyn?" Malik asked.

"Loki's wife."

"Why would she help us?" Quinn said, raising an eyebrow.

"It was Loki's fault their son was killed. She spent a very long time helping him by collecting the dripping snake venom, and for her trouble, he abandoned her. Besides, she is Aesir. She will fight on the side of the gods at Ragnarök."

"Prophecy?" Quinn asked.

"Yes," Odin answered, his eyes narrowing.

"Well, we also need to watch Bright Falcon and the jotnär," Quinn said. "And I think Bright Falcon being an island makes it just about perfect for me to keep an eye on."

Odin nodded.

"Presumably, that leaves me with the jotnär. Again. How exciting," Malik said.

After a warning look from Quinn, he added, "Not that I mind the Frost Giants. They're very…sparkly."

Cornelia arrived with a tray, bearing tankards of mead, salmon for Quinn, and roast meat for Odin.

"Thank you, Cornelia," Quinn said, then quickly looked at his food. Knowing how she'd been brutalized, he was almost afraid to talk to her, finding it difficult to strike a balance between friendly and distant without coming off as patronizing.

"Are you well, my dear?" Odin asked her.

She nodded, smiling shyly. Then she removed one more thing from the tray and set it on the table.

Odin laughed. "Clever girl!" he said.

Quinn looked at the object. It was a stoppered glass jar filled with a deep red liquid.

"What is that?" he asked.

"Bodin," Odin said, nodding for emphasis.

"And what is a Bodin?" Malik asked.

Odin looked disappointed by the question. "It contains some of Kvasir's blood, of course!"

Quinn grimaced.

"And that would be useful in what way?" Malik asked.

"Kvasir was able to find Loki when no one else could," Odin replied.

"As enchanting as a bottle of his blood may be, how does that help us?" Malik asked.

"Like this," Odin said.

He pulled out the stopper and poured a few drops into his drink and another into Quinn's.

"Oh, I really wish you hadn't done that," Quinn said.

The taste of human blood had always made him nauseous. The smell of it was bad enough, when Odin opened the jar, but having it in his drink was too much.

"What's wrong with a little blood?" Odin asked.

Quinn recalled the blood sausages that Halle had eaten with gusto the last time he was here, and the salmon in front of him suddenly lost its appeal.

"The blood of Kvasir makes you very clever, perhaps smart enough to catch Loki," Odin said, then drained his tankard.

"I don't think I can drink that," Quinn said.

"Of course you can," said Odin, his voice stern. "Would you risk bringing on Ragnarök because you're afraid of a little blood? What kind of monster are you?"

An image of Marti and Cassie, smiling and happy, unaware of a boiling wall of water rolling up behind them, flashed into his mind. Quinn picked up the tankard and glared at Odin. "I am *not* a monster."

Then he drank the blood-laced mead in one draught. He gagged a little afterward, but it stayed down.

"What are you looking at?" he snapped at Malik, who was unsuccessfully suppressing a smirk.

Odin guffawed and pounded his fist on the table. Cornelia shrank away from him, and he turned and softly said something to her.

Quinn did not understand what he said. Perhaps because he wasn't really listening. He suddenly felt strange, like his mind split into halves. One half was looking out of his eyes and was inside the Three Sisters with Odin and Malik. The other seemed to be looking out of a completely different space in his skull, perhaps even above it. Information from other channels was flooding in, overloading his brain. He couldn't make sense of anything, so he closed his eyes and rested his face in his hands to block out the stream.

"I see a flood
Sound, knowledge, and sight
Drinking Kvasir's blood
Has caused this blight," Quinn said.

"What did you just say?" Malik asked, incredulous.

"Poetry," Odin answered, "is sometimes a side effect. Kvasir was known for it, you see." Laughter was in his voice, even if it wasn't on his face.

Quinn shook his head, but remained silent.

Cornelia removed Bodin and carried it away on her serving tray, leaving the men to eat and plan.

Even with his hand over his eyes, Quinn couldn't stop the flow of information. Where was it all coming from? Was it the thoughts of other people?

"I now see double
And speak in rhyme.
Need to stop this vision trouble.
Will be poet for all time?" Quinn said.

"The rhyming should stop in a day or two, as you start to adjust," Odin replied. "The third eye vision is not permanent. Usually. You will have to learn to focus on one stream or the other. With practice, you can learn to narrow it, although I do not think it is possible to shut it off altogether. It rarely lasts longer than seven years, or shorter than seven days."

Quinn gave up covering his face – it wasn't really helping anyway. He picked at his salmon, and speared a caper with his fork. He put it in his mouth.

He had the sense of growing, hot sun shining on his skin, his body swelling, getting ready to burst. Being picked from the branch, washed and sunk in vinegary brine, with a thousand others just like him. He was the caper.

Quinn blinked and shook his head. He was back to himself. Curious, he took a bite of the salmon. He felt himself swimming up a river, battling the chilly currents, twisting and leaping up rapids. On the one hand, he felt bad for eating it. On the other, it would have lost its life for nothing if he spurned it now. More out of duty than hunger, he ate every bite of it, even a few of the bones.

As he chewed, he tried focusing on Odin, who had been talking the whole time.

"In Asgard, I can retrieve my horse, Sleipnir. I will send word ahead for him to be fetched. Once I have spoken with Sigyn, I may have a better feel for what Loki is up to. I can send word by my ravens, Huginn or Muninn, to both of you, if need be. Then I will return to Lake Amsvartnir where Bright Falcon now stands on Lyngvi Island. And I will bring reinforcements," Odin said, between mouthfuls. When he finished he wiped his greasy hands on the tablecloth and grunted.

"Malik, would you be good enough to zap us to where we need to go?" Quinn asked.

A breeze twirled around the three of them, and Quinn found himself alone on the banks of what Odin knew as Amsvartnir Lake.

Quinn pulled his coat around him more tightly. He walked nearly half-way around his side of the island, looking for a good place to enter the water where the view from Bright Falcon was obstructed. Gratitude for Odin's gift of the ability to keep his clothes on between shifts made him smile. Quinn didn't fancy the idea of running around naked on the chilly beach, and the idea of putting on frozen underpants made him shiver. He looked around, on the off chance that there was anyone watching. He was standing in a swale, and mostly hidden by large rocks. He hoped he wouldn't have to do anything other than shift to maintain the clothes, and he wondered if they would be wet or dry when he came out of the water. He was about to find out. At least changing into his normal form would get his mind off his poetry predicament. Kelpies didn't speak.

He took another look around and ran out to the lake, wading in and swapping one form for another at the same time. The cold water was sharp and refreshing. It felt good to dive deeply and swim hard. He paddled, all underwater but his head, around the island. There was a helipad and some large radio and satellite antennae on the far side of the building. A kennel, with twelve dog runs that Quinn could see, stood empty. He suspected he knew why. If you have one giant dog, why do you need any smaller ones?

Chapter 12
Hard Time and Hardware

Hadrian frowned at the pad of paper on his desk, tapping it with the end of his pen. "How can that be?" he asked the technician at the other end of line.

"Maybe he has a twin?"

"Maybe. I'll have to look into that. Thanks, Penny. I owe you lunch for getting this back so fast."

If she was keeping track, he probably owed her twenty lunches by now. "Sure thing," she said, and hung up.

He tapped the Bluetooth set on his ear and looked at his notes. CODIS had identified the DNA in the blood sample he'd taken from the wall outside the Tenth Sphere as belonging to a felon named Terrance Ogilvey. The only problem with that was that Terrance Ogilvey's last known address was in Forest Glen Cemetery in northwest Houston.

Starting with arrest records, Hadrian traced Ogilvey's short life. He'd started out as a juvenile, minor stuff – malicious mischief, trespassing, breaking and entering. But as he got older, he became more violent. Aggravated robbery, assault with a deadly weapon, and multiple counts of grand theft auto. He'd been a busy boy to rack up all of that by twenty-three.

After his last stint in County, his parents had sent him to a residential treatment program for disordered personalities, run by a Dr. Grigori Pavlov. Unless that was more than one psychiatrist named Grigori Pavlov, that would be the doctor who was killed last week in a hit and run traffic accident. With Marti Keller's car. Curiouser and curiouser.

Unfortunately, the week after he'd been released from the program, Terrance Olgivey's car was found crashed into a bridge abutment. According to the medical examiner's report, Terry had suffered extensive head trauma and probably died instantly. His body was identified by his clothes, a wolf tattoo on his hand, and a class ring that he always wore.

Hadrian next hit vital statistics. And he also hit a wall. Terrance Olgilvey had been adopted, and his records were sealed. It would take some time to get a court order, and he considered requesting an exhumation while he was at it. He had only been dead three years, so viable DNA should be recoverable. He was beginning to suspect that instead of a twin, Terry had a ringer. A dead ringer, that was. A DNA identification had not been run on the corpse, and with the massive body trauma, a match was the only way to prove whether the person in Terry's grave was actually Terry. Before he started on the paperwork, he would call Terry's parents and see if there was, indeed a twin. Maybe they'd tell him enough that he wouldn't need to get the records unsealed. Still, he hated making those kinds of calls, so he put it off for a few minutes by taking a restroom break.

"Hello?" a man's voice said.

"Mr. Ogilvey?" Hadrian asked.

"Who's this?" the words were curt.

"Sir, I am Special Agent Hadrian Galanti. I'm trying to find out some information about your son, Terrance."

"Terrance is dead."

"Yes, sir. And I'm very sorry for your loss."

"I'm not. Don't tell my wife I said that. That kid was nothing but trouble from the get-go. I told her we should have gotten a baby, and not a three year old."

"I'm sorry you had that experience." Sometimes the best way to get information was to sympathize and shut up.

"He had something-or-another Attachment Disorder. Whatever it was, he was a psychopath. After he set the house on fire, I wanted to send him back to Russia, but my wife wouldn't hear of it."

"That must have been hard for you. Do you remember where in Russia he came from?"

"Does it matter?"

"Well, it's important for a case that I'm working on. I need to find out if he has a twin brother."

"God help us all if he does. I really don't know. He wasn't introduced with one, but that doesn't necessarily mean anything." Ogilvey thought for a moment. "The name of the place in English was Three Grannies. I don't know what that translates to in Russian."

Hadrian did. It was Tri Babushkas. "Thank you, Mr. Ogilvey. You've been extremely helpful."

"Sure, no problem. If there's another one like Terrance running around out there, I hope you get him."

"Yes, sir."

Hadrian tapped the Bluetooth and hung up.

Why don't I get interns like Sara does? he wondered as he started on the exhumation request. And when he was done with that, he needed to shovel through the mountain of paperwork on his desk. At the top of his list was getting a surveillance warrant for the cozy little group at the Tenth Sphere. He needed to know why supposedly dead Odessa gang members were hanging out there.

Aside from the household staff, Irina and Sveklá were alone in the massive villa that dominated Boris' one and a half acre fiefdom.

"Shall we watch a movie?" Irina asked, pouring two shots of vodka. She handed one to Sveklá, and her fingers brushing his almost caused him to drop the glass.

"I suppose," he replied, turning away from her so she wouldn't notice the effect her touch had had on him.

She turned the television on and turned up the volume. The house was bugged. Her husband trusted no one. Still, all of the security cameras were at the estate's gate and perimeters. It was just as dangerous for Boris to risk being photographed with some of his business associates as it was for them to associate with him.

Irina sat down on the white leather couch next to Sveklá, a little too close for his comfort. He drained his glass.

"How are the children, Sergei?" she asked, her low voice barely audible above the blaring television.

"Coming along well. Feliks broke into Latvian bank last week without detection. His fighting skills need work. He is almost ready. Others, doing good for age."

The thinnest of smiles lifted the corners of Irina's mouth. "I have heard from Vitali," she whispered.

"And what does Vitali say?" he whispered back.

Vitali had not run away from Babushkas with them. He had been sick, and too thin, too weak, to make the escape. The three of them only barely survived the ordeal, frozen and starved nearly to skeletons by the end. But with Vitali, they shared a bond that could only be forged at a place like Tri Babushkas. He had stayed in Russia, and built a thriving business smuggling military hardware out to the highest bidder.

"The opium cartel in Afganistan wishes to counter any drone incursions over their poppy fields. They are very interested in obtaining a MiG-35. Vitali can acquire one in India. We would get a twenty percent finder's fee."

What she was suggesting amounted to treason. If she had planned to tell her husband, she wouldn't have used the TV to cover their voices. If Sveklá knew what was good for him, he would leave the room now. "Twenty percent of how much?" he asked.

"Thirty-five million, for just the plane. Forty with pilot."

Sveklá sucked in his breath. He could retire and live quite well on his share of that. No more killing. He was getting too old for it, anyway.

"We could leave here. Together. Perhaps bring Feliks, and start our own organization."

"We could never leave. Every hired killer in world would be after price our heads. And it would be huge price, bol'shoi price."

Irina's large eyes filled with tears. "I don't care. Death would be better than this gilded prison. I am tired of being humiliated and mocked, treated worse than dog."

Sveklá's jaw clenched, holding in the white-hot flash of anger. He could not bear to see Irina so miserable. "Perhaps, then, we should not be the ones to leave."

"Oh, Sergei! You are my hero."

Pleasure shot through Sveklá's body, melting him like a bolt of lightning as Irina suddenly straddled his lap and kissed him hard, her warm tongue parting his lips.

Chapter 13
Doggone

"Bruce?" I called hopefully into the backyard.

A bird flicked through the shrubs. At least I think that's what it was. What else would it be, so close to the birdbath? But that was the only response to my call.

It's not like he's an ordinary dog, running off to chase cars and get run over. But he was still gone, and I had no idea what had happened to him. Knowing that there was a demon after him, it made me nervous about his welfare. *What if Balcones had come and snatched him right out of my house?*

Surely he would have left a note if he had been called away. I had a good look around, checking the fridge and all of the mirrors, the kitchen table, my pillow, any place where I thought he might leave a note. If he had, I couldn't find it.

Cassie had been asleep for a couple of hours, and I was trying to distract myself with the TV. It wasn't unusual for Quinn to disappear for days at a time, but it was unusual for him not to tell me he was going.

There was a quiet knock on my back door just after ten. I flipped on the light and saw Halle standing there, blinking in the sudden glare. I opened the door, nervous that she was bringing bad news.

"Halle? What's up?" I tried to sound casual as I moved out of the way so she could come inside.

She didn't move. "Quinn had urgent business – there was news about the jötnar situation."

"I see. Did he say when he might be back?"

Halle shrugged. "I do not know if he will be back. He also has some family obligations he needs to attend to."

"Family obligations," I echoed. *What kind of family obligations?*

"Yes. I saw your light on, thought you might have some concerns, since he just took off and left you." She shook her head ever so slightly, almost as if out of pity.

"I was surprised he didn't at least leave a note," I said out loud, although it was less for Halle's benefit than for mine.

"You didn't find one?"

"No."

Halle shrugged again, then dodged out of the way of a fat June bug on a kamikaze mission to the porch light.

"It would be best for you to recognize that this relationship could never have worked. Be glad of the memories, but move on to someone more suitable for you. A fellow human, perhaps." She nodded and patted my shoulder. "Time for me to leave," she said. "Sleep well."

She stepped off the deck, out the anemic circle of light, and was swallowed by the darkness.

Time to leave the conversation, or to leave town? I wouldn't be unhappy to never see her again, but on the other hand, Quinn wasn't around to protect us from Balcones, either. *English is not her first language. That's all.*

But what about Quinn's "family obligations?" That could mean a lot of things, I assured myself. Like maybe visiting his sick mother in the hospital. But supposing it meant taking his wife out for her birthday. Had I misinterpreted the cues he was giving me? It had seemed pretty obvious that he was available and interested in being with both me and Cassie. I reminded myself that both Lulu and Delilah had said, over and over, "You can't trust a shifter." Had I really been so stupid?

I told myself I wouldn't cry. No reason to jump to conclusions. I wanted to hear it from Quinn's own lips, if we were finished. If he came back. After all, I had known him for only a few weeks. And he had saved my life. More than once. But maybe he was just acting in a professional capacity. Nick, and Ryan, when he was alive, saved damsels in distress all the time, and it didn't mean they wanted to run off and live happily ever after with them. I was a little unclear on what, exactly, Quinn's job was, but I did know it was all about catching demons and righting wrongs. Maybe my thinking that his protecting me was personal was a mistake. Although, when he kissed me, that was far from professional.

I dabbed at my eyes with a paper towel and blew my nose.

Well, at least Lulu and Delilah would be happy to hear he was gone, and maybe never coming back. I guess I could tell Aiden and Kyle that someone had left the gate open and Bruce had run away. It wasn't really a lie.

Dammit. How could he do that to Cassie and me? Was it something I did (or didn't do?), or was he just a jerk? Or was this just a big misunderstanding?

I snapped off the TV and got in the shower. I shampooed my hair, then stood under the showerhead until the hot water was gone. I was still emotionally fragile after Ryan's death, even after almost two years. This was not helping.

On Wednesday, I found I had no real appetite, for either food or doing things. I fed Cassie and gave her a bath. But we skipped our morning walk. I almost never watched daytime television. But I did today. Theoretically, I just had it on while I was folding a basket of laundry, but it took me all day to fold Cassie's clothes.

I should have taken a shower on Thursday before I went to work. But I didn't. Didn't go for a walk, either, so it probably evened out.

"Are you okay?" Lulu asked when I walked in the door. "You look peaked, honey."

"Yeah. Think it might be a virus or something. Just felt kind of pep-less the last couple of days."

Lulu chewed on her bottom lip as she studied my face. "Do you think you'll be up for Circle tonight? It might make you feel a lot better."

"Doubt it. Childcare issues."

"Belinda would love to stay with Cassie. Her grandkids are all at camp, and she's missing them something awful."

"Fine. Have her come by about a quarter of so I can show her where everything is."

The shop wasn't Saturday morning busy, but it was really busy for a Thursday afternoon. That was good — kept my mind from dwelling on Quinn.

Belinda showed up on my doorstep at 6:30. Cassie was delighted to see her and started babbling away as soon as Belinda stepped inside.

After I had given her the grand tour, and she and Cassie settled in the living room, Belinda turned to me and said, "So…where is Bruce?"

"Good question. There was some movement on his case, and he had to go check on it. Or something like that." I was still feeling a little touchy about Quinn leaving without so much as a Post-it note on the mirror. I doubted "news about the jötnar" was likely to be such an emergency that he had to drop everything and go that instant.

"I see," she said. "Is he coming back?"

"Not sure."

Belinda hesitated before responding. Perhaps measuring her words, perhaps having a conversation with someone I couldn't see. I had no idea whether Belinda could see ghosts or not, but I assumed she could.

"Whatever happens," she said, finally, "it will be for the best."

"I hope you're right. My cell, my mom's numbers, and Emily and Nick's numbers are all on the fridge, if you need anything at all."

"We'll be fine. Don't you worry about us." Belinda smiled so confidently that I couldn't help but believe her.

"Okay. I'll see you soon." I gave Cassie a hug and a kiss and headed out.

Although Lulu had done the cleansing ritual and earthy sage smoke lingered in the air, the energy in the room was prickly and unpleasant. Lulu seemed particularly distracted. I don't know if was more about Benjamin's predicament, or Ellen's deteriorating condition — she'd looked awful when she came by the shop Tuesday.

Our focus tonight was on table tipping. As far as I knew, that was something that was popular during the Spiritualism movement of the nineteenth and early twentieth centuries. And I also thought that many, maybe most, of those séances were famous for being based on trickery, so I was a little puzzled that Lulu would have us do this.

There were two round wooden tables, and Lulu put five folding chairs at each one. I ended up being awkwardly sandwiched between Marilyn and Hunter Greene. Again. She was clearly trying to flirt with him — she kept bumping into him, touching his hand, and based on the way he was squirming, his knee. He, just as clearly, wasn't interested.

Two other women had joined our table. I'd seen them before at Circle, but didn't really know them.

"Hi, I'm Melissa. I don't think we've been formally introduced," the older of them said.

"I'm Marti," I replied.

Hunter stood up and extended his hand to Melissa. "I'm Hunter — I just moved to Houston from Virginia. I was really surprised to find a group like this just down the road from me."

"Welcome to town, Hunter," the other woman said. "I'm Savannah. Melissa's my mom."

"Would you believe he just moved in across the street from me?" I asked, mostly to needle Savannah for ignoring me.

Even so, the image of Hunter standing in his garage, sweat glistening on his naked chest, popped into my mind.

"You don't say," she replied, unimpressed.

"Alright, ladies and gentleman," Lulu said, standing up at her table. "Let's get started. What I want everyone to do is put their hands on the table, palms down. Your pinkies should touch the pinkies of the people on each side of you. I'll lead this table, and Melissa, if you wouldn't mind leading the other table?"

Melissa nodded.

Lulu dimmed the lights so that it was nearly dark. A candle flickered in each corner of the room, casting uneven shadows that danced on the walls and slid eerily across the faces of the people at the tables. Hunter's hand was warm against mine, and I missed Quinn. Marilyn's hand was icy, and it reminded me of Halle.

"I know that Marilyn and Savannah have done table tipping before. How about you two?" Melissa asked, looking from Hunter to me.

I shook my head. I had played *Light as a Feather* at a slumber party once and gotten totally creeped out when Sara Grace Jackson really did seem to levitate. But I didn't want to talk about it.

"My sister and I used to try it, with some of her friends. But it was a long time ago, and we never really had much success," Hunter said.

"I see. Good to know," Melissa said. "Now, Marti, what's going to happen is that I'm going to ask for any spirits who would like to communicate with us to come and move the table. Sometimes, the table jumps around like a March hare, and sometimes, nobody shows up. You never know how it's going to go until someone, or something, manifests."

Melissa took a deep breath, then exhaled dramatically. I didn't know what her day job was, but it seemed that she was a natural for the theater.

With eyes closed, she said, "Are there any clean spirits here who wish to communicate with us? Those with harmful intent are not welcome here. We are seekers of truth and light."

Delilah, arms crossed, appeared behind Melissa. She rolled her eyes and her head swiveled ever so slightly from side to side. If I didn't know better, I might have thought she was listening to music.

"Girlfriend, you know this is almost as bad as using an Ouija Board, right?" Delilah said.

How's that?

"You wouldn't go to the mall and ask random strangers to come on over to your house, now would you? That's what most people do with Ouija Boards. This ain't a whole lot different. If you're not real careful, ya'll'll have lower astrals all up in this place. And they're a bitch to get rid of, worse than roaches."

I shuddered. Anybody who's spent more than twenty four hours in Houston has probably encountered the two inch long flying cockroaches that like to play chicken by swooping right at people's faces.

Why don't you do something then, so that Melissa quits calling for someone to come?

"Fine. You ought to be real grateful, girl, for the stuff I do for you."

"Up!" Melissa demanded. "Up!"

Marilyn and Savannah joined her in chanting "Up!"

I looked at Hunter. He gave me a slight shrug and joined them. As weird as it felt, I added my voice to the mantra.

I felt the table vibrate as Delilah reached out and grabbed the edge of it. She jerked it up and down a few times, then moved to the other side, between Marilyn and I, where she lifted the table slowly for an inch or two and held it.

"It's working!" Marilyn said. "I can feel the spirit moving around us!"

"Shhh! We have to keep the focus on the table. Up!" Melissa said.

Any updates on Bertram Kounis? Or is he still cocooning? I thought at Delilah, hoping that there might be some news.

"No. He's still the same. He –" Delilah stopped suddenly.

I followed her gaze across the room. A shadow, clearly defined by the candlelight, stood against the wall. I suddenly felt cold. There was no one standing up to cast the shadow.

"Now see? That is exactly what I meant. It probably ain't strong enough to cross Lulu's barrier she laid down with that smudge stick, but we better keep an eye on it all the same."

We?

"Yes. I'm busy tippin' tables, remember?"

Delilah jiggled the table around for the next twenty minutes or so, until Lulu turned the lights back up. I watched the shadow prowl around the outer edges of the room, but it never approached the tables.

Lulu broke the circle, and we all filed downstairs. The hibiscus iced tea she had made for refreshments was just what I needed. I was eating a lemon gingersnap cookie bar when Lulu pulled me aside.

"Are you available to work an event on Saturday a week?"

"Maybe. What is it?"

"Charity fundraising gala. Benefits orphans. It should be a really big event, and I think it will take all three of us."

I brushed crumbs off of my chin. "Wow. But I don't have an outfit, if I can't borrow Belinda's."

"Oh, honey. I have the perfect outfit for you. I think you'll like it much better than Belinda's, anyway. And," she said, "your share would be $500.00. Plus tips."

"I'll see if Mom is available."

Conversation disappeared with the tea and cookies. The Circle attendees drifted out of the shop, until only Marilyn, Hunter, and I remained.

"You know, Hunter," Marilyn said, twisting a lock of hair around her finger, "I'm going to see that new play at Mainstreet Theater tomorrow. I think there might be a few tickets left, if you're interested in going. Maybe we could even meet for dinner before the show." She pressed a slip of paper with a phone number on it into his hand.

He held onto the paper, too polite to throw it away, yet unwilling to put it in his pocket. "I'm sorry, Marilyn. I already have plans for tomorrow. Hope you enjoy the play."

Looked to me like he needed an intervention.

"Hey, neighbor," I said.

"Hey."

"I was just wondering, since it's a little late, and you live just across the street, if you wouldn't mind walking home with me?"

"No problem. I don't mind at all. Just let me know when you're ready."

"I'm pretty much ready now. Just let me get rid of my trash." I threw my paper cup and plate into the bin.

I smiled at Marilyn. "Good night. See you next time."

She gave me the stink eye.

"Night, honey," Lulu said. "I'll come pick up Belinda in a few minutes. Hope Miss Cassie hasn't worn her out."

Lulu locked the door behind us, and Hunter and I started back into the neighborhood.

"You looked like you needed a rescue," I said.

"I did." He chuckled. "Thanks."

"Just one of the many services I offer."

"Excuse me?" He said, shooting me a quizzical look.

"Wow. That came out totally wrong." I hoped the streetlight wasn't bright enough to show how red my cheeks were. "My other services include sarcasm and general wisecrackery."

"Good to know." Hunter smiled, and I hoped that it wasn't because he was trying not to laugh at me.

"So where are the best places to get a quick bite around here? Sometimes I work late and I don't have time to cook."

"You cook? What's your specialty?"

"My specialty? Hmmm. Not sure I have one, but I make a mean pumpkin gnocchi."

"Not sure I've ever had pumpkin gnocchi."

I liked Hunter's smile, I decided.

"Maybe I'll bring you some next time I make a batch. My original college major was hotel and restaurant management, so I went to cooking school."

"Does that make it hard when you go out to eat?"

"Sometimes."

"Well, there's a pretty good cluster of restaurants on the south side of I10 and Highway 6. Most people don't realize what all is back there, but the food is good, and they stay crowded. You just have to know when to go, if you want to get in."

"Maybe you can show me sometime."

"Sure."

I noticed that we were almost at my house. "I guess this is my stop. Thanks for walking me back. See you around."

Hunter waved slightly. "Yeah. Take it easy."

I fished around my purse for my keys. They weren't in their normal pocket. Instead, I found them underneath my wallet. Suddenly, I stopped. *Had I just agreed to go to dinner with Hunter?*

Chapter 14
A Woman Scorned

The sky was a serene cerulean and the weather was shatteringly crisp when Quinn heard a couple of horses approaching at the gallop. He turned his head toward the sound as the riders came flying down to the lake. There were two riders, but only one horse. Odin's grey horse, the eight-legged Sleipnir, carried them both.

Quinn swam up as close as he comfortably could to the beach. The grey horse stopped and snorted, all four forelegs splayed and head raised.

"Easy, Slippy," Odin said. "He's a friend."

The horse looked unconvinced, with his nostrils flaring and ears pricked forward. But he made no effort to bolt. Odin kicked his right leg over the horse's neck so he was facing Quinn and slid ungracefully to the ground. He turned to help the woman, who was tucked behind the saddle, to dismount.

She was tall, at least six feet, and her shoulder-length blonde hair was dull and flat.

"This is Sigyn," Odin said. "Wife of Loki."

Quinn dipped his head. Kelpies did not smile, and even if they did, the result would be far from reassuring.

Sigyn looked at him impassively. Her eyes were the same feldspar grey as the surrounding rocks, and just as lifeless.

Odin touched her arm. "Please tell Quinn what you have told me."

She sighed slightly, resigned to do as she was told.

"As you may know, when my husband Loki was bound, a serpent was suspended over him to drip venom onto his bare skin. It burned him, so I caught it in a large bowl, to lessen his suffering. From time to time, the bowl would fill up, so I had to empty it.

"In the beginning, I just poured the venom into a ravine, but after so many years of doing so, a lake has formed. Nothing can survive there. The trees and grasses are blasted, and even birds which fly above it succumb to its vapors. Skadi has much to answer for tapping the venom of such a pernicious serpent to torment Loki."

Odin shifted his weight slightly away from her, perhaps feeling the heat of her anger at the Aesir.

"There was a group of men," she continued, "climbers they called themselves, who stumbled across my path. I was unaware that they had followed me. But while I emptied the bowl, the bitter liquid dripped down from the serpent's jaws upon my bound husband," and she said the last word through clenched teeth, "and such was his torment that his screams echoed from the rocks far and wide. Even as I returned and held up the bowl to catch the serpent's poison, they came creeping from behind the rocks.

"'Free me!' Loki begged of them.

"He knew that as mortal men, they were not bound by the enchantment that prevented the bonds from being severed by either Aesir or jötnar.

"'What will you give me?' asked their leader.

"'Life. And wealth. You will survive Ragnoräk, and I will show you hidden hordes of treasure.'

"The climbers spoke amongst themselves in a tongue that was foreign to me.

"'I know who you are,' said the leader. 'I have heard the legend of the great god Loki who was bound with the entrails of his son for insulting the gods, and who shakes the mountains in his pain. But I also know you are a trickster. You offer us treasure for your freedom, but how can we be sure you will keep your word?'

"'Take my wife as a hostage,' Loki replied.

"He offered me up as a hostage without the bat of an eyelash, after I had spent centuries aiding and comforting him," Sigyn said, her voice edged in bitterness.

"'I have heard your reputation for many infidelities, and I fear I cannot trust your dedication to your wife,' the leader replied.

"'Release me, and I will ensure you each have a berth on the ship Naglfar when the world drowns.'

"The men talked among themselves, and finally accepted this pledge. They used their climbing axes to cut the bonds that held the great serpent and set it free to slither into the rocks.

"Then they released Loki. He laughed, and the sound of it was wild and fey. Even the crows roosting in the valley flew shrieking into the air with the fear of it.

"'Now,' Loki said, 'shall I have my revenge! The prophecies foretell that my Fenrir shall swallow that loathsome Odin and put an end to him.'

"He turned and spat upon the rock on which he had long been chained. 'Time to go.'

"The men left me on the mountain without so much as a backward glance from Loki. All these years," Sigyn said. "I stayed with him and sacrificed everything, trying to ease his misery. And this is how he repays me?"

Her eyes were pink-tinged and puffy. It was obvious that she had shed all the tears she was going to over him.

"And his plan?" Odin prompted.

"Of this he has spoken much during his confinement. He said that to sever Gleipnir, the impossible chain, he would need an impossible blade. He would seek out the dwarves who created Gleipnir and offer them a price to secure its undoing. He is most likely searching for the impossible items they have tasked him with retrieving."

"It is a pity," Odin said, "that you have no idea what those items might be."

Sigyn bowed her head.

"I am sending Thor to the dwarves that are most friendly to us, so see if they can ken what these impossible items might be," said Odin.

Quinn wished that he could ask Sigyn what the climbers looked like, so he might recognize them if they came to Bright Falcon. He shook his head in frustration. Since he couldn't speak, he tried focusing his enhanced perception on Sigyn. The ability was starting to fade, and it was already diluted in his kelpie form, but it might be enough.

He closed his eyes and breathed in deeply, slowly. An image filtered into his consciousness: five men dressed in various colors of snug spandex shirts, cargo pants, mountaineering harnesses, helmets and gloves. One of the men was in front of the group, clearly the leader.

He was certain that one would be Balcones, in his smarmy human form.

But he was wrong.

Boris Cherngelanov was the last person he expected to see as the team leader. Which begged the question: If Boris was the one who freed Loki, what was Balcones up to with the Frost Giants?

Chapter 15
Sucker Punch

It was Friday morning, and Hadrian wasn't sure where he was. Then he smelled perfume, Sara's perfume, and he knew that the deliciously warm body next to him was his girlfriend. He'd felt out of sorts after the table-tipping session at Circle last night. It felt good to not feel like a freak, even if it was just for an hour.

Hadrian eased himself out of bed to go to the restroom. It was 5:00 AM. If he hurried, he'd have time to fit in a run before he showered and went to the office. He could see the indistinct form of Sara's face, lit by the alarm clock. He decided not to wake her up — he already felt bad about making what amounted to a booty call last night.

He took his clothes and dressed in the bathroom, blowing Sara a kiss on his way out. He swore softly as he tripped over something on the floor near the front door. Banging his shin on the end table was unpleasant, but what he felt when he touched her laptop was worse.

He knew then, why Sara hadn't introduced him to Matt, the intern. She was sleeping with him.

Was it an affair? He and Sara had been dating for nearly five years now, but neither had made any promises about exclusivity. Perhaps she was fond of him, but he was a much a booty call for her as she had been for him last night. He was surprised by how much that idea hurt.

A run would clear his head. Maybe. He let himself out into the muggy July morning.

The run had not helped. He refused to allow himself to be upset. He had too much work to do. But he was supremely unhappy about the situation. So unhappy, in fact, that he could barely stop himself from yelling at the judge who denied his request for the exhumation of Terrance Ogilvey, whose blood he found on the wall of the Tenth Sphere's back alley.

He spent his entire lunch break, and then some, at the gym, pounding on the heavy bag until he could hardly lift his arms. It hadn't made him any less angry, but at least he was too tired to hurt anybody. All afternoon, he alternated between wondering if it was his fault, and wondering if Matt was the first. Nothing drives home the you-are-so-not-special point like a cheating significant other.

It was Friday afternoon, and his head was just not in the game. He regarded his mile long to-do list with dismay and decided he had enough for the day. He left on time for a change, and it felt like he was playing hooky.

At 5:30, Sara texted Hadrian. *Dinner?*
Not feeling well
☹ *Feel btr soon, Blackbird*
Thx

He was still feeling like someone sucker-punched him in the gut. Maybe it was his own fault. If he wanted her to be only his, maybe he should have asked her to. But was that fair? To either of them? Whether or not he had a right to be hurt, he was. He needed some time to sort it out.

Chapter 16
The Magician

   I thought it was pathetic to just mope around the house on Friday, so Cassie and I went for our usual morning walk. Afterwards, I called my mother.

   "Marti. I was just about to call you."

   "What's up?" *Was something wrong with Dad? Emily?*

   "I guess you know that Tropical Storm Denise looks like it's going to hit Mexico. But there's a system in the Caribbean that I have a bad feeling about. I just wanted to make sure you are stocked up on water and non-perishables. And batteries. You've got batteries for your flashlight, right?"

   My mother had an uncanny ability to predict storms. I always told her that the Weather Channel would pay her beaucoup bucks to work in their hurricane center. She said that if she charged people money for her gift, God might take it away, to keep her humble.

   "I think I'm good, thanks. I'll keep an eye on it." I took a breath to compose myself. "Not tomorrow, but the next Saturday, I've been offered a job working at a charity gala – they're raising money for orphans." I knew my mother would never turn down orphans. "I was wondering if you could look after Cassie for me?"

   "Of course I can. Polly is coming over to play dominoes, but I'm sure she'd just love to spend some time with that precious baby girl. Now, Cassie's party is only two weeks away – you have invited some of her friends from school, right?"

   "Mom, she's one year old. She doesn't have any friends."

   "It's never too early to start. You and Sara Grace Jackson knew each other since before you could walk, and you were best friends all through school."

I was startled when my mom mentioned Gracie. I hadn't seen her since high school, or thought about her in years, not until last night at the Tenth Sphere.

"Oh, and call your sister, dear. I think she's feeling lonely."

As the morning waned, there was still no sign of Quinn, or even Halle, for that matter. I called Emily, and she invited Cassie and me over for lunch.

"I was wondering," Emily said between bites of macaroni salad, "if you could possibly chauffer me to Dr. Pavlov's funeral on Monday. I'm still not allowed to drive, and Nick will be at work."

"They're just now getting around to the funeral? He died, what, two weeks ago?"

"Medical Examiner's office had a backlog. Also, the Feds wanted their hands in the investigation. Took longer than usual."

"You said he was going into the Witness Protection Program. What was that about?"

"Since he's dead, I don't suppose it matters if I tell you. My case involves a juvenile accused of stealing credit card numbers on the internet. He has some mental health issues, and since Dr. Pavlov is one of the foremost authorities on Reactive Attachment Disorder, I wanted him as an expert witness. He had agreed help out just before he discovered that a Russian criminal gang was exploiting children with disordered personalities for criminal acts. So, naturally, the gang didn't want him to talk about it."

"I'm sorry. I had no idea when I called him. I was just trying to find your doctor. But if his location was so secret, why did you have him in your contact list, for anybody to see?"

"I normally use an encryption device whenever I make calls to clients or witnesses. I took the password off my phone because I'd been feeling so foggy, I was having trouble remembering it. My thought process was that if I, or one of the boys, had to call 911, it was better unlocked. Sometimes I wish we hadn't gotten rid of the landline."

I spent the weekend pretending I was fine. If I stopped moving long enough, I found myself alternating between sad and angry that Quinn had seemingly abandoned Cassie and me. I also chided myself for not listening to Delilah and Lulu when they warned me that this would happen. As long as I kept busy, I did okay, although I really didn't have much appetite.

While Cassie slept in the afternoons, I played around with the Tarot cards Lulu had given me. I remained skeptical about divination, per se. But I had seen Lulu give some uncannily accurate readings.

Lulu had told me to study the pictures on the cards. There was nothing extraneous – everything on the card meant something. If I could remember that water, for instance, was about emotions and the subconscious, any time I saw water in the picture, I'd understand that as part of the meaning. That might be easier than trying to memorize each card. But with this deck, that only applied to the Trumps. The nine of swords had nothing but nine intertwined swords on it. For that, I had to remember that the suit of swords represented defense and protection, and the number nine represented things earned. And the court cards were something altogether different. There was definitely an art to Tarot reading, and I had begun to despair of ever mastering it.

Dr. Pavlov's funeral on Monday was not particularly well attended. Maybe two dozen mourners sat in the first few rows of pews. Emily and I sat in the back. I wasn't eager to encounter Dr. Pavlov's son again, not after Halle broke his nose. I suspected that the three men in dark suits across the aisle from us were FBI agents, probably watching to see who showed up and hoping the killer was in the gathering.

Not unsurprisingly, the casket was closed. It was a lovely dark green, almost black, with brass fittings. A spray of white roses draped across the top of it, and ferny wreaths of lilies and roses surrounded it. The organist played a song I didn't recognize, and a priest began speaking in a language I didn't understand. I glanced down at the program and noticed the letters were Cyrillic. That would explain it. The only Russian word I knew was *borscht*.

Near what I believed to be the end of the service, I leaned over and whispered in my sister's ear, "Meet you at the car."

I was anxious to get back to the house. Kyle and Aiden were at Briar Ridge Montessori, but Mom was taking care of Cassie, McKenzi, and Dad. I listened to the radio while I waited, tapping my thumbs on the steering wheel. As my feet got involved in the tunes, I noticed some paper on the floor.

Not wanting to leave any trash in Ben's car, I leaned over to pick it up. Two pieces of paper had been stapled together and tucked under the floor mat. It wasn't mine. However, it was a copy of the bank statement for Lulu's Homeowner's Association, and there were a couple of line items highlighted in yellow. Odd that it would be in Ben's car. I'd just give it to Lulu tomorrow, when I went to work.

"You still look peaked, honey," Lulu said when I walked in the door. "Are you feeling alright?"

"I'm fine. Just a little tired, that's all. How's Ben?"

Lulu nodded. "I see." She sighed. "Ben's okay. Or at least as well as can be expected. The good news is, the lead homicide detective doesn't think he did it. Ben had blood on his shoes, but it was all on the soles. The detective thinks the killer must have had blood on the top. The bad news is that the prosecutor is desperate to get a conviction for the murder, and he doesn't seem care whether or not Ben is guilty – he had motive, means, opportunity, and an eye-witness put him at the crime scene, holding the murder weapon. The judge won't even set bail."

I shook my head. "It doesn't seem fair, does it? If only there was a way to show them what Bert Kounis showed us."

"Tell me about it."

Business was slow today. I dusted the counters and the shelves. Lulu re-arranged the jewelry.

"Have you been working with your cards?" she asked.

"I have, actually. I'm not sure I'll ever figure it out, but I've been studying the guide book that came in the box."

"Excellent. It just takes some practice."

She pulled a cardboard box from under the counter. When she opened it, I saw it contained several different Tarot decks.

"It's good to experiment and find the deck that suits you best," she said as she rummaged through the box.

She pulled out a pack of cards that looked just like mine, with the very medieval stained-glass pictures.

"Have you been doing any layouts?"

"Not really," I said, putting the duster down. "I've been mostly trying to learn the meanings."

"Let me teach you the Celtic cross. That's one of the easiest and most common ones. Shuffle the deck and cut it with your left hand."

When I had done that, she said, "Some readers like to choose a significator card to represent the querant – that's the person being read for. It's usually a court card, like the Queen of Swords, or the Knave of Disks. I normally only use it if I'm reading over the phone."

She tapped the deck. "Take the first card and lay it on the table."

I did. It was the Two of Cups.

"This card represents the present situation. What do you think it means here?"

"Well, the two has to do with comparing options. And Cups represents, um," it seemed to be on the tip of my tongue, tormenting me. Cups can hold water. "Emotions?"

"Possibly. In this particular deck, cups have to do with interactions. If you think of two people clinking their cups together, saying 'Cheers!' it might be easier."

I couldn't help frowning. Lulu patted my hand.

"Reading the cards is about learning to trust your intuition. I might have a little different interpretation than you, but both could still be right, because they reflect different aspects of the problem." Lulu smiled, encouraging. "Now, take the next card, rotate it 90° and lay it on top of the first."

I did. The second card was Trump II – The Magician.

"This is what crosses you, usually a problem or obstacle. But it could also be strength or skill you're having trouble harnessing."

I considered The Magician. According to the booklet that came with the cards, he could be a shaman or a con man, a hero or a villain – someone adept at deception. Well, that sounded just like someone I knew.

The cowbell on the door clattered, and a customer entered the shop. Class was dismissed for now.

Belinda watched Cassie again for me on Thursday night. The focus of tonight's class was psychometry. Lulu had brought a variety of objects which we had to hold in our hands and see if we were able to pick up any information about their owners. She knew the history of each one, so she had an idea of our accuracy.

Lulu divided us into groups of three. Except for one group, mine, that had four, since there were ten of us. Hunter, Ellen, Marilyn, and I sat on the floor facing each other.

Ellen looked like death warmed over, and I was less suspicious of Lulu's assessment that her soul was separating from her body. It made me a little sad.

Presumably for Hunter's benefit, Marilyn had chosen a particularly snug, low-cut blouse. It was like a car accident – I didn't want to see it, but I had trouble looking away.

Hunter must have come straight from work. The top two buttons of his crisp Oxford shirt were unbuttoned, his sleeves were rolled up to his elbows, and his hair was just a little mussed. Doing my best not to make it obvious, I inhaled deeply. I don't know if was his aftershave, laundry detergent, or what, but that man smelled good. I smiled to myself as it occurred to me that he seemed to have fallen out of an ad for designer cologne.

"Since this is the biggest group, I'm going to start here," Lulu said.

She pulled a silver locket on a chain out of her bag and handed it to Ellen. She gave Marilyn a pencil and a few sheets of notebook paper.

"Focus on the object and relax. Let any images, sounds, or words come to you," Lulu said. "Make sure those perceptions get written down. We'll compare notes at the end, and I'll tell you about the objects."

Moving on to the next groups, she produced a watch, and then a smooth black stone. She started moving around the room, and I looked at Ellen.

"I see an image of a young woman with long, black hair. She's very pale," Ellen said. "I don't have the energy to try for any more."

Marilyn traded the paper and pencil for the locket. The pencil scratched across the paper as Ellen wrote down her description.

Although I can't be certain, because I don't know what Marilyn did for a living, I think she may have missed her calling. She needed her own daytime TV talk show, a la Jerry Springer. She made a show of breathing in ultra-deep breaths and expelling them. After several long moments, she said, "I hear children laughing, and the wind."

She was careful to brush her fingers against Hunter's hand when she passed the locket to him. While he was quietly contemplating the necklace, she was busy writing her observations in blocky handwriting that marched across the page and took up too much room.

Hunter frowned. "All I am getting is a white porch swing."

He handed the locket to me. It was still warm from being in his hand. Marilyn coughed to get his attention, then handed him the paper.

I looked at the locket, turning it over in my hand, then opening it. There was a picture of a young man in a military uniform inside. Suddenly, I was seized with a heart-rending sorrow. Tears welled up and trickled out from under my closed eyelids. I hadn't felt this way…since Ryan died.

"Are you okay?" I felt Hunter's warm hand on my shoulder.

The connection was broken, and I dropped the locket. But I couldn't stand for him to touch me right now. The pain was too sharp, the reminder of that loss too fierce.

"I need a tissue," I said, getting up.

After I returned to my group, Lulu took the locket and brought us the black rock. Ellen and I felt nothing, but Marilyn dramatically exclaimed that it had something to do with the death of someone important. Hunter had a sense of red roses.

I found the watch to be very comforting, like a bowl of hot soup on a cold day. Ellen got a picture of a walrus moustache. Marilyn was sure it had belonged to a famous movie director. It reminded Hunter of rocking chairs.

"Has everybody had a turn with each object?" Lulu asked.

She looked around the room. No one objected to moving on. The stone was the first object she held up. "This rock has been in my driveway for years now. I just picked it up on my way here tonight. If it has any history, it is from prior to eight years ago.

Marilyn sniffed.

Lulu held up the watch. "This belonged to my grandfather. He loved to sit out on his porch and smoke his pipe. He was famous in our family for his corn chowder recipe."

She looked at me when she held up the locket. "This belonged to my grandmother's sister, Rebecca. Her young husband was killed on Normandy Beach in the war. She was pregnant when he left, but then she was in a car accident and lost the baby. She never remarried."

Hunter walked me home again. As it turned out, Lulu had red roses around the sides of her garage, and her grandfather had an antique rocking chair that he sat in to smoke outside on the porch.

"You did pretty well on seeing the surroundings that Lulu's objects came from, Hunter."

"I did okay. You nailed the emotional bits. Quite impressive."

I considered telling him about my ability to see ghosts, but decided against it. Since he was attending mediumship circles, he would probably be accepting of the idea, but somehow, it didn't seem right to share just now.

"Thanks. I have some very sensitive areas." *How is it that everything I say to this man sounds dirty?*

"Do you now?" I could hear amusement in his voice.

"I meant areas of expertise. You seem to be good at environment, and I'm good at feeling."

Hunter laughed softly. "Good to know."

"Okay. I'm just going to shut up now. My mother always said 'If you're in a hole, quit digging.' I think that's probably rule number ten or twelve."

"Your mother sounds like a smart lady."

"I think so." I was hoping to turn the glaring spotlight off of me. "Your mother must have a pretty good sense of humor. She married a man named Forrest Greene and then named her children Kelly and Hunter."

"I don't know. I never met her."

I should just give up talking to him – I put my foot in at every turn. "I'm sorry. I didn't realize."

"She had pre-eclampsia. The high blood pressure caused an aneurysm in her brain to rupture. There was nothing they could do to save her, but they had her on life support while the doctors performed an emergency c-section to get us out." He paused and I had the impression that he was holding his breath. He exhaled, and continued. "I sometimes wonder if she was there watching, waiting to see if we were going to stay here or go with her, before she went to heaven. Or wherever people go when they die."

"I am so sorry. I had no idea."

"Tell him she was," Delilah's voice said next to my ear. I jumped.

"Are you okay?"

"Yes, thanks. Do you believe in guardian angels, spirit guides, and stuff like that?"

"I don't disbelieve in them. I think this is your stop."

We were, indeed, in front of my house, so we quit walking and began loitering.

"What if I told you that I was able to talk to my spirit guide?" I started picking at my thumb with my ring finger.

"I would wonder if you were sure that is who or what you were talking to."

Oh, good. Now he thinks I might be schizophrenic.

"Well, whether it is a spirit guide or voices in my head, she says that your mother was there, watching you and your sister, when you were born."

"That's not what I meant. Just that maybe not all entities are who they say they are," Hunter said. "Thanks for telling me."

"Sure."

"You see them, don't you?" he asked. His voice was soft, not much above a whisper.

"Maybe." I wasn't sure if he was trying to find out about ghosts, or determine whether or not I was crazy.

Hunter sighed. "I always wished I could. When I was little, my sister always saw things. Or said she did. I could never be sure that she wasn't just teasing, because no matter how much I wanted to see what she saw, or how hard I tried, I could never do it."

"Be careful what you wish for."

"Good advice. But that looks like Lulu's car coming this way to pick up Belinda. I should go."

I so very nearly invited him in for coffee. But I thought better of it and said, "Good night. See you around."

"See you."

Hunter Greene, you are an enigma. Why is someone who spends all day crunching numbers interested in something as abstract as ghosts?

At 10:30 on Saturday morning, my mother called me in a panic.

"Calm down, Mom. What is this about?"

I heard her breathing deeply, in and out, to get a hold of herself. "The deepfreeze in the garage died last night. Everything in there is starting to thaw out. What am I going to do with all this food? Do you have any room in your freezer?"

"Not much." I thought for a moment. "Why don't you have a block party? Cassie and I can go knock on doors and invite whoever's available. Maybe they could bring desserts or something."

"You know," she said, "that is a fantastic idea. I think there are a couple of new families in the neighborhood, and I know Polly's always up for a party. Nick's off today, and it would do Emily a world of good to get out in the fresh air and let him mind the boys. I knew there was a reason I called you."

"What time do you want me to say?"

"I'll need to run to the store for some marinade and rib rub, but the meat should be ready to start cooking in an hour or so. It's barely frozen now. I'll call Nick and get him to come over and help Drew move the barbeque into the front yard so he can get the charcoal going."

After I hung up with my mother, I turned on the computer. Cassie was busy with her activity table, giggling every time she pushed the yellow button and it played a horse whinnying sound.

I opened my word processor and typed: "Block party at the Schmidts! 1005 Sheldrake Ln. Bring a side or dessert or beverages. Any time after 2:00." I put that text in each quadrant of the paper and printed four sheets. I figured I'd leave them on doors if people weren't home. Sixteen should be enough. I tore the papers into quarters, smeared sunscreen on us both, and strapped Cassie into her stroller.

I went door-to-door, seven houses past my parents', across the street to those houses, down and around the cul-de-sac, and started working my way to the houses on the other side of mine. Hunter was out working in his yard. His damp shirt clung to his body, highlighting his shape. I hoped he didn't notice me noticing.

"Hey," I said, popping Cassie's stroller up onto its back wheels and wobbling it around. She was getting tired of messenger duty.

"Hey, ladies," he said, setting down the branch lopper. "You out enjoying the sweltering heat this morning?"

"Enjoying may not be the word. My mom is having an impromptu block party this afternoon, and I told her we'd let everyone know. You can bring a side dish or dessert. Or if you prefer, drinks. Cold water's always good. Or, it may give you an opportunity to show off those cooking skills you were telling me about."

Hunter's face broke into a huge grin. "You're right – I promised you pumpkin gnocchi. I suppose these bushes will still be here tomorrow."

"Did you hear that?"

"Hear what?" he asked.

I was certain that I heard a relieved sigh, but there wasn't anyone around except Cassie, Hunter, and I, and neither of them made the noise. I shook it off. Bound to be a bird or squirrel – squirrels are always making unexpected and weird noises.

"You can't miss it – my parents live next door to me, and they'll drag the barbeque out into the front soon."

"Sounds fun."

"We have to go knock on some more doors. See you in a little bit."

In the end, I only needed half a dozen of my mini-fliers. I stuck one on the bank of mail boxes on the corner, and one on the gate to the community pool for good measure.

It has taken us almost an hour, and Cassie and I were both starving. While I made us a quick lunch, I scoured my kitchen for side dish and/or dessert ingredients. Of all the ideas I came up with, the only one that I had all of the necessary components for were chocolate chip cookies. I made four dozen while Cassie was napping. While I was scooping dough onto cookie sheets, I wondered if Halle was right. Perhaps there was no future for Quinn and me, and I would be best served by finding a fellow human.

I could smell Dad's barbecue before we even got out the door. I was surprised to find Hunter already next door, beer in hand, chatting with Nick.

"I see you've met Hunter," I said, setting the tray of cookies on Mom's rickety card table.

"Yep," he replied, with no elaboration.

"Nick's my brother-in-law," I clarified. Although it might have been better to let Hunter wonder about our relationship.

It was a nice afternoon, mixing and mingling with the neighbors. Most of them showed up, even some I hadn't expected. And it had solved the problem of Mom's deceased freezer. If only everything in life was so easy.

When I left at eight to put a grumpy Cassie to bed, the party was still going strong. I left the screen door closed, but opened my front door so I could hear if she woke up, and sat out on my porch. The gathering had bled over into my yard anyway.

Nick came up to the porch. He wasn't exactly drunk, but he was merry.

"I know," he said. "Let's play 42."

"42? You hate dominoes," I replied.

"That's true. But it seems like we ought to do something."

Somehow, Nick, Miss Polly, Hunter and I ended up playing Blind Man's Bluff Poker on my porch until after midnight. I couldn't remember the last time I'd done something like that. By the end, I'd gotten so tired and punchy that just about anything started me giggling. I couldn't stop laughing, and Hunter couldn't stop patting me on the shoulder.

And once again, I wondered if maybe, just maybe, if Halle was right.

Chapter 17
Bargain

Quinn enjoyed swimming in the deep lake, although some of the sturgeon were close to being as long and heavy as he was. Perhaps his wariness was hardwired from hundreds of millennia in the past when their ancestors might have eaten his. The third eye sense was still with him, although modified, in his kelpie form. He'd never thought much about fish before, just ate them if he was hungry. But as the sturgeon swam by him, he could sense them, ancient, cold, aware of nothing but food or potential mates. Sometimes, he even envied the fish for their lack of troubles.

True, it was summer, but he was in mountains north of the Arctic Circle, and this windy part of the world did not get far above freezing, even with the midnight sun glaring off the snow. It was difficult to keep track of time with twenty-four hours of daylight, but Quinn reckoned it was early on the twelfth day since he met Odin. So far, he had seen nothing but a helicopter, which came with five men and left with two. The occasional guard appeared behind the razor wire, Kalashnikov slung across his back, to smoke or talk on a cell phone, but the raw wind usually drove them back inside quickly. Odin's ravens came every morning for news, and every morning it was the same. Nothing.

But then, Quinn noticed a plume of white smoke rising off to the west. He decided to take his dog form and scout around on dry land to investigate. The jötnar had no use for fires, but their allies might. There could be an army gathering behind the high ridge to the west and north of the island, and he'd never know it, not if he stayed in the lake.

He swam into the shallows, changing into Bruce as he came on shore. He paused to look back at the island, but if anyone had noticed the black dog trotting among the rocks, they made no sign. Bruce shook himself, and droplets of water flew in all directions. Steam rose from his warm, damp body into the frigid air as he picked his way through the stones and out towards the rising smoke.

It was not far, as the dog lopes. The smoke led to a decrepit shack nestled against a cliff. Rusty wire and rotting wood - a sad parody of a fence - drooped around the tiny house. Bruce cautiously approached the little hut, but there didn't seem to be anyone inside. He sniffed the ground, exploring in a hundred meter radius around the hut and on top of the overhanging cliff.

He had just about decided that this was a false alarm when his ears caught the sound of a diesel engine rumbling in the distance. He paused to listen. The sound got louder - it was coming closer, from the direction of the lake. Bruce bounded through the snow. He was not a small dog, and his stride was long, but he still had a mile to run. By the time he arrived back at the lake, he saw a soldier climbing into a snow cat and slamming the door. The machine growled away, tossing snow off its treads as it went. He followed it for a little distance, but while he was fast, it was faster. Enough time had been spent away from Bright Falcon, he reasoned, and he'd better get back. The machine was large, but not large enough for Fenrir to climb inside. It was going away, so it hadn't brought Loki. Or so he hoped. If he was wrong, he'd just failed the most important mission of his career.

As soon as Quinn got back in the water, he dove deep and plowed through the water to the island. He circled it, head just out of the water, until the sun skimmed low on the horizon. Finally, he changed his pattern and swam away to rest. As far as he could tell, nothing had changed at the prison. Still, doubt gnawed at him, and his repose was fitful. He eventually gave up on it and decided to hunt for a meal. This task should have been an easy distraction, but he found it difficult to concentrate enough to catch any fish for his breakfast.

The day wore on. As Quinn scanned the lakeshore, he noticed a large white bear. It stood on its hind legs, tilting its head from side to side, probably trying to figure out what Quinn was. It suddenly dropped to all fours and loped off.

Scaredy cat, Quinn thought smugly.

Until he heard the screaming.

He was horrified to see a figure in a long skirt and blue kerchief on her head standing on the bank. The polar bear was galloping right at her. Using a cane, she hobbled into the water. The bear could easily outrun her on land and outswim her in the water, and if the bear didn't get her, hypothermia would.

Quinn launched himself like a torpedo, heading for the old woman.

She had frozen in fear in chest-deep in the lake. The bear was splashing in after her when Quinn's head broke the surface of the water, then kept going up, rising on his long neck, well over the woman's head.

The bear stopped and growled. Quinn flashed a mouth full of sharp teeth and hissed. A roar, he thought, would probably be more effective, but he didn't' want to alert all of Bright Falcon to his presence.

Still trying to claim its prey, the bear danced from side to side, looking for an opening to attack. Failing that, it stood on its hind legs and snarled. Quinn hissed at it again.

They stared at each other, two well-armed mouths displaying fearsome teeth. Quinn could feel the vibrations in the water as the old woman shivered in front of him.

Glowering, the bear dropped down on all fours and moved back onto the bank. It did not leave, however. There was something about that bear, though, that just didn't seem right.

The easiest thing for the woman would have been for Quinn to shift into his horse form and carry her back to wherever she came from. Through his heightened third eye perception, he had a sense of a small wooden hut, nestled against the craggy base of a cliff – the same one he'd visited the day before.

But a horse couldn't hope to out-swim a polar bear, nor outrun it in four feet of water. Perhaps the bear sensed his dilemma, because it sat on its haunches and licked its black lips, abyssal eyes glittering with hunger.

The woman started to sigh and groan. Too-cold muscles were failing, and she would slip under the water and drown if Quinn didn't do something right now.

He dived, his head searching for its target between her ankles and under the full skirts that billowed around her like wildfire smoke. He scooped her up with his neck and she plopped onto his back with a heavy squelch.

The woman wobbled a little bit, numb fingers unable to get a handhold on Quinn's slippery skin, so she just threw her arms around his long, slender neck. He couldn't swim as fast on top of the water as he could underneath it, but he went fast and far enough to put sufficient space between him and the polar bear. The poor old woman was nearly washed off his back by the rushing water, and even as she tried to tighten her grip on his neck, he shifted into horse form and came out of the water.

With his newfound the third eye sense, he could use the old woman's thoughts to get his bearings and make his way to her little hut. As windy as it was today, there would be no plume of smoke from her chimney to follow. The dilapidated fence was little hindrance as he trotted into the tiny yard. He used his teeth on the makeshift bar handle to tug open the poorly fitted door.

The woman slid off his wet back and landed in a heap next to him. He nudged her, and she said something he couldn't understand, her words slurred together. All he could sense about her was blackness. Hoping it was not too late to help her, he nudged her inside, where he could see low flames wavering over nearly-consumed sticks in the hearth.

He was starting to shiver himself. Being a kelpie in the frigid lake wasn't uncomfortable; being a wet horse in near-freezing weather was. He pushed the door closed, to try and contain the heat within the hut. There wasn't much else he could do for her at this point, and he was anxious to get back to his post, so he trotted back to the lake and slipped into his true form.

Nothing seemed to have changed at Bright Falcon. He didn't believe he had been gone for more than ten or fifteen minutes, surely not long enough for Loki show up, row a boat out to the island in strong wind, then drag it inside the building. Even so, unease prodded him. His minor diversions hadn't seemed to have done any harm. He only hoped that nothing had happened when he'd been distracted.

He wondered about the old woman, living all alone in a rickety shack on a snowy mountain. What did she eat? Where did she get wood for her fire? She might have been some type of unfamiliar fae; although the polar bear looked interested enough in eating her. It seemed odd to him that for someone living this part of the world, she didn't seem to know much about polar bears. Quinn racked his brain to recall the different types of non-human people in this area, but other than Valkyrie, Aesir, jötnar, dwarves, and elves, he came up short. If she was non-human, it might explain why he was having difficulty perceiving anything about her, even with his heightened psychic sense. Still, he had bigger things to worry about, such as the location of Fenrir.

The day after he rescued the old woman, she came back to the lake. He was swimming on the far side of Bright Falcon when he saw the dark figure moving across the bleak shoreline. He hadn't recognized her until he'd gotten closer, swimming with only his nostrils and eyes above the icy water. Still, her eyes followed him, and Quinn was even more convinced that she wasn't human, at least not entirely. And then he remembered another entity that lived in this region – the dreaded Maras, or werewolves. That made sense to him. As a wolf at night, she could easily hunt and bring down reindeer, so she'd have no problem getting food. The Maras were cunning and dangerous, and he'd have to be on his guard. For all he knew, there was a whole pack of them lurking nearby. He approached the old woman warily, and did not come so close to shore when he raised his head above water and breathed in deeply. She smelled like cardamom and lemon cookies, and if his belly hadn't already been stuffed with the salmon, it would have rumbled in anticipation of a sweet treat.

"Hallo," she said. "Thank you for helping me yesterday, Mr. Nøkken. That bear and I have some history, and it gets sneakier every day."

Quinn dipped his head toward the water. He could not speak when he was in kelpie form. He also used the opportunity to sneak a glance back at Bright Falcon. Nothing seemed out of the monotonous ordinary.

"I brought you something," she said, pulling a package wrapped in white fabric out from under her shawl. She set it on a flat rock near the edge of the water and unwrapped it.

Cookies.

Again, he bowed his head.

The woman smiled, then turned and headed back toward her cabin.

They smelled wonderful, even to a kelpie. But Quinn knew that eating food offered by any fae creature was risky. And if she was indeed a Mara, there was no telling what enchantments might be on the cookies. He did, however, move them to the other side of the lake and hid them under some rocks, so as not to insult her.

Not a thing appeared to change at Bright Falcon. It gave Quinn a lot of time to think, and it was a good thing he was in kelpie form, because in human form, he would have driven himself crazy. As a kelpie, his senses were ultra-sharp, but his emotions were dull. As a human, it was the other way around. There was one thing that appealed to all of his shapes: Marti's hair smelled like lemon blossoms. It made the man think of warm spring days and cool nights and firelight. It reminded the kelpie of lengthening days, more food, and mating. He hoped that Halle, Eoin, and Aleksei were keeping her safe. He also wondered what Balcones was up to. He would not put off his schemes just because Quinn was involved elsewhere. *Why couldn't Loki just get on with it?*

There were parts of the day when the sun skimmed the horizon, but never dropped below it. Dark embraced the rest of the world at these times, and Quinn had trouble getting enough rest. His mostly nocturnal nature did not function well with only daylight. The day was getting brighter, so Quinn reasoned that Huginn and Muninn would be by for updates soon.

He could smell the warm blood sausages and oat bread long before he saw the old woman making her way to the lake with a wicker basket.

Quinn watched her approach, his head and just some of his neck above the water, searching for the rock where she had left the cookies. She set the basket down and looked out on the lake. She could surely see him.

"Would you like some breakfast, Mr. Nøkken?" she called out over the water.

Quinn remained where he was.

"I am just an old baba, and I mind my own business. Have you heard? It seems that accursed trickster, Loki, has been loosed upon the world again. I have a certain jewel that he wishes to possess. He came to bargain for it, but I would not let him have it. It is a small thing, of little value, though it is special to me. Now he's set that wretched white bear against me. For all I know, it is Loki himself. It grows bolder by the day, and I fear I shall be overwhelmed by it."

She opened the basket, and the oily smell of sausages became stronger, turning Quinn's stomach queasy.

"If you are willing to help me, please come to my cabin. I'll surely pay you for your trouble. I hope you arrive before the bear does."

She pulled her shawl tighter around her shoulders and hobbled back up the trail.

This could be a golden opportunity. Or it could be a trap. Could he risk missing a chance to capture Loki as he came for Fenrir? Odin's ravens should come for news at any moment.

He would send word with them. If things went well, Odin and company would be the first to know. If they went badly, at least Quinn would know the cavalry was on the way – if he failed, perhaps they wouldn't. And with any luck, they'd even arrive in time. It briefly crossed his mind to ask Malik to come and help him, but if he pulled him off of surveillance for something frivolous and Balcones slipped through their hands, he would never forgive himself.

Huginn and Muninn took their sweet time arriving. Quinn couldn't really blame them – there'd been precious little to report. He told them about the old woman – she'd come after they left yesterday – and what he planned to do.

Quinn remembered exactly where the crone's hut was, and it took just about half an hour traveling over the rough terrain in human form to reach it. It might have been an easier trip as a horse, but he thought it might be safer not to shift at the woman's house. In that moment between forms, he was highly vulnerable.

He raised his hand to knock, and the door creaked open.

"Come in," said the old woman. "Would you care for some tea?"

"No thank you, grandmother. Please excuse my bluntness, but I have other pressing business. How is it that I can help you?"

The crone laughed, then gave him a head to toe scan. "If we are being uncouth, your man-form is pleasing to the eye, Nøkken."

Quinn squirmed inwardly.

"And as you can see, I am old and frail."

She was probably much older, and not nearly as frail as she looked.

"I cannot hope to slay such a beast as a polar bear," she said. "It is all I can do of late to stop it eating me for its supper. I have an idea that its skin would make a fine blanket for my old bones, though."

"So you want me to kill the bear for you?" Quinn asked. "If it has been forced against its will to stalk you, that hardly seems fair. And if it is Loki in bear form, I don't suppose it would be possible to slay it."

For a small, drafty house, it was stiflingly hot. Quinn took off his coat.

"Perhaps not. Disenchant it, cage it or kill it as you will, but this bear will be the death of me if nothing is done."

"Have you considered a sojourn to a place it cannot follow?"

"Is that your solution? To move my dry old bones every time some greedy hand comes grabbing for my meager belongings?"

"I'm sorry. If I do this for you, what is my payment?"

The woman scanned through dusty bottles on a shelf, until she came to one with a pink label. "What would you like? A charm to win the heart of your true love?"

"If she is really my true love, I wouldn't need a charm."

She looked through more bottles and packages. "A ship, then?"

"A ship?"

"It is large enough to carry all the Aesir, and it cannot be sunk. And," she leaned forward, nodding, "it can be folded up as a cloth and carried in your pocket."

Although Quinn had no need of a ship, if he and Odin failed to stop Ragnarök, he could think of at least two people who would.

"Okay, how is this for a bargain? I will catch the bear. If you give me this ship, and I like it, I will give you the skin. If the ship isn't suitable, I'll let the bear go." Quinn didn't relish the thought of killing the polar bear, but he would do what he had to do to save Marti and Cassie.

"As you wish," she replied.

Chapter 18
Lunch

The weekend sprawled in front of Hadrian like a bowl of wet papier-mâché: lumpy, grey, and unpleasant. He tried to distract himself from his personal life by rehashing every detail of his professional one. If he hadn't been watching both Marti and Lulu, he would never have gone to something like Thursday Circle at the Tenth Sphere. But there, maybe he should have lied and said he didn't get anything when he held Lulu's objects. Or just made something up. Like he should have done afterwards, when he walked Marti home. His ability, blessing or curse, was his deepest secret, and it felt good to have it acknowledged and accepted. It was a brand new experience for Hadrian, to be around people who wouldn't regard him as a freak for even entertaining the possibility of psychic abilities, much less actually possessing them. But there was a problem in associating this newfound personal liberation with Marti.

He'd allowed himself to get too distracted by her. She was a surveillance subject, he told himself harshly. Not a friend. Not a lover. A subject. And he would do well to keep that in mind. His cover ID didn't have any real details about his childhood, just a generic history. He'd made a terrible mistake telling Marti the truth about his mother's death. And he did have a twin sister, only her name wasn't Kelly, it was Sabina. That's what happens when the sole parent is a professor of ancient history. Kids get named things like Hadrian and Sabina. No one would have blamed her if she stuck an 'r' in between the 'b' and the 'i.' But she never did. No one would have blamed him, for that matter, if he chopped the 'h' off of Hadrian. But he never did that, either.

That's why it was such a perfect opportunity when Marti knocked on his door and invited him to her mother's house for a block party. Instead of surveilling his targets one at a time, he could watch them all together – Marti, and Nick and Emily Benson. Well, most of them. Lulu wasn't at the party. Of course, if they were working with the Odessa Group, and they figured out who he was, it could all go pear-shaped in a hurry. But that is why he loved this job – the feeling of walking the edge of a knife, balanced between victory and annihilation – now that was a rush.

Hadrian had never gone to cooking school. But he could make gnocchi. It was time-consuming, though not difficult. But it was even easier to slip out to Carmine's and get a family portion to go.

It was the stupid dumplings that pricked his conscious. Compared to the enormous lie regarding his identity and what he was really doing in the neighborhood, whether or not he made the gnocchi, or bought them, shouldn't even be a blip on the veracity radar. Funny how it was always the little things that caused the most damage. Even though he couldn't be absolutely certain, he was pretty sure that Marti and her family were not involved with Odessa. They seemed so salt-of-the-earth real. Still, he knew that people were nothing if not surprising – after all, no one ever suspected Ted Bundy of being the sadistic monster that he was. Marti's mother had acted like she'd known him for years. Nick was very protective of his sister-in-law, which made Hadrian smile. She definitely deserved a man of her own, though. Unfortunately, even without the prohibition on physical relationships with subjects by his job, he knew he couldn't trust himself to be around her alone. It would be too easy for him right now, freshly wounded by his discovery of Sara's liaison, to use Marti to dull the pain.

Hadrian never really took off his Special Agent hat, but he sometimes wore it at a rakish angle. The impromptu party had been one of those times. He'd let go a little and really enjoyed himself. He would be sad when the assignment was over, and he left the neighborhood.

He yawned and stretched, and found himself humming one of the songs that was playing on Marti's phone last night. She didn't have a very fancy phone, and it didn't have a lot of storage capacity, so she only had about eight songs in it that played over and over again. The songs were on shuffle, and they'd incorporated a bet on which song would come up next into their card game. He smiled to himself as he got out of bed. While he was making coffee, he checked his phone for messages, and saw that he'd missed a call from Sara. While she was sitting in his apartment.

Irina Cherngelanov arranged the final details of the Child Advocacy Partners Luncheon with The Houstonian's banquet manager. The guests would start arriving in twenty minutes. Representatives from the District Attorney's office, Child Protective Services, all of the local law enforcement agencies, a select few child and adolescent mental health professionals, and the local branches of children's welfare nonprofits had been invited. Her assistant had told her there were one hundred three RSVPs.

Boris may have been the brains and financial brawn behind the Cherngelanov Foundation, but beautiful, charming Irina was the public face of it. She and Boris had no biological children, but they considered the residents of their RAD residential treatment center to be their own. They did what they could to heal starved and battered bodies and scarred souls. To help them make their way in the world, they taught them the family business and inducted them into the hierarchy when they were trained and ready. Family was not necessarily blood, but who had your back when the chips were down. Besides, they all had a common lineage. Tri Babushkas Orphanage, and its awful sisters, was their bitch of a mother.

Irina loved the open, airy banquet facilities in the hotel. With floor to ceiling windows and indoor plants, it was just like having a garden party, only in the air conditioning and out of Houston's brutal summer sun and energy-sapping humidity.

She heard her name being called and turned around. "Sara! You are a little early, my friend."

Hadrian's girlfriend crossed the room, she and Irina air kissed each other.

"How have you been?" Sara asked.

"I am well. And yourself?"

"Fine. Keeping very busy."

Irina smiled "Good. And your handsome boyfriend? You should have brought him."

Sara had once let it slip that Hadrian worked for the FBI. It wasn't classified information, but it was usually best not to advertise it. When Irina found that Hadrian worked for the gang task force, she couldn't believe her good fortune. Hadrian never told Sara any of the details of his work, but she certainly knew when he was available and when he wasn't. Irina had passed along that information to Boris, who'd used it as something of a heads up that an FBI operation was underway, and to lie low. Sara, the unwitting mole, had helped Boris sidestep law enforcement at least three times.

"He's sick," Sara said with a little pout.

"I'm sorry to hear that. I hope he is better soon. Please," Irina said, "have a drink, a glass of wine perhaps?" She gestured toward the bar set up near the dessert table. She pretended to be slightly embarrassed. "I must go to the powder room while I still have the chance." She would text Boris while she was there.

After the luncheon, Sara decided to stop by Hadrian's apartment to check on him. He didn't answer the door. She let herself in, but he wasn't home. *He probably ran out to get some cold medicine*, she told herself. She waited for a little while, checking her email and Facebook on her phone. After half an hour, she gave up. She tried calling him, but he didn't pick up. She started to wonder if maybe he was working, after all. Usually, he just told her he'd be out of touch, so it was odd that he would claim to be sick.

Before her ruminations got any darker, her phone rang. She hesitated to answer it. It seemed wrong to answer a call from

Matt in Hadrian's apartment. But there was a chance it was work related. She tapped the "Answer Call" button and quickly let herself back out of the apartment.

Chapter 19
Open Door Policy

There had been an ozone warning today, and the Air Quality Index was 108. Usually, I was fine, but when the ozone was this high, my head plugged up and my nose dripped like a faucet. I normally kept chewable Benadryl in the medicine cabinet, just in case. I took some right before I left my house, and put another couple of bubble packed tabs in my purse.

I dropped Cassie at my parents' house and headed for the Tenth Sphere. When I arrived, Lulu forced a garment a bag into my hand. "You're late. You did bring the shoes, right honey?"

I held up a plastic bag.

"Good, good," she muttered, hustling me into the shop and towards the dressing rooms.

She and Belinda were already wearing their Gypsy fortune-teller outfits. A slight queasiness swirled around my stomach. I really hoped they weren't planning on me being dressed as a chicken or something utterly ridiculous. The door squeaked as I swung it open, and hung the garment bag on one of the hooks. Taking a deep breath, I unzipped the bag.

"Lulu? Are you sure this is the right costume?"

"Yes. Hurry up, honey. We don't want to be late."

I slipped into the dress and stepped into my heels. "How do I look?" I asked, opening the saloon-style door.

"Fabulous," Lulu said, glancing at her watch.

"That color suits you," Belinda said, gently nodding.

I looked at myself in the full-length mirror. Harsh fluorescent light glittered off red sequins. The stretchy fabric was form-fitting, rather than tight, and it hugged my décolletage like a needy blind date. It wasn't a micro-mini, but it was shorter than I was comfortable with.

I balked. "I don't know. I think it looks a little slutty."

"Honey, if I could get away with wearing that, I'd do it in a heartbeat. Although," she said, looking at my wrist, "I'm not sure that bracelet goes with the outfit."

"I'm not taking it off. Quinn gave it to me."

Lulu's eyebrows raised.

"It's supposed to ward off demons." At least he'd left me with something. Maybe. I hadn't seen any evidence of demons since I'd been wearing it, anyway.

Lulu shrugged. "You're going to be passing out goodie bags to the guests — the bags are already at the party. Also, you'll be giving out a Tenth Sphere coupon with each bag, then telling them where we're set up. They don't have to pay for readings — the host has already covered it, if they ask. We really need to go."

I would need to carry a tab of Benadryl with me, just in case. Once it started cooling off and the ozone levels started dropping, I was usually okay. Usually. I wouldn't be carrying my ginormous purse around while I was passing out goody bags. For lack of anywhere better, I tucked it into my bra. I also tucked my cell phone under my extra-wide nursing bra strap, just above the cup. It took a little adjusting to that it didn't stick out, but it was hard to see the lump under the glittering sequins.

I clambered into the back seat of Lulu's car, and struggled to find a place to put my feet and legs. Her folding table took up most of the floor board, and her decorations and supplies occupied an uncomfortable percentage of the seat. I grunted as a basket of silk daisies toppled into my lap.

"Could some of this go in the trunk?" I asked.

"Have you seen her trunk?" Belinda replied.

I sighed. Actually, I had. There was no room in there, either, as Lulu kept it packed with "emergency" supplies, like her smudge sticks and runes.

Fortunately, it was only a half hour drive to our destination, and only one of my feet fell asleep on the way.

A guard at the gate checked our names off his list. The house wasn't *in* a gated community, it *was* a gated community. I'd stayed at smaller hotels than the main house, and there were at least three guest cottages that I could see from the driveway. An enormous swimming pool with a waterfall and its own pool house sparkled in the sun. I could see what appeared to be a full bar, complete with bartender, through the partially open French doors. Behind that, a fieldstone building, with a brass sign that read 'OFFICE,' nestled between the pool and a putting green.

As soon as the car stopped, a grey-uniformed valet trotted out to open Lulu's door. His mouth twitched a little when he looked at the vehicle. I guessed that he was expecting an all-you-can-eat buffet of Mercedes, Lexus, and BMW.

"We need to unload, hon," Lulu said, somehow sounding overly-pleasant.

The words had hardly left her lips when his fellow valets swarmed around the car and started removing things from the back seat. The one who helped me out of the car and then to balance on one leg while I tried shaking out the pins-and-needles from my slumbering foot didn't look old enough to drive. It made me doubly self-conscious that he did a poor job of concealing his apparently positive assessment of my wardrobe. *I wasn't corrupting a minor, was I?*

A man in a tuxedo vest, shirtsleeves rolled up to his elbows, and an undone bowtie dangling from his collar, came out of the cut-glass and mahogany double front doors.

"Ah!" he said, grasping Lulu's right hand in his own and squeezing her shoulder with his left hand until she winced. "The entertainers are here. Welcome! I will show you place for set up."

I knew I'd seen him somewhere before. It took me a minute, but I realized that he was the guy I saw on TV the other day who took in RAD orphans. *What was his name? Boris something?*

"Yes," Lulu said. "Thank you." She gently pulled away from his grip. "I'm Lulu, this is Belinda, and our gift bag passer-outer here is Marti."

Boris smelled like cigarettes and expensive cologne.

"Excellent! Is good to meet you," the man said, vigorously shaking each of our hands in turn. "You call me Boris, da?"

He led us, followed by the laden valets, to a large conservatory which gave us an excellent view of the pool and outdoor kitchen.

"Miss Marti, if you would come with me? I show you where gift bags are located."

Lulu grabbed one of the shopping bags with her supplies. "Hold on a sec, honey." She rooted around inside it, finally coming up with two boxes of business cards. "Don't forget these."

I took them from her and followed Boris back into the foyer.

Boxes, stacked several layers deep, held row after row of red iridescent gift bags. I estimated that there were about two hundred of them.

"Please to hand each lady gift as she enters," Boris said.

I nodded. "Will do. I saw you on TV the other day. I think it's cool, what you're doing with the orphans."

Boris beamed at me. "Thank you, Miss Marti. These children are very special, even if most people cannot understand them."

"I'm sure."

"I must finish dressing – guests will be soon arriving. Is powder room there," he said, pointing to a closed door, discretely tucked almost out of sight underneath the grand staircase, "if you need to refresh yourself."

"Thank you."

Boris started up the stairs, two at a time. I thought I'd check out the powder room, more out of curiosity than necessity.

The walls were papered in a deep red velvet-flocked damask pattern. All of the fixtures were highly polished black ceramic, the tile was black, and even the countertop on the vanity was black granite. Dim recessed lighting kept the place from being cave-dark, but the mirror above the sink was lit up almost painfully brightly. Bottles of expensive perfume were lined up neatly on one side of the sink, and other bottles – hair spray, mousse, and powder commanded the other. It was almost like being in the ladies' lounge at an expensive department store. *If I'm going to get those goodie bags stuffed with Lulu's coupons, I'd better get a move-on.*

As I came out of the bathroom, I nearly knocked over a woman in a teal ball gown.

"I'm so sorry!" I said, touching her elbow. She was looked waifish – prominent cheekbones underscoring large, sad eyes.

"And who are you?" she asked, her grey eyes narrowing.

"My name is Marti. I'm here with the Tenth Sphere – the entertainers – and I'll be passing out gift bags at the front door."

She nodded. "It is good to meet you, Marti. I am Irina, and I am married to Boris." Something about the way she said it - perhaps because there was no spark in her eyes when she mentioned his name, or perhaps it was the way her thin shoulders squared themselves when she said her own name – that made me think that her marriage was more of a business arrangement than a love affair.

"Oh. It is nice meeting you, Irina. I hadn't realized that Boris was married."

"Didn't you?" she said, her lips pursing slightly.

Ohhhh. Did she think that I was interested in Boris? No worries there, sister.

"I must go and check on the catering, Marti. You enjoy the party."

"Thank you," I said as she swept away into the depths of the mansion.

The party had been going on for just over an hour, and I was out of gift bags. I decided to go find Lulu and Belinda to see what else I could do to help out.

Suddenly, Boris was at my elbow. "All finished with the gifts, Miss Marti? Very good. There is one more box in wine cellar. Anna can help you – she will be in kitchen." He pointed off to my right.

"Okay. I'll go find her."

It was weird, snooping around a stranger's house. But he had sent me off with only a hint of direction. Surely the kitchen couldn't be too hard to find. Maybe.

I followed my nose, and only made one wrong turn. Several hairnetted women dressed in white loaded either hors d'oeuvres or glasses of champagne onto serving trays, which were promptly whisked away by black uniformed waiters. Through the picture windows, I could see expensively frocked guests milling around the pool, the servers moving like shadows between them, delivering tidbits of food and champagne flutes without a sound.

"Hello?" I said to the busy ladies. "I'm looking for Anna?"

"I am Anna," a bruiser of an older woman said, her deep voice gruff. She did not appear to be pleased about being interrupted.

"Boris said you could help me get the last box of gift bags in the wine cellar."

One disapproving eyebrow raised above the other. "I am too busy now. Go through that door, then turn right. The door to the wine cave is in the hallway." She turned back to her canapés.

"Alrighty, then. Thanks."

She waved me away without looking up.

I opened the door she had indicated, and found myself in a softly lit corridor with plush carpet and cherry wainscoting on the walls, and a solid wood door about midway down the hall. This part of the house was quiet, away from the party, which seemed to be scattered over most of the property. I turned the knob and the door opened with a soft click.

Basements in Houston are cost-prohibitive, what with the high water table and unstable gumbo, so it is a rare thing to find one here. I had half expected a dank, dark concrete room. But this one was cozy. A lush Persian rug protected the marble tile from a heavy oak table in the middle of the large room. A cabinet with every shape and size of wine glass stood opposite me, and the rest of the walls were covered with floor to ceiling wine racks. A wrought iron stepladder stood in front of one of them. Curiously enough, a white painted door with a frosted glass window loomed near the glasses cabinet. It didn't match anything else in the cellar, and was jarringly out of place. I assumed that it led to another wine storage area, but I found it oddly disturbing.

There was no box of goodie bags anywhere to be seen. I walked around the cellar, just to make sure. I tried the white door, and discovered that it wasn't actually a door at all, but a trompe-l'oeil. Which made it even stranger.

Boris was mistaken about the box of gift bags. It was chilly in the wine cave, and I wasn't unhappy to head back up the stairs.

But the door to the hallway was locked.

I knocked politely, thinking someone must not have realized I was down there and closed the door I'd left ajar. "Hello? Can anyone hear me?"

Apparently, no one could.

I tried pounding harder on the door. "Hello! I'm locked in!"

Still no response.

I pulled my cell phone out of my bra strap and dialed Lulu's number. It went straight to voice mail. I tried Belinda's, with the same result. I pounded on the door again.

Nothing.

Probably no one else in the entire world goes to a gala fundraiser and finds a way to get locked in the wine cellar. I really, really hated to do this, but I didn't see what choice I had.

I dialed Nick's cell.

"What's up?" he asked.

"You're not going to believe this. And I wouldn't have bothered you if it wasn't an emergency. But I'm locked in Boris' wine cellar."

"Who is Boris? Where are you?"

"Boris is the guy hosting the fundraising gala at his house in River Oaks. My job was to pass out gift bags to the guests, but I ran out, so I came to the wine cellar to get some more, but there weren't any more, and somehow the door locked behind me. I tried calling both Lulu and Belinda, but their phones are turned off."

Nick was polite enough not to laugh out loud at me, but I could hear the amusement in his voice. "I see. And what, exactly, is it you want me to do?"

"I don't know. Can you call the house and tell someone to come let me out?"

"What's the name?"

"His first name is Boris. But his last name is tricky. It's Russian and starts with a 'C.'"

"Considering that the number is almost certain to be unlisted, it probably doesn't matter that you can't spell it. I can call one of my buddies to stop by there – his beat is close to that part of town."

"No! You can't send a car with uniformed officers here. Are you kidding me? The Society Page reporter is here, along with probably the two hundred richest people in Houston. I'm sure your friend doesn't want to be famous for being the cop that raided the biggest social event of the summer." I paused for breath. "I know it's a lot to ask, but could you just come and tell the security guard at the gate to let someone know I'm trapped down here?"

"Marti, I –"

"Please, Nick?"

He breathed out heavily. "Fine. I'll be there soon."

"Thank you so much." I gave him the address.

"You owe me big time for this."

"I know."

There wasn't much to do while I waited for Nick to send someone to rescue me. I plodded down the stairs and sat at the wooden table. *I'm such an idiot.* Since the cell was still in my hand, I decided to kill some time by reading an ebook. That lasted for all for three minutes before my battery died.

I left the phone on the table and walked around, reading the labels on the wine bottles. Surely the 1758 on one label of port must refer to when the winery was founded, not when that wine was bottled. Although, it was dusty enough. I might be able to believe it was over two hundred and fifty years old. Still, I suppose really old bottles of spirits show up from time to time, and if Boris was an avid collector, he certainly had the money to buy such things.

At long last, I heard the doorknob turn upstairs. "Hello?" I said, getting up to meet my rescuer.

"Marti? You okay?" Nick called down the stairs.

"Yeah, I'm fine. I-"

I couldn't believe it. Nick was on the third step down, and behind him, on the landing, stood a short, bull-necked man with a port wine stain birthmark on his head.

Bertram Kounis' killer.

"There is problem?" he asked.

"N-n-no, nothing's wrong," I stammered. "I'm just a little surprised that Nick came all the way into the house to look for me."

The killer's eyes glinted wickedly under the safety light. He stepped forward.

"Nick!" I yelled, just as he leaned over to give Nick a vicious shove.

He managed to catch the handrail, but momentum caused him to stumble, too quickly, down the stairs.

"What was that about?" he snarled at the short man.

"Is how we deal with spies," he replied with a smirk.

"What are you talking about?" I asked

Nick and I looked at each other, perplexed.

The man shrugged. "You deny it now. Boris wants to know where girl is getting information. But you, you are unnecessary. We play game, eh?"

"What information?" Fear made my voice shrill.

"You helped Boris track down old friend. And, by the way, your clutch needs adjusting."

"Your clutch?" Nick asked.

It took me a minute to work out what he was telling us. *Your clutch needs adjusting. Clutch.* Nobody would know that. Unless he'd driven my car.

"You. You killed Bertram Kounis. And Dr. Pavlov."

The short man grinned, then pulled an evil looking knife from his boot.

"Why me?" I asked. "Why would you go to all that trouble to steal my car and run over Dr. Pavlov? How did you even know where I'd be?"

"Boris wanted to use your car to kill traitor to send you message — you are next. Do not play innocent. The two men who were following you last week. What did you do with their bodies?"

"I have no idea what you're talking about."

"On Thursday last week, two men, two good men, follow you to devil shop. No one sees them again. What did you do to them?" He shook the knife.

I tried to think of what had happened over a week ago, but details were hard to recall while being threatened with a Bowie knife. Halle had been with me all day. She disappeared while I was at work. We went to Circle. When I came out after I'd forgotten my phone, she had dirt on her face. She's bound to know something about it.

"I did nothing to them. I didn't even know they were there. Maybe they quit."

The man with the port wine stain scowled and moved closer.

Nick had put himself between me and the killer. But it should have been the other way around. I wasn't in any danger, at least not for the moment. It was Nick he was planning to kill, right here, right now. He now knew things he wasn't supposed to. And apparently, so did I.

I backed away from the approaching man, tugging gently on Nick's shirt as I went, to keep him moving with me. Not sure where I thought I was going, but it seemed a good idea to do something other than stand and be slaughtered.

The wine glass cabinet got closer, and so did the painting of the white door. Not realizing how fast the wall was coming up, Nick backed me into it, and I grunted. The wall switched from cold to warm, then solid to liquid, the un-door opened, and we tumbled through the wall into the dark.

Chapter 20
Under Cover

Crap. Hadrian wasn't sure what to tell Sara, but he had to tell her something. He tapped his phone against his forehead, struggling with what to say. He opened his call history and touched her number.

"Hello?" Sara answered, her voice thick with sleep.

"Hey, babe. Sorry I missed your call yesterday. I had the ringer turned off so I could sleep, and I forgot to turn it back on."

"Hey, Blackbird." She only sounded half awake.

"Did I wake you?"

"Yes, actually."

Hadrian thought he heard the soft thump of a door closing in the background. Was she with Matt?

"Yeah," Sara said, her voice a little clearer. "I got a little concerned when I went to your apartment and you weren't there."

"I had gone out to get something to eat." That much was true. He'd eaten far too much at the Schmidt's block party, spent too much time with Marti.

"Oh. You feeling any better? Do I need to get my mom to make you a pot of chicken soup?"

Hadrian laughed. "That's okay. I'm a lot better now. So…you up for doing anything later?"

"Like what?"

Hadrian's competitive nature had kicked in. He wasn't going to let some kid waltz in and take his place with Sara. That, and he really needed to stop thinking about Marti Keller. "I don't know — maybe check out the IMAX at the Museum, and go to the Butterfly Center. Don't they have a new exhibit that just opened? Spy gear or something? We could grab something to eat after."

Sara laughed. "If they do have a travelling spy gear exhibit, you'd better give me the guided tour."

"I can do that. What time do you want to meet up?"

The spy gear exhibit consisted of items used during the Cold War – hollow nickels, carrier pigeon gear, a robotic fish. It was interesting to have a look at some of the old school methods. Sara seemed distracted, and Hadrian decided it was high time to distract her back towards him. The Egyptian Hall was extraordinarily dark. They must have taken a page from the Gem Vault. The brightly lit displays that made the dark seem even darker by comparison, made it easier to sneak in a public display of affection or two. Hadrian stood behind Sara as she looked at a sarcophagus.

He was too close, not quite touching her, but close enough to feel the heat of her body. He caressed the side of her neck as he placed one hand on her shoulder. He could feel her shiver under his touch. That was a good sign. He hoped.

It was Saturday night, exactly one week before the charity gala, and Sveklá had way too many things to do.

But, instead of doing them, he stared at the ceiling in the dark. *What have I done?* His body still buzzed from the deft application of Irinia's array of sensual skills. Her head rested on his shoulder, her bare flesh soft against his. He could not remember a time in his life when he had not wanted her. But now that she had given herself to him, no, more like taken him by storm, he felt awful.

He was betraying the one man who had always stood up for him, always protected him as a child at Babushkas, and gave him a job as an adult. The only two people in all the world that he cared for were waging war against each other, and he was being mangled between them. If there was a way to tear himself in half, so he could be loyal to both, he would do it in a heartbeat. But as it was, he would have to choose.

"Sergei?" Irina asked. She stroked his chest with her fingertips.

"Mmm?" Regardless of what his mind wanted, his body craved her. Again. Even though he knew if Boris found out, it would be the death of both of them. Perhaps that was part of what made the high so high.

"Do you know where Boris is now?"

"Out."

"He is at a hotel with three women. He texted me a picture." Her voice sounded soft and bruised. "I'll show you."

She got out of bed, and fumbled with her clothes on the floor. Sveklá was disappointed that it was too dark in the room to see her clearly. At last, she found the pocket that contained her phone. When she turned it on, the screen illuminated her face. A thin tear clung to her eyelashes as she opened her text messages. She slipped under the covers next to Sveklá, and showed him the photo.

It was hard for him to look at. Boris was grinning like a drunken teenager, with a gravity-defying set of enormous breasts hovering over his head. There were two other women with their heads in his naked lap. Sveklá could not bear to look at it. He turned the phone onto its face and set it on the nightstand.

He rolled over, scooping Irina into his arms and pulling her on top of him. "I am sorry, Irina. I do not know why he does these things."

"He does not wish to share power. He wants to break me. I think," Irina breathed in sharply, "that he is planning to kill me."

Sveklá caressed her cheek. "No, Irina. That cannot be so. Do you remember, when we left Babushkas, how Boris protected us? He would not have fought so hard to keep you alive, only to kill you himself now."

Irina sighed. "He fought for us because we belonged to him, not because he loved us. You have never understood that about him, Sergei. I think because you are not like him."

"I am certain that he loves you."

"I am certain that he does not. He is not capable of loving anyone. He is always playing chess in his head, and people, they are the pieces. You, Sergei, you are a rook."

"If I am rook, then you are queen."

"But Boris is still the chess master."

Sveklá stroked her hair. "Why you think Boris is planning to kill you?"

"I caught him taking some of my jewelry to give to one of his women. He laughed at me, told me that he bought it, and he would do what he liked with it. He said he would leave me a few pieces to wear at my funeral. I slapped his face, and he almost broke my wrist. He suggested I get a prescription to deal with my suicidal depression."

"But you are not depressed. Are you?"

"No. Angry. Very angry. But not depressed."

He knew that Boris was capable of appalling cruelty. But he found it hard to believe that he would kill Irina. "Perhaps he was just angry you found what he was doing," Sveklá said, but the words sounded hollow as they came out of his mouth.

"You are a good man, Sergei, to believe in your friends so." Irina traced a finger across his cheekbone and down his jaw.

He kissed her fingers, then her palm. She curled her legs up, knees against his ribs. When she sat up, she was straddling his hips. He let her guide his hands up her body. It wasn't that Sveklá had not been with a woman before. He had, many times, just never with one he loved. Irina was tough on the outside, but he knew she was fragile on the inside. Things that should never happen to anyone, much less his beautiful Irina, had happened to her. It was important to him that she was in control of their coupling, so that it wasn't too rough or painful for her. He couldn't repair the damage, but he could stop it from getting any worse.

He'd made his choice.

Chapter 21
Bright Falcon

Nick landed nearly on top of me when the wall opened up and we fell through it.

The floor was rough, bare concrete, and it snagged a few of the sequins off my dress. They stood out against the stark grey floor like glistening droplets of blood.

"What the hell?" Nick asked, scrambling to his feet.

We were in a cage, 12 x 12, I estimated. A guard in a khaki uniform and furry hat barely gave us a second look, as if he'd been expecting us. There was a large control panel in front of him, and directly opposite us, a large observation window, blinds tightly shut.

"*Zdravstvuĭte. Dobro pozhalovat' v yasnyy sokol.*" he said.

Nick and I looked at each other.

"I forget my manners," the man said with a thick Russian accent. "Welcome to Bright Falcon."

"I still don't understand," I said.

"You just arrive Kola Correctional Colony. We call it Bright Falcon. Boris will be with you when all party guests leave."

"Boris? The philanthropist, with the orphans?" I asked. I hugged myself and rubbed my upper arms. It was awfully chilly in here.

"Boris is man with many hats," the guard replied.

Nick grabbed the bars and tested them. Set in concrete, they weren't going anywhere. He scowled. "I'm not familiar with anything called 'Bright Falcon' in Houston, much less in River Oaks."

"Bright Falcon is in Kola Peninsula. Not so well known outside of Russia," the guard offered.

"It is not possible to walk through a door in Houston and come out in Russia," Nick said.

The guard shrugged. "But here you are."

"I don't believe we're in Russia. This is a trick. You've just cranked the AC all the way down, or maybe we're in an industrial cooler."

"Suit yourself," the guard replied, then tapped some text into his cell phone.

I tested the wall, just in case. But it was as solid as, well, a brick wall.

"Why are we here?" I asked. We may or may not have been in Russia, but we were certainly locked in a cage.

"Information," the guard said.

"About what?" Nick snapped.

"Is not for me to say."

Nick turned his back to the guard. "You've got your phone, right?" he whispered.

I patted my bra strap. It was flat. "No. I left it in the wine cellar. Battery was dead, anyway."

A hint of a frown floated across his mouth. "When I get a chance, I'll use mine."

I nodded.

"To save you troubles," the guard said, "there is no cellular service here. You need satellite phone."

Just to be sure, Nick checked his phone. Instead of bars, he had an icon of a phone handset with a line through it.

I'm not sure how long I'd paced around that cell, partly to keep warm, and partly because I couldn't sit still. Nick was conserving his energy by sitting cross-legged on the floor, back against the iron bars. If he was cold, he didn't show it.

I felt relieved that at least Cassie was safe at home with Mom. If anything happened to me, at least she would be well taken care of. I wished I could get word to Quinn, but then I wondered if he would bother coming, if I did. Hunter, on the other hand, might come to rescue me, but I wasn't sure this was a job for a statistician. Guilt for dragging Nick into this washed over me. If I'd just been more patient, surely Lulu and Belinda would have noticed I was missing. But that did give me an idea.

I closed my eyes and silently called for Delilah.

"Girlfriend, you done put your foot in it this time."

I opened my eyes to see her standing on the other side of the bars.

Where are we? Are we really in Russia?

"Oh, yeah," she said, "you're in Russia alright."

I don't understand. How is that possible?

"The fae, and some of them demons, use portals. Kind of like mini wormholes, you know?"

Not really. But I'll take your word for it. How do we get out of here?

Delilah tugged at her earlobe. "That's a tricky one, girl. I'm not going to lie – there's some bad shit coming down on you just now. But when everything is on the line, if you trust your heart, you'll be okay."

Her words left me more agitated than comforted. *When everything is on the line?*

"You're stronger than you think," Delilah said. Then she patted my arm with her ghostly cold hand and vanished.

Dammit. I'd wanted to ask her to tell Lulu where Nick and I were, and to send help. But then I realized how ridiculous that was. No one would believe we stepped through a magic portal and ended up somewhere in Russia. And what would she do? Call the consulate? I had no idea where in Russia we were. The only one who could help was Quinn, and I had no way of contacting him.

We didn't have much longer to wait. Next to our cell, the wall shimmered translucent. First Boris, and then Irina, walked through it. Boris grinned, but there was cruelty rather than warmth behind it.

"Miss Marti, is good to see you again," he said, as if we had just run into each other at Starbucks.

"Why did you bring us here?" I asked.

"It is not obvious?" he asked.

"No," Nick said. I could hear the slow burn of controlled fury in his voice.

Boris continued to smile, but Irina hovered dourly behind him.

"I want to know how you found out about Dr. Pavlov. What else do you know about his work?"

"I don't know anything else. He was just a name in a contact list when I was trying to find my sister's doctor. I didn't know anything at all about Pavlov until that short guy with the birthmark on his head stole my car and ran over my sister's sequestered witness. She told me he was supposed to be going into the witness protection program immediately after the trial."

"She sequester him, so we monitor her calls. Smart girl, normally scrambles communications. One call, not encrypted. When you call Pavlov. We triangulate signal. Easy. Did she tell you what was reason for his protection?"

"No. She just said that he was an expert on attachment and conduct disorders. She was defending a kid with RAD – "

I stopped myself. Pavlov was an expert, probably *the* expert on RAD. And Boris took in RAD orphans.

"What did Pavlov know about you?" I asked him.

Nick's thumb was starting to tap on his knee. I knew he was used to being in charge and taking action, but right now, he wasn't able to do either. I could feel his agitation crackling in the air around us like heat lighting. It put me on edge, but Boris either failed to notice or disregarded it.

"Grigori was my oldest friend – I knew him from my time at Tri Babushkas. He worked for me after I started the Foundation, worked with the children. He did not understand, as I do, that these children were truly special. Grigori, he wanted to 'fix' them, make them more like normal. But they are fiercely loyal to their family, their brothers and sisters from Babushkas, and no one else. Many of them, they have excellent skill on internet. I teach them how to get money. Support themselves when they grow up."

"How much do you keep for yourself?" Nick asked, his staccato words bouncing off the cement like sonic bullets.

Boris chuckled. "Very good, friend of Miss Marti. Yes, I have expenses and I must be reimbursed. But they keep most of their earnings."

"What earnings are you talking about?" I asked, confused.

"He means he's teaching them to be cyber criminals. Isn't that right, Boris?" Nick said.

"That sounds very harsh," Boris answered. But he didn't deny it.

Irina leaned forward, on tiptoe, and whispered something in Boris' ear. He nodded. "Let us bargain. You know my secrets, so you cannot leave this place. If you tell me name of everyone who knows about me, I will break your necks before I feed you to Fenrir."

"What is a Fenrir?" Nick asked.

Boris laughed out loud, and even gloomy Irina smile a little. He nodded to the guard, who pressed one of the buttons on the console.

Each slat of the vertical blinds rotated from being parallel to the window to being perpendicular to it, then they all slid down the tract and disappeared into a recess. Pale yellow light flooded a skylight probably a third the size of the room and fell on what appeared to be a large pile of furs in the middle of the room on the other side of the glass. Then one of the pile's eyes opened, glowing electric blue.

I gasped.

The creature's other eye opened. I backed against the wall. Nick reached for his absent sidearm.

Then the beast stood up. It looked like a white wolf, fur edged in grey. Only it was the size of a Clydesdale, maybe even bigger.

"What do you want, Boris?" it asked, its tone equal parts boredom and annoyance.

"I was asked, 'What is a Fenrir?'," Boris said. "I am answering question."

In the furthest corner of the wolf's room, a door opened. A very tall man, I guessed seven feet or better, in leather pants and a cloak entered the room.

"Have you got it?" Fenrir demanded.

"No, my son. Be patient for a little while longer," the man said.

The wolf's lips pulled back in a semi snarl. "So close," he said. "I can feel it coming. My freedom. And when I am loosed, I will eat up every living thing I can find. None shall be safe! It will be payment for the thousand years' torment of being shackled to this wretched stone."

It seemed to me that he eyed Boris, in particular, when he said that nobody was going to be safe.

Nick started to laugh.

"I get it now. This is a dream. What else could it be? A magic wall that opens up and sends you from Houston to Russia? A giant, talking wolf? It's funny, though. I don't remember going to bed. But here I am."

"Nick, this is not a dream," I said.

"Of course it is." He uncrossed is legs and stretched them out.

"Okay, Nick. Okay. If this is a dream, why can't you walk through the bars? Or fly?"

He shrugged. "Not that kind of a dream."

Fantastic. If he thinks this is all a dream, no telling how he'll react when Boris tries to feed us to Fenrir. He might try to get away, but he might just fling both of us right into the wolf's maw. He might try jumping off a cliff or something.

"You seem to have problem," Boris said.

I glared at him.

Through the window into the other room, I could see the tall man leave the room. Moments later, three men, shackled and chained together, shuffled in. They wore what I guessed were poorly matched uniforms. As soon as they saw the monstrous wolf, they began screaming and cowering against the wall.

"It appears to be feeding time for Fenrir," Boris said.

"What?" I asked, unwilling to comprehend what he'd just said.

Fenrir grinned the way a fox grins at a mouse, and pounced on the first prisoner, jaws clamping around his body with a sickening, wet crunch. Bright blood spattered Fenrir's snowy muzzle. I turned around and slid down the bars as my knees gave way. I was afraid I was going to vomit.

"I wasn't expecting that," Nick said.

"Nick! You're not asleep!"

I rose to my knees and slapped him hard across the cheek. I got in his face, almost nose to nose. "You. Are. Not. Dreaming."

He slithered sideways to get away from me.

"This is real," I said.

His brow furrowed and he shook his head. "No," he said, but he seemed less convinced than he had been before.

"That's all very touching," Boris said. "But I do not suppose it much matters, at this point, what you do or do not know. You will die, whether or not you tell me. Fenrir has just been fed. Think about that. It will be your turn tomorrow."

The tall man who had been in the room with Fenrir came through the door near the guard's control panel and approached Boris and Irina.

"How much longer?" Boris asked, his words polite, but his tone brusque.

A single eyebrow arched above the man's icy blue eyes. "Soon."

The same color blue as Fenrir's I decided. After all, he had called the wolf "my son." How he came to have a canine offspring was more than I was interested in knowing. He was physically attractive, in an unconventional way, but there was something about him, a treacherous vibe perhaps, that also made him repulsive at the same time. To be fair, at least part of his physical attraction was that he smelled delicious – like cardamom and lemons.

"I do not understand what is delay, Loki. When you were set free, you said it would be no problem." Boris said.

Loki's eyes narrowed dangerously, and Boris took a step back. "I do not understand what is problem, Boris," he said, in perfect mockery. "When you unbound me, you said you knew that finding seven impossible things would take some time."

"How can you find even one impossible thing, much less seven?" Irina asked.

"That is the beauty of magick," Loki said, smiling. "To create a chain that Fenrir could not break was impossible. So the clever dwarves made a chain of six impossible things – the sound of a cat's footfall, a woman's beard, a mountain's roots, a bear's sinew, a fish's breath, and a bird's spittle. To break an impossible chain, an impossible blade, made of seven impossible things, is needed. To my dwarvish allies, I have already given a glass of burning water, dust from the grave a living man, a serpent's leg, hair from a babe birthed of a man, spider silk milked from a goat, and a vial of Kraken venom. The seventh item, the jewel from the gallbladder of a Nøkken, is proving more difficult. A great many of them seem to have died off since my imprisonment."

"What is a Nøkken?" I asked, forgetting I wasn't part of the conversation.

Irina's eyes widened, but a small, greasy smile oozed up the corners of Loki's mouth.

"A Nøkken is a large creature that lives in ancient lakes. It has a long neck, like a swan, and flippers, like a seal. And more teeth than the Orca. There was once one in Lake Seljordsvatnet, but it seems to have moved on. They are very rare and difficult to catch. Some say they are nothing but a fairytale, told to keep children from straying too close to the water's edge."

Nick snickered, although Loki's entrance had seemed to generate nothing but apathy from him.

I was familiar with lake monsters. Like Nessie. Or Quinn. I felt the breath catch in my chest. Wasn't he supposed to be in Scandinavia somewhere, watching Frost Giants?

"Sounds terrifying," I said, hoping that he hadn't noticed that my heart just skipped a beat.

He continued to look me in the eye, much longer than was comfortable or polite. His head tilted slightly to one side, then he turned abruptly and walked out. Irina and Boris followed him, although Boris paused to speak to the guard in Russian. I didn't like that he kept glancing over at Nick and I as he spoke.

I resumed my pacing, trying to keep warm. I would have traded my sparkly sequin dress for thick sweats and a hoodie in a heartbeat. I missed Cassie, and wondered what she was doing right now. I hoped she was sleeping soundly in her bed. I fretted about my sister, home alone with the twins and new baby, perhaps wondering where her husband was. What if I couldn't get Nick back to her? What if I died and left Cassie an orphan? I tried to avoid going down that road by distracting myself with thoughts of Hunter Greene, and his raven tattoo. I tried to focus on the details of sweat glistening on his chiseled muscles. The inky embrace of the raven's feathers around his shoulder, the pumpkin gnocchi, walking me home from Thursday night Circle. But try as I might, images of Hunter were pushed out by thoughts of Quinn – how he loved entertaining Cassie, his sizzling kiss, and his knack for showing up in the nick of time. The tiny little boat of my emotions rose on waves of anger, then dropped into troughs of sadness. I was actually glad when the guards came and opened the door to our cell.

There were three of them, the one who was there when we arrived, and two more. "Come with me," the original guard said. Even armed with machine guns, I might have been willing to challenge them and attempt an escape, if only Nick was with me. He was in complete denial about the very mortal danger we were in. He could not entertain the possibility that this was anything other than a dream.

We were escorted out of our cell and down a dilapidated corridor. White paint hung in strips from the ceiling, and pale blue paint flaked off of concrete walls. The air grew colder as we approached a double exterior door. The English-speaking guard punched in a code, and there was a loud click. The other two guards each pushed open a door, and we found ourselves on an island in the middle of a large lake. Beyond a razor wire-topped chain link fence, a dingy bobbed at the end of a decrepit dock. Seated inside the boat was an elderly woman, head covered with a bright blue kerchief, shoulders wrapped in a lacy shawl. A gnarled walking stick lay across her lap. She didn't seem to be suffering from the cold, although I was already shivering uncontrollably.

A gate in the fence was opened, and we were led out to the pier.

"In," the guard said, motioning toward the boat.

Lacking any better alternatives, I got in, followed by Nick. One of the guards also climbed aboard. The boat was well over capacity, and rode alarmingly deep in the water. The original guard stood, feet apart, arms crossed across his chest and watched us while the remaining guard untied the boat. When we had cast off, he picked up his machine gun and trained it on us. The guard in the boat began rowing us toward the rocky shoreline.

It didn't take very long to reach our destination five minutes or less, I estimated. The rowing guard hopped out and hauled the boat out of the water, then helped the elderly lady out. He just nodded toward the shore at Nick and me. When we reached terra firma, he stood behind us, Kalashnikov at the ready.

The elderly lady beckoned, and we followed her up the ridge. As we neared the top, I could hear the sound of a diesel engine running. Sure enough, down below was a snow crawler – a peculiar vehicle that appeared to be an unholy union between a truck and a tank. The large blocky chassis didn't appear to have any official insignia or identifiers, and it was painted with a snow camo pattern. Instead of wheels, it had treads. Two armed men jumped out of the back and prepared to receive their prisoners. Us.

The ride was bumpy and jarring, but at least the cabin was heated. It was the first time I'd felt warm since Nick and I fell through the wall. We drove for a while, perhaps as long as an hour, before we stopped. The door opened and the guards gestured with their rifles towards it. I started shivering again before I even reached the opening.

Note to self: don't wear stiletto heels to the beach next time. I had never been to the seashore this far north before. A colony of taupe-colored seals, all sporting ragged cream-colored spots on their fur, looked in our direction, but didn't seem too bothered by our presence.

We appeared to be free to go. But that seemed too easy, and I was reluctant to believe it.

I was right.

"There has been a change of plan," the old woman said. "Boris has decided to give you a sporting chance. On my recommendation, of course."

She pounded her cane into the beach three times, then started chanting in a language that I didn't understand. I tried to walk away from her, but my feet were rooted to the ground. The seals began to bark and call to each other, then stampeded into the water.

My skin began to itch. Then I felt cold and hot at the same time, almost like someone was pouring hot water on me, then rubbing my skin with ice. I gasped as my back was suddenly stretched and my ribcage felt like it was being pulled open by opposing elephants. My arms and legs began to swell, and my skin tightened and stretched painfully. I was startled by a ripping sound, then looked down and realized that my clothes were starting to tear apart.

My fingernails fell off, and were replaced by heavy black claws. Rough pads extruded from underneath my curling fingers and my palms. The same thing happened to my feet. By now, my beautiful dress was nothing more than a tragic and sparkling corpse on the beach, and my unmentionables weren't any better off.

It was at least as bad as childbirth, maybe worse, as my skull stretched and reshaped itself. I groaned as my jaws began to widen and extend. My teeth fell out. I couldn't help but to cry out as huge, sharp fangs pushed through my gums. I could smell my blood before I tasted it, as the wicked teeth forced their way out.

The itching intensified until it was unbearable. I needed to scratch, but I was unable to move. I whimpered out of frustration and dismay as fluffy white fur sprouted from my skin. That was the undercoat. Glossy guard hairs appeared next. When I opened my mouth to say something, a roar fell out instead of words.

My stomach growled. Nearby was an overpowering aroma. And it was delicious. I turned towards the source of it.

I was horrified to discover that as I was being turned into a polar bear, Nick was being transformed into a seal.

It was a struggle to restrain myself. I was so hungry, and he smelled so good. But I managed. I desperately studied him, hoping to find some special mark, or clue that would distinguish him from the hundreds of other seals in the colony. I just hoped that not too many of them had jagged white triangles on their left flippers.

I couldn't blame him for being afraid of me. Right now, I was afraid of me. Soda commercials notwithstanding, polar bears are huge and scary.

Nick finally flopped his way into the water, and I stood growling at the old woman. She smiled at me, and one of the men helped her back into the snow cat. Once he had climbed in himself, the engine growled as it churned its way up the slope. I snarled again with impotent rage.

Long after the noise of the machine faded into the distance, I sat on the beach and watched the seals. My stomach twisted and rumbled with hunger. I was unwilling to try to catch any of them, for fear of harming Nick – it would be hard to find the flipper pattern without catching the seal first. What had I done? How could I have gotten him involved in this? Would I ever see Cassie again?

A movement on the horizon caught my eye. Raising my head and scenting the air, I realized that there was a polar bear approaching. A male. I didn't want him hanging around – sooner or later, the seals would have to come back on shore, and I didn't want him anywhere near Nick. It was hard enough for me to resist eating him, and the other bear wouldn't care in the slightest that he was my brother-in-law.

I watched the other bear approach, loping across the snow. He stopped about a hundred yards from me, and stood on his hind legs, sniffing the air.

Unfortunately, I had no idea what polar bears did to claim their territory. I supposed that on their own, they probably clawed up trees and left scent markings of one type or another. But when directly confronted by another bear? I just did what a mother bear would do to protect her babies. I stood on my hind legs and roared. The sound was deep and harsh, nearly otherworldly. The other bear dropped to all fours. He didn't respond, but he didn't leave either. I took an awkward step towards him and roared again. He stayed put. Possibly, his hunger was stronger than his fear.

The seals were not on the beach, and therefore, not any easier for him to catch that they were for me. I suppose he realized this, because he began to meander down the beach, away from me. I watched until he disappeared, where the shoreline and the sky became indistinguishable.

I felt satisfied with myself for chasing away the other bear without any blood being shed, especially my blood.

Then I heard the splashing.

Seals leaped out of the water as an enormous black dorsal fin broke the surface.

Crap.

The seals wouldn't come on the beach if I was sitting there. But they couldn't stay in the water with the killer whales, either. I only saw one, but I knew they often hunted in packs.

Nick, if you get eaten by a polar bear or an orca, I'm going to kill you.

I trotted up the slope, away from the beach, so the seals could get out of the water.

If I had any chance of helping Nick, and myself, I couldn't just sit around looking at the delicious seals. First, I had to get something to eat. Then I had to find the old woman.

Chapter 22
When Life Hands You Lemons

The scent of the old woman – cardamom and lemons – was easy to follow. It lingered on the stones and floated in the air, when the wind wasn't whisking it away.

I followed her to a cabin, a hut, really, in the shelter of a cliff.

That was the good news. The bad news was that I was starting to feel light-headed from hunger. If I came across anyone right now, human or animal, I might not be able to control myself.

I stood up on my hind legs and breathed deeply, hoping to find something, anything edible. It was windy, but off to my left, I smelled water. Fresh water. Perhaps there would be fish.

I followed the smell of water until I came to a lake. There was something odd about it. An island in the middle reeked of fear and death. Even I feared being in sight of it.

But then there was another scent. Not fish. Not seal, but animal, and of the water. I crept towards the lake, wary, testing the air with each step.

And then I saw the long neck, rising from the water. The head that topped it wasn't large, but the mouth was filled with daggers. Could it be Quinn? How many others of his kind were there?

I reared up again to get a better view. The creature saw me. I wanted to get closer, but then a flash of color caught my eye.

There, to my left, the crone in her bright blue kerchief approached the lake. I had to catch her. No telling when I'd get another chance. I bounded towards her, moving as fast as my hunger-weakened legs would go. Cold seared my lungs, and spurred me on.

I saw her turn her head to look at me, and I could swear she smiled. Right before she started screaming.

I was closing in on her, and she waded into the water. *What was she thinking?*

A dark ripple plowed under the clear surface of the lake, streaking towards the woman. *Oh, great. He was protecting her. Fantastic. Who does he think she is, anyway?*

I might be able to reach her first. I started into the water, but the kelpie got there before me. He raised his head high above her and hissed. I knew there was a possibility that this beast wasn't Quinn. But what if it was? Surely if he only knew what this old woman had done to Nick and me, he wouldn't be protecting her. I growled in frustration. Wondering how much maneuvering room the kelpie had, I moved from side to side, trying to see if he was resting on the bottom. I couldn't tell, so I reared up on my back legs. That didn't help, either.

"Listen to me!" I shouted at the creature.

But my voice only came out as a gravelly roar.

He hissed again, and we stared at each other for a lengthy moment before I retreated to beach and sat down, not wanting this confrontation. His neck was long and vulnerable, easily snapped by my strong jaws and sheer weight, if it came to that. But, if I missed, he had his own armory, and I suspected that his six inch teeth could penetrate even my heavy skull. I didn't want either of us to get hurt, even if that thing wasn't Quinn. On the other hand, I was hungry enough to eat a human, and it just might be that if the old woman died, her spell would be broken. At least, that's how it worked in the movies, anyway.

The decision was made for me when the kelpie dived underneath the old woman, scooped her up and swam off with her. I didn't try to pursue them. I had to eat, or I wouldn't be able to help anybody.

Using my nose when the wind died down, I eventually picked up the scent of something goaty. I followed it to a partially stripped reindeer carcass. The flesh was tough and stringy, but it was food. I cracked its long bones and ate the marrow, as well. Not much of a meal, but better than nothing.

After I finished with the carcass, I looked around the area for something more. As I walked, I noticed something curious. Sprouting from vines creeping along the ground were red and orange berries. They looked like unripe blackberries, but I was hungry and didn't really care if they were ripe. Those berries were everywhere, and I walked along, nose almost to the ground, scooping up the little snacks as I went. It took a lot of them to fill me up, but there were countless numbers of them. It was difficult to tell how long this had taken – there was never any nightfall, only a bright twilight. I finally felt ready to get back to my hunt for the crone.

Going to the old woman's hut and watching for her to come out seemed like the obvious choice, but the area around her house was strewn with black rocks and the snow was thin, due to the hovel being in the lee of the cliff. Being a large white bear made blending in to the background difficult without much snow. No, I had to find a way that she wouldn't see coming until it was too late. I just hoped Nick was okay – he had as much experience being a seal as I had being a polar bear. I wasn't doing so well, and nothing was trying to eat me.

Grazing on berries the whole way, I found my way back to the old woman's shanty. I went around, far out of my way, and came up on top of the sheltering cliff. I couldn't see the shack, but I could see anyone approaching it. It was too high for me to be able to jump down without breaking my neck. I wished there was a big boulder I could roll down on top of it, but there was nothing larger than a basketball. If I had any reason to expect accuracy, that would be more than enough. That was an awfully big if, though.

I had just decided to go back the way I'd come when I saw something moving in the distance. I lay down, making myself as flat as possible, near the edge of the cliff. I could observe without being observed.

Quinn approached the cabin. The wind blew his dark hair back, away from his face, and his eyes squinted against the fresh breeze. I found it hard to believe he would just run off and leave Cassie and me without bothering to say goodbye, but here he was. But why? Was he in cahoots with the old lady? Did he know all along this was going to happen? Or was he walking into a trap? I wasn't sure how to feel, so I just sat and watched until he disappeared from my line of sight. After a few seconds, I heard a door open and shut. I could hear voices, but not well enough to make out words.

I got up and trotted back to where I could climb back down the cliff and go to where the shack huddled against the rock face.

While I didn't expect much success with a direct attack, I was so angry, both at what the old woman had done to me and Nick, and at seeing Quinn strolling around nonchalantly, that I grabbed a corner of the little building in my teeth and worried it like a terrier with a rat. The hut was surprisingly sturdy, and I accomplished even less than I had expected. I roared at the hovel. It shuddered and a few pebbles from the top of the cliff rolled down, ricocheting off the roof. One hit me in the face, and I let go of the corner.

The door had fallen ajar when I tried to demolish the little structure. I looked in the crack. Nobody was in the house. However, I could see an orange glow coming from an opening in the rocks where the shack clung to the cliff. Curious.

I thought my energy could be put to better use than being a Peeping Tom, so I started searching for the hag's spoor. There were traces of her all around, but none of them were fresh. Would it be worth my while to go search for Quinn? What would I do if I saw him? Roar? He could hiss back at me. Wouldn't that be a nice conversation?

No, what I needed was a plan. How was I going to catch the old woman? What was I going to do with her when I caught her? Knowing where she lived helped me far less than I had thought it would. It seemed to me that in so many stories, breaking the wand or staff of the wizard was always took away his power. She had a walking stick. Was it the same thing? The only sure thing was that if I didn't do something, I was never going to get back home to Cassie.

While I was coming up with a plan, I decided that I would go get a drink at the lake and see if I could find something to eat. The berries were wearing off.

I thought I was being careful. The only signs of life I saw on the way to the water were a couple of ravens. Those freeloaders were probably just hoping I'd kill something so they could get the scraps. I ignored them.

In the mud near the water, I noticed something. Tracks. Some were from horse shoes. Some looked human. Most of the ground was rocky, and didn't take footprints, but this little soft spot was covered in them. There seemed to have been two people here. One very large, the other smaller, but not small. I wasn't a tracker, but my guess was that unless Sasquatch had started wearing shoes, the larger tracks belonged to someone the size of a professional basketball player.

I sat down.

The only seven footer I'd seen in this area was Loki. And he was hunting for a kelpie. Even under my thick fur undercoat, I suddenly felt cold. Quinn was in danger, and there was nothing I could do to warn him. In fact, it may already be too late.

I studied the muddy area again. The big tracks didn't go into the water, and I could see no indication that something large had been dragged out of the lake.

A rock scraped against another rock, and I whirled around.

There was the kelpie, undulating up behind me. He'd been coming from upwind, so I hadn't smelled him. I dodged out of the way as his wicked jaws snapped shut on the space my head had just occupied. Reflexively, I raked at his face with my claws, drawing blood. He yanked his head out of reach. I backed away, out of range of his long neck. I took my eyes off of him for a second, when I noticed a patch of blue where there shouldn't be one, near all the footprints. The crone was watching us, her hideous mouth gaping open in a frightful grin.

I almost paid dearly for my moment of distraction. Quinn had swung his head at me like a wrecking ball and missed by inches. I felt the breeze of it as it flashed by me.

I couldn't bring myself to attack Quinn. But I wasn't about to sit around and let him kill me, either. Quinn's strength in that form was water, so I made sure to put as much distance between me and the water as I could. He could move faster on land than I'd originally given him credit for. But he wasn't as fast as me.

This ungainly dance up the slope of the beach was a draw. He'd swipe at me, I'd dodge and back out of his way. The effort it took for Quinn to move quickly on land was starting to show. His strikes were slower, easier to avoid. I didn't have a way to communicate with him. If he only knew who I really was, he would stop. I was sure of it. But how?

The gravel beneath my paws suddenly gave way. I tumbled down on my back and started to roll over. Faster that I thought possible, Quinn was partially on top of me, pinning my hind legs and trapping one of my forelegs underneath my body.

The snakelike neck reared back, and the jaws opened wide, poised to deal the death blow. There was nothing I could do but look into his eyes as they came at me like an on-rushing locomotive.

His teeth were blade sharp against my throat, and I could feel his breath on my jugular.

But he froze.

To my utter amazement, he pulled away. He looked at me, tilting his head from side to side. Did he realize who I was?

Pebbles crunched together and I saw the old woman streaking towards us, cane raised. I grunted and he looked around.

He jerked out of the way, the end of the cane grazing his neck before it hit the ground with enough force to break it in two.

The hag stood glaring at us, so angry she was foaming at the mouth. She leapt at Quinn, and I grabbed her blouse in my teeth. So much for my theory about the broken cane.

A horse whinnied in the near distance. The ground vibrated with its footfalls as it galloped towards us at twice the speed of a normal horse.

"Loki!" the man riding the horse roared.

The crone began laughing. And growing, stretching up taller and taller. Now, instead of the bent old woman, the tall man I'd seen on the island stood in her place.

His laughter deepened as he pulled a gleaming ax from his belt.

"You're too late, Odin!" he shouted back, raising the axe and angling it toward Quinn.

He might have been seven feet tall, but I was taller. I raised myself to my full height and put my front paws on his chest, pushing him back. Then I roared in his face and grabbed his forearm in my mouth, biting down hard until I hit bone.

He screamed and dropped the axe. In a flash, he'd turned himself into a crow, slipped through my teeth and flapped away, cackling.

I dropped back down to all fours. Odin pulled up his horse. It took me a moment to realize that the thing that looked so wrong about it was that it had eight legs instead of four.

"Are you harmed?" he asked.

Quinn and I looked at each other. The side of his head where I'd scratched him earlier was already almost healed. I felt I was in one piece.

Odin put his hands on either side of my head and I suddenly felt drunk. My eyes closed and I swayed, but he held me up. It seemed like a tornado was whirling inside my body, and every single molecule was caught in the vortex. The motion slowed, and I opened my eyes.

The first thing I saw was my hands.

Hands! Not paws. I was back to my normal self. Odin had the foresight to generate some clothing for me as well, because I was dressed in white pants, a white sweatshirt, and a thick white parka.

Quinn scooped me up in his arms and crushed me against him.

"I'm sorry," he said. "I'm so sorry. I almost killed you."

"Can't…breathe." I managed to wheeze.

He let go and cupped my face in his hands. "What are you doing here? Where's Halle?"

"I have no idea where Halle is. Isn't she with you?" I asked, my enjoyment of his touch suddenly tempered.

"No. She said she would look after you while I was gone." Quinn shook his head.

While I was gone. That implied that he had intended to return.

"You could have at least left a note." I wasn't going to let him off the hook that easily.

"I did."

"There was no note."

"I left it stuck on the fridge with a magnet."

Odin cleared his throat and looked up at the sky.

"Never mind," Quinn said. "I think I know what happened to the note. Hurricane Halle."

That made sense. "How did you know?"

"Know what?" he asked. His mouth smiled, but his eyebrows furrowed slightly.

"That it was me. That I wasn't just any ordinary polar bear."

Quinn brushed a stray lock of hair out of my face. "From the first time I saw that bear, I knew there was something different about it. When I got close to you, I caught a whiff of lemon blossoms. Your hair always smells like lemon blossoms."

"This is very charming," Odin broke in. "But we are running out of time. And you," he pointed to Quinn, "do not, for any reason, shift into the form of the Nøkken."

Odin scanned the horizons. "Our reinforcements should be here soon."

Without warning, there was a tremendous *Boom!* and fire shot out of one of the windows of the main building on the island. Men screamed and shouted. Then there was silence.

"What's happening?" I asked.

A plume of black smoke billowed out from another part of the building. A wolf howled, and it was such a deep, chilling sound that I involuntarily took a step backwards.

"Fenrir has been unchained," Odin said grimly.

Chapter 23
Loyalty Among Thieves

That smoking island in the middle of the lake was the last place I wanted to go.

"We have to save Nick," I said.

"Nick? What is he doing here? And how did you get here?" Quinn asked.

"I'm not sure we have time for this," Odin said.

I looked at him and gave a demi-smile. "Long story short, I was working at a party, got locked in the wine cellar, called Nick for help, and we fell through a door painted on the wall and ended up there," I pointed to the island. "The old woman, who turned out to be Loki, turned me into a polar bear and Nick into a seal. We have to change him back, before something happens to him."

"Understood," Odin said. "But we need to see what is happening at Bright Falcon, first."

"We don't have a boat," I said.

"We don't need one. We have Sleipnir."

Odin sprang into the saddle, Quinn lifted me up behind him, and then he vaulted up, sitting practically on top of the poor horse's hips. Sleipnir didn't seem to mind, and he half-reared as Odin spurred him. He galloped over the water just the same as if it had been land, then leaped up onto the island where it rose from the lake.

"That's a neat trick," I said.

Odin smiled. He put his hand to the gate and the locks snapped open. Quinn and I followed him into the prison yard.

"That's strange," Quinn said.

"What?" I asked.

"I've been calling Malik ever since Loki escaped, but he hasn't responded. He's supposed to be watching the jötnar, not far from here. He should be well within range. He heard me last time with no trouble."

"Hmh," said Odin.

We dismounted and left Sleipnir in the shelter of an empty vehicle shed. We made our way into the prison. Bloody corpses – some guards, some prisoners – were strewn everywhere. Steam rose from a broken radiator pipe. There was a massive hole in the wall to the windowed room which had contained Fenrir.

"This is the work of the jötnar," Odin said with a scowl.

A deep-throated howl echoed off the bare concrete. Not the howl of a wolf, but the howl of a man who has been wounded down to his soul. Quinn put his hand on my shoulder.

We picked our way through the glass and debris, moving towards the source of the sound. A reinforced door on the other side of Fenrir's enclosure hung from one hinge. Another howl reverberated out of the darkness behind the doorway.

Odin led the way into the murky corridor. Light from the collapsed roof shone on the far end of it. There was a figure there, a very large figure, standing against the wall, arms in the air.

"What trouble have you gotten yourself into now, Loki?" Odin asked, crossing his arms over his chest.

Loki's arms were manacled above his head. An ax was poised at his throat, ready to lop off his head if he moved his weight from a brick that held down the other end of the heavy gauge wire. The edge of the brick was narrow, and Loki's feet were large. If he lost his balance, his head would roll.

"Those traitors, Boris and Irina, have stolen Fenrir and done this to me. I will grind their bones to dust when I catch them! The man with the serpent's eyes cannot long protect them. I never thought my kin, the jötnar, would allow such a thing to happen," Loki fumed. The brick rocked back and forth as he talked. "Release me!"

Quinn's face went a shade or two paler.

"Is Fenrir loosed then?" Odin asked.

"He is still bound with Gleipnir, but Gleipnir is no longer bound to the rock."

"I see no reason we should do anything other than leave you here," Quinn said.

I felt bad for Loki, but I didn't disagree with Quinn, either. Loki had just turned me into a polar bear and Nick into a seal, then he'd pitted Quinn and I against each other in a duel to the death. I had no doubt he would kill Quinn at the first opportunity, to get the Nøkken's jewel, if he was released.

As I looked at Loki a little closer, I realized that there was a note pinned to his chest with a shard of glass.

"What's that?"

Odin removed the note, scowled at it and thrust it at Quinn. He scanned it, then closed his eyes for a moment and swallowed hard. His shoulders slumped a little.

"What does it say?" I asked, reaching out for it.

A spidery handwriting crawled across the paper. I read it out loud. "Do not think I have been unaware of you watching me, fay. I warned you not to meddle in Balcones' business. Now, I have the ultimate weapon. There is no end to Fenrir's appetite, and he cannot be killed by any mortal man. Between him and the Berserkers provided to me, courtesy of the jötnar, I am an unstoppable force. Now, where shall I test my new weapon? Perhaps at the Model NATO Student Diplomat Festival in Geneva tomorrow. A shame so many bright young people and their families should end up as wolf fodder. Or perhaps I should start with your girlfriend's house. It worked so well the last time. Decisions, decisions."

Quinn looked like someone had whacked him with a 2x4. "I knew the Frost Giants were involved. But not Balcones. I had no idea."

"Do not let him goad you into doing something rash," Odin said. "He may only be guessing, trying to trick you into betraying your hand."

Quinn's eyes went kelpie black, and he kicked a piece of wreckage. Loki jumped at the sound, and nearly fell off his brick.

"Of course you knew Balcones was involved. You've been chasing him for weeks," I said.

"No. I knew the Frost Giants killed Siobhan. She was on my team. We...had a relationship. I had no idea Balcones had anything to do with her death."

"I'm sorry," I said. I took his hand, and he squeezed my fingers gratefully. "Do you think he will really hurt Cassie?" I asked, trying to push down the rising panic. "And my parents?"

"Not if we stop them first," Loki said. His voice was butter-smooth. "Please. Release me. I can help track him down. I want my son, Fenrir back at least as much as you want Balcones."

Odin reached out and took hold of the ax at Loki's throat.

"What are you doing?" I asked, unable to believe he was just going to let him go.

Odin shook his head. "The Prophecy cannot be unmade. It is fated that Fenrir shall be unbound and unfettered, and he shall swallow me alive. Still, my son Vidar will break his jaws and Fenrir will be slain. It is not what I would wish, but it is what must happen. Loki will no doubt track Fenrir like a hunting hound if he is paid for it with my blood."

"He still needs the Nøkken's jewel," I reminded him. I glanced at Quinn, but I didn't miss the fleeting gleam in Loki's eyes when I mentioned the jewel.

"He can only take it if I'm in kelpie form," Quinn said.

Odin released the haft of the ax from its improvised trigger. I didn't trust Loki as far as I could throw him, but I seemed to have precious little choice in the matter. Odin touched the manacles, and they clanked open. Rubbing his wrists, Loki stepped off the brick.

"I have upheld our end of this evil bargain, my brother," Odin said. "Now, find Fenrir."

"As you wish," Loki replied with an unctuous smile.

Ahead of us lay a tunnel that sloped gently downward. It wasn't well lit, and sounds of dripping water, sizzling, and the occasional metal clanging made it even less inviting. Loki started down it. Odin hesitated, then whistled for Sleipnir. The horse was reluctant to follow, but did as he was asked. His nostrils flared and he snorted the entire way. The slope bottomed out, went level for a time, then changed direction. We all seemed to be walking faster, hurrying to get out of the frightful place.

Finally, we came to the top of the grade. A ruined steel door lay a few yards away from its frame. But I think we may have jumped out of the frying pan and into the storm. The wind was howling, and the sky was a strange color, a swirl of purple and green. A few glowering grey clouds scudded by on the fierce wind.

"It has begun," Odin said. He looked to the sky. Two black dots, high up, came hurtling towards us. Huginn and Muninn landed on Odin's shoulders. "Tell the host to meet us on the battle plane. We are traveling there with all haste. Time is short. Fly!"

The ravens took off, back in the same direction they came from. I looked towards my right, and there was what looked like a pillar of smoke coming from the horizon.

Odin followed my gaze with a grim smile. "The Valkyries are coming."

I wondered if that included Halle. I had a few choice words for her when this was over. I stood and watched the cloud approach. It reminded me of watching the bats come out from under the Waugh Street Bridge during the summer. Loki raced around like a demented bloodhound, looking for clues as to which direction Fenrir had gone.

Most of the Valkyries circled overhead. One started dropping down towards us. I bet I knew exactly which one it was. Although I hadn't expected her to be riding a huge black horse with wings, fangs, and glowing yellow eyes. This must be where the word "nightmare" comes from.

"Odin," I said. "We have to rescue Nick. He doesn't know the first thing about being a seal. Something is going to eat him." *If it hasn't already.*

"Halle can take you," he replied. "Be swift."

As soon as her scary black horse's feet touched the ground, I said, "We have to go get Nick."

"Where is he?"

Quinn boosted me up onto the horse's broad back, behind Halle. He kissed me on the forehead while he was doing it. "For luck," he'd murmured. Then he gave Halle a hard look. "Leave Nick alone. He doesn't belong to you."

"What do you mean by that? Of course he doesn't belong to her." *Weren't there enough complications already without Halle trying to poach every man she met?*

"I am a Valkyrie. Do you not know what Valkyries do?"

The horse shifted, and I had to grab Halle so I didn't fall off. "I don't know. Walk around in bronze bikinis and horned helmets? Can we just go and get Nick now?"

Halle clucked to her horse. "Rädsla, up!" The black mare leaped into the air. Even holding on to Halle, I nearly slipped off Radsla's butt.

"Valkyries are choosers of the slain. We choose the very best warriors to go to Valhalla, to fight with Odin on the day of Ragnarök. It is our choice who lives or dies during battle."

"Don't. You. Dare. I'm sure Nick would be flattered to know that you thought he was one of the very best warriors, but he has a beautiful wife, two young sons, and a brand new baby. It seems totally unfair for you to involve him in this. He never did anything to you."

I had to close my eyes because I was getting a terrible case of vertigo. I never even liked to go on glass elevators. My other senses automatically sharpened when I shut my eyes. I could hear the whuff, whuff of Rädsla's wings beating the cold air. I was sharply aware of the warm horsey smell rising around us and masking the crisp, snowy scent of arctic breeze. The mare's back was relatively steady, but her ribs moved in and out a lot with each breath, making my legs unsteady. It had been a long time since I'd ridden a horse. When we lived out in the country, we weren't too far from Gracie. She competed in barrel racing, but there was always a quiet horse around their farm that I could ride when I came over, which was often. Riding a horse isn't quite the same as riding a bicycle – you do forget if you haven't done it in a while.

I was thankful that Odin had set me up with such a warm coat. It was cold up here. I wished I could relax and enjoy the view. The trouble was the view made me nauseous, and I couldn't relax because I was concerned about my family being eaten by a giant wolf. That niggling worry edged everything in my mind.

"Where did you see him last?" Halle asked.

"That's a good question. They drove us in a snow truck from the island out to the beach."

"Landmarks?"

"Being kidnapped, held at gunpoint, and turned into a polar bear kind of put a crimp in my enjoyment of the landscape."

"A polar bear? What are you talking about?" Halle asked.

"On the beach, I didn't know if they were going to shoot us or just leave us out there, but Loki turned me into a polar bear and Nick into a seal."

Halle made a noise, that if I were feeling charitable, would say was her clearing her throat. Otherwise, it was suspiciously like a stifled laugh. "That sounds like Loki."

My eyes were still tightly closed. I opened one part-way. The view was stunning, but my head swam and invisible hands seemed to be clutching at my stomach, squeezing and twisting it.

I decided to try focusing on the panorama over Halle's shoulder and not look down. I still kept one eye closed.

"I think I've found the seals," Halle said.

Rädsla began her descent. It wasn't a steep bank, but it was enough to make me queasy.

It did not help that three tall black dorsal fins rode high in the water. I would never forgive myself if Nick got eaten by a killer whale.

"How can you tell which one is Nick?" Halle asked.

"There's a whitish triangle on his left flipper."

"That doesn't help much, unless you know a way to ask the seals to all line up on the beach for you to examine."

The black dorsal fins ominously disappeared. *Please, please, please be okay, Nick.*

"Can you get low above the water? Maybe I can call him."

Rädsla dropped down until her hooves were skimming the waves.

"Nick!" Halle and I both called out, over and over.

Halle guided the horse in an increasingly larger spiral around where we'd last seen the seals.

"If we do not find him soon, we will have to try again later," Halle said, glancing toward the sky. The Valkyries were a diminishing swarm in the distance.

"We can't leave him! Nick! Please come out!"

I caught a flash of movement near a rocky outcropping on the beach side of the spiral.

"What's that over there?"

Rädsla banked in that direction. We found a group of five seals on the rocks. A very large orca had them cornered. He was whistling and clicking to call his pod over. The outcropping was narrow, and it wouldn't take much effort to yank the poor things into the water.

"Nick?" I called.

The largest of the seals, also the one who was closest to the edge, looked up.

"Halle, I think that's him."

Rädsla circled the seals, and sure enough there was a whitish triangle on the seal's flipper.

Unfortunately, I hadn't given much thought to the logistics of lading a one hundred fifty pound seal onto the back of a horse that was hovering over the ocean. The outcropping wasn't solid enough for Nick to travel all the way to the beach, and jumping in the water with the killer whale was not likely to end well.

There was a loud whooshing, and an animal a little larger than a Chevy Suburban appeared near Rädsla's head. It almost looked like it was smiling at us as we were abruptly at eye-level with him.

I thought that breaching was an odd thing for the whale to do. But then I realized why it was so clever. When he landed back in the water, he created a wave which nearly washed the seals off the rock. A small seal would have been pushed over the edge, if the largest hadn't put his bigger body in the way. That was definitely Nick. A second orca came up on the other side of the rock and missed Nick's tail by inches. "We've to get rid of these killer whales! If they can't get the seals, they'll start going for Rädsla next."

Halle muttered something I didn't' understand. Rädsla screamed with rage. The next dorsal fin that popped up, she caught in her teeth. Not horse teeth, but the sharp, wolfish fangs I'd glimpsed earlier.

Blood ran down the sides of the dorsal fin, and the orca started to dive. I wasn't sure if Rädsla was trying to keep the whale on the on the surface, or if her fangs were stuck in the cartilage of the fin. Two thousand pounds of marine mammal in the open water was a definite advantage over fifteen hundred pounds of flying horse. Gravity was on the whale's side. My feet, then lower legs went into the water as the orca pulled us down. Again, Halle shouted and the mare let go. I wasn't sure if I was shaking from the cold or from fear.

"Get a little closer to the rocks so we can get Nick."

Tall dorsal fins circled the outcropping, but the orcas didn't surface. It was not easy to watch them and tug Nick onto Rädsla's back between Halle and myself. He was slippery, mostly inflexible, and didn't offer much in the way of handholds. At least he wasn't a walrus. We finally managed to drag him up and lay him precariously across Rädsla's back.

"Nick, don't move. If you fall off the horse, there isn't going to be a way to catch you. We'll get you to Odin, and he'll change you back. Just hang on, okay?"

The flying horse began to rise slowly, gently into the air, and I supposed that she would stay as low as she could, at least partly because of the extra weight.

The killer whales had gone, and I'd assumed that it was because of Rädsla's attack. But I noticed that the water around the rocks was quickly retreating, as if someone had pulled a plug somewhere on the ocean floor, and it was draining away. I felt the hair on the back of my neck rising.

"Tide's awfully fast around here," I said.

"That isn't the tide," Halle replied.

I had remembered reading somewhere that before a tsunami, the tide goes out both much faster and farther than usual, and at the wrong time. I looked out toward the water. There seemed to be an island forming a couple of hundred yards away from us.

"Rädsla! Up! Up!" Halle shouted. "Hold on tight," she added as an afterthought.

"Halle, what's happening?"

"Jörmungandr is rising."

"I don't know what that is," I replied through clenched teeth. I was holding on to Halle with one hand and Nick with the other. His weight was pushing me backwards, due to the steep angle Rädsla's back had suddenly acquired.

"Jörmungandr is the Midgard Serpent, Fenrir's brother, and Loki's son. He lies under the ocean and circles the world, clasping his own tail in his jaws. When he lets go of his tail, it is the time of the world's end."

Chapter 24
Contracts

Boris did not trust the Frost Giants. But Balcones, he had made an offer Boris couldn't refuse. Loki had wanted to release Fenrir just to get revenge against Odin. The end of the world was merely an unfortunate side effect, collateral damage. Balcones had a plan. In the developing world, kidnapping was a common tactic to raise cash fast. But why settle for kidnapping individuals? With a weapon like Fenrir, entire governments could be held for ransom, or toppled for a generous fee. For his cut, all Boris had had to do was free Loki and let him collect all the materials to set the wolf loose.

Boris had known, all those years ago when he'd stumbled onto the chained Fenrir, that he was sitting on lighting in a jar. He hadn't known how to harness what he had, but he'd had plenty of money to lubricate the palms of local officials to award the contract for building the Kola Correctional Colony to his own company. Feeding Fenrir would make him grow, and what better food source than the cast-off dregs of humanity? People whom would not be missed or mourned. Of course, the original proposal for the colony came at Boris' request as well. He thought of the provincial governor whom he'd persuaded to submit the request. The governor had killed himself soon afterward. Boris had been disappointed that his asset had put himself out of play, but he had shrugged it off. If one has skeletons in one's closet, one should not participate in public office.

He stood smoking a Black Russian cigarette at the edge of the ice cave, and pulled his coat tighter around himself against the wind. He didn't understand why Balcones had insisted on taking Fenrir now. Loki still had one element left to find. He would rather have kept the beast in Bright Falcon, where he could easily come and go through the portal. Being stuck in this freezing cave brought back too many bad memories and made him cross.

And speaking of things that made him cross, he should probably ask Sveklá to kill his wife. He knew that the man was quite fond of Irina, but he was also an excellent lieutenant, and always did as he was told. Irina had been necessary when the three of them had escaped from Babushkas. When they'd finally made their way to St. Petersburg, he'd sold her by the hour to pay for food and shelter. She was already so damaged at that point that he didn't think it would do her any more harm. Besides, everyone had to pull their weight.

She was very clever, and she made a lovely figurehead for the Cherngelanov Foundation. Still, he'd grown tired of her, even though she always did things he craved, like arranging not one, not two, but three prostitutes for him last week on his birthday. She'd even taken a photo on his phone to remember it by. Perhaps he should just give her to Sveklá as a bonus for a job well done.

Fenrir lay sleeping at the far end of the cave. It was never dark in the cave, but never truly light, either. The sun shone through the ice with an unsettling blue light. He was tied by the flimsy chain – Boris had seen thicker jewelry chains – but the monster either couldn't or wouldn't break free. He was guarded by one of the Frost Giants. As he watched, he saw Irina appear from the depths of a tunnel in the ice and began a conversation with the giant. After a while, the Frost Giant left, leaving Irina in charge of the wolf.

From where he was standing, Boris could not hear anything Irina said, but he did see one of Fenrir's great blue eyes open. Irina talked some more and the other eyelid raised.

Boris thought it would probably be in his best interest to join the conversation. It could be dangerous to talk to such a creature as Fenrir, and Irina might need protecting. Or at least monitoring. Dragons are said to have irresistible, hypnotic voices. Perhaps Fenrir was the same.

He took a final pull on his Sobranie, and flicked the shiny gold filter out of the cave. His stride was purposeful as he made his way to where Irina and Fenrir were talking. Boris exuded confidence from every pore. He kissed Irina on the cheek, a gesture of ownership rather than affection.

"Pah!" complained Fenrir. "This one stinks."

"I'm sorry for that. But he is well fed." Irina answered.

"I can see that," Fenrir said, eyeing Boris in a way that made him take a step backward.

"Irina, darling, what are you talking about?" Boris asked.

"You, of course, darling Boris. Is not everything about you?"

Boris was taken aback. It seemed uncharacteristic of Irina, to be so bold. Perhaps he should have Sveklá kill her, after all.

"I do not like this arrangement with Balcones," she continued. "We have housed and fed Fenrir all these years, at great expense, I might add. He's grown even larger than when you found him. Why should Balcones step in and take all of the money?" As she spoke, Irina had backed away from Boris, slowly, almost imperceptibly, one tiny step at a time.

"He is not taking all money!" Boris snapped. He didn't like her insinuation that he had made a bad bargain. Was she calling him a fool? Perhaps he wouldn't bother Sveklá, and just kill Irina himself.

"I have made my own deal," She untied the knot that fastened Fenrir to a large rock. "Goodbye, Boris," she said, then disappeared back down the tunnel.

In an instant, Fenrir was on his feet.

"Hello, Boris," he said with a wicked grin. Frothy slaver dripped from his wide jaws.

Before Boris could turn to run, Fenrir was on him Bones crunched and tissues squelched as the great wolf swallowed Boris head first, like a python swallowing a rabbit.

Chapter 25
Plain of Vigrid

The various Aesir had been filtering into the camp as soon as it had been made. There were a lot of tall, blonde goddesses that were hard for me to tell apart, both from each other and the Valkyries. Thor was easy to remember because of his hammer, and Tyr had only one hand. They stood talking to Nick, who was still a little rubber-legged after having just been turned back into a man from having been a seal for days. They were comparing hero notes, I supposed, although it looked like Thor was doing most of the talking. His fingers traced the tip of the engraved war horn that hung from his belt, as if he was anxious to blow it and get the battle started. I shook my head. Portals and giant talking wolves, Nick couldn't accept. But add a few muscle-bound warrior gods, and he's all over it.

There had been minor earthquakes all morning, and smoke poured from what must be a volcanic mountain top maybe ten miles away.

I hated this.

This was not my fight, but Balcones had threatened my family, my baby, and I could not just go home and pretend everything was fine. Because it might not be. I had to stay here and make sure that Fenrir was dead, see it with my own eyes, before I could believe it. Odin had assured me that the prophecy foretold Fenrir's death. As well as his own. But prophecy is a slippery thing.

Nick had been bewildered to find that the person whom he was so sure was a low-life criminal and drug user at the camp.

"Try and think of it as an undercover operation. There really was a Marc McLeod – I just borrowed his identity. He didn't need it anymore," Quinn said.

"The real McLeod is dead?"

"Yes."

"Did you kill him?"

"No. He'd chosen a high risk lifestyle," Quinn said, but didn't elaborate.

Nick nodded, but I think it was less that he accepted Quinn's story, and more that he believed that junkies tended to have short life expectancies. That was probably the only thing that made sense to him.

Quinn scowled.

"What's wrong?" I asked.

"I've been trying for days now to reach Malik. He doesn't seem to be able to hear me. I hope…I hope he's okay." he trailed off.

Odin had found woolen shirts, chain maille, leather armor, and shields for Nick, Quinn and myself, and given each of us a spear, axe and bow. My axe was the lightest, and I still needed both hands to lift it. Nick wasn't used to old school weapons, but found he liked the chain maille. It looked strange on him. Not bad. Just not normal.

"Maybe I'll start wearing this instead of my Kevlar," he joked.

"The Renaissance Festival is coming up," I reminded him. *Assuming we survive this.*

He seemed to be taking this in stride now, considering that earlier he steadfastly maintained that the whole thing was a dream. I didn't want to ask if he'd changed his mind, or if he'd just decided to play along.

Because I was a nurse, and Nick was not trained in using Viking weapons, it had been decided that we'd stay at the camp and tend to the wounded. Most of the wounds were likely to be mortal, so I suspected that it was Odin's way of keeping us from getting underfoot.

Quinn was going with the Aesir. Where Nick's mail and leather looked anachronistic, his suited him. I had no way of knowing if it was faery glamour, or just him, but he looked incredibly sexy, all kitted out for battle. Part of me hoped that we both lived long enough to do something about it. He put his arms around me, but the stiff leather armor was an uncomfortable barrier between us. Then he raised my chin up with his fingers.

"In case I don't see you again," he said.

Then he kissed me, warm, soft and slow. My body felt like it was on fire, melting and reforming. I could feel my heart beat, pulsing pleasure through every corner of my body.

Nick cleared his throat. Loudly. Twice.

Quinn pulled away from me, and I suddenly felt cold. I knew it wasn't his fault that Halle had stolen the note he left, but there were still some rough edges, and I found it impossible to go back to exactly the same place I had been before I believed that he had abandoned Cassie and me. Although, if he kissed me like that another time or two, it might not be so difficult.

Over Quinn's shoulder, I could see a Valkyrie's black horse spiraling down towards the Earth. Halle and Rädsla approached the camp. Odin gestured to the Aesir and they came to listen to her report. Nick came and stood near me, warm in the seal-colored coat that Odin had dressed him in when he transformed him back into his normal shape.

"The jötnar are gathering. There are also dwarves, trolls, and wargs. Curiously enough, Quinn's demon is with them. He wears a red anorak, and has the ear of the jötnar leader."

"How many did you count?" Thor asked.

"It seems as if all of Jötunheim has been emptied onto the Plain of Vigrid," she replied.

A roar went up behind us.

I turned to find a legion of men pouring out of a rift in the cold, clean air. Behind them, I could see what looked like a gigantic mead hall. The men were semi-transparent, and dressed in furs and leather – ancient Vikings.

"The warriors of Valhalla have been summoned," Odin said.

The smoke coming from the mountain changed from white to black, obscuring the sun. Another earthquake made the ground shudder and jump under our feet. It was the strongest one yet. Nick caught me as I stumbled.

Drums sounded from the other camp. *Doom. Doom. Doom.*

"It is time! To horse!" Odin called.

Horses were brought for the Aesir and they mounted up. Odin raised his spear. "It is a good day to die!"

Thor put his war horn to his lips and it bellowed out the call to combat. Odin's spear came down and the battle cry of five thousand warriors echoed off the mountains. They charged past us, an angry tide of death and destruction.

The ground shook under the massive jötnar as they ran to join the fray, and the two armies clashed in the middle of the plain. Swords clanged together, and the dull light glinted off maille and weapons. Axes flashed as they sliced through the air. Men shouted battle cries, and the wounded screamed in agony.

How casualties were meant to arrive from the battle field to the camp, I wasn't sure. Odin had been a little unclear on that. Behind us, on the sea side, I heard a loud hissing, like a gigantic kettle was boiling away.

A shadow fell across us.

I turned to see an immense snake, as big around as a house, rising up behind us from the water. That must be Jörmungandr.

"Nick, run!" I screamed into the wind.

We scrambled to get out of the way, but he was slithering back and forth, and it was near impossible to tell which way he was going next. He saw us, finally, although we must have been like flies to him. He raised his head to strike. I have never seen anything so big in my life. The open mouth hurtling at us was bigger than my living room. The serpent was beautiful, in a terrifying sort of way. Each of his scales, about the size of a pickup truck hood, was translucent, shades of green and blue. The scutes on his creamy underbelly gleamed in the near twilight like white opals. He was going to either swallow or crush Nick and I, and there didn't seem to be anything I could do, other than stand there admiring him.

I never saw them coming, but somehow, both Quinn and Thor were there. Thor swung his hammer at the snake. The snake spat venom at him. Quinn found one small bare spot on the snake's side where a scale had been broken. He shifted into kelpie form and bit the snake's tender flesh. The snake twisted and rolled, trying to dislodge him, but he held on like a tick. In his thrashing about, Jörmungandr put his huge head in exactly the right position for Thor to land a killing blow. Green blood ran from Jörmungandr's broken head, spattering Thor and steaming on the cold rocks.

The war god laughed, turned, and took nine steps towards us. His knees crumpled and he went down. Nick and I ran to him.

Was the snake's blood toxic, or was it the venom he'd spat earlier? Thor's eyes were swollen shut. His lips were also swollen, and bluish. He wheezed and squeaked as he struggled for air. Anaphylaxis. *Damn, I'd kill for an EpiPen.* But I didn't have one, and if I didn't find a way to get some oxygen into him, and soon, he would die. What I did have was a spear and a war horn. Something in my bra poked me. And Benadryl. It wasn't an EpiPen, but it was better than nothing.

I grabbed at the leather thong that held the horn and yanked it out of Thor's belt.

"Nick, you hold the spear handle. I'll guide the point," I said. He wasn't entirely sure what I was up to, but he complied.

I located Thor's Adam's apple, then found the next bump down. Carefully, I guided the tip of the spear to cut through the cricothyroid membrane, giving Thor an emergency tracheotomy. The only thing I had to intubate him with was the war horn, so I inserted the narrow end of it into the incision to keep the airway open. His chest heaved as air suddenly reached his lungs. Then I fished the bubble card out of my bra, popped out the pill, broke it and put it under his tongue. He just might live, after all. I found some animal pelts in one of the tents, and covered Thor as best I could. I also propped his feet up on a rock. If he went into shock, all of our heroics would have been for nothing.

"Is he dead?" Quinn asked.

He had escaped being drenched with Jörmungandr's blood, although he surely must have come in contact with it when he bit the serpent.

"He's alive, but not by much," I replied. I looked at Quinn. "You're wearing clothes."

"He just turned into a freaking sea monster and back, and the only thing you notice is his clothes?" Nick said. He'd taken a few steps backward, away from Quinn, Thor, and me.

I shook my head. "I've known about this for a while. If I had told you that my dog, Bruce, that freaking sea monster, and Quinn – whom you think is some junkie named Marc McLeod, were all one in the same, would you have believed me? You've seen it with your own eyes and you can't believe it."

"Wait. He's also Bruce? Bruce, that my kids have played with?"

Quinn shimmered, turned into Bruce and wagged his tail, then returned to his human form. "Odin helped out with the clothes thing." He raised his chain maille and wool shirt to reveal an odd tattoo around his navel.

Seeing Bruce made me yearn for Cassie. I hadn't seen her in days, and I just wanted to hold my baby. She adored Bruce. Now, I was homesick.

The battlefield sounds changed. Nick and I looked towards the plain. Combatants on either side were running away from an enormous beast wading out into the middle of them. It was Fenrir, and he had grown to the size of an elephant, or, perhaps given the climate, a woolly mammoth. A lone figure stood in front of Fenrir.

Odin.

Sword raised and blue cloak unfurling in the wind, he refused to let Fenrir pass. The monster wolf raised his head and snarled. Still, Odin held his ground. Fenrir shook his great head from side to side.

There was something, a fleeting glimpse of dark red, behind the monster wolf.

"Quinn, do you see that? Is that Balcones?" I asked.

"I think so," he replied.

Nick looked up, too. "Looks like someone in a red parka." He obviously didn't want any part of this scenario, but his training had kicked in, and he couldn't help himself.

Balcones jumped around, arm in the air, as if he was trying to catch something that floated around Fenrir.

"What is he doing?" I asked.

"Looks like he's trying to grab Gleipnir. If he thinks he can use it as a leash to control Fenrir now, he's a bloody fool," Quinn said.

The Aesir had fallen back towards the camp. The Valkyries swarmed the air above them. The jötnar had re-grouped, and watched Fenrir, possibly waiting for the slaughter of Odin as their signal to attack.

Now, it appeared that Fenrir and Balcones were having a conversation, but I couldn't hear it.

Apparently, Quinn could.

He shook his head. "Balcones is trying to convince Fenrir to join him. Fenrir is having none of it. He doesn't care about money or power. The only thing on his mind is revenge."

Balcones continued to argue his point, his arms extended in supplication. Fenrir lunged at the demon. But there was a loud BANG and the wolf's immense jaws snapped shut on smoke and air. The wind carried the smell of rotten eggs down to the camp.

"Dammit!" Quinn said. "We've got to find a way to stop the demons from getting those percussion portals."

I checked on Thor. The prophecy had predicted that he would die. What if he didn't? What if keeping him alive had changed things just enough that the whole prophecy didn't happen? I looked back toward the battlefield.

Fenrir turned his fury on Odin, and swallowed him whole.

I was stunned. I had not expected it to be that easy, expecting some epic, hard-fought battle to the death.

I checked on Thor. He was still breathing. Changing his fate had not altered the prophecy, as far as I could tell.

The jötnar surged around him, and Fenrir ran through the warriors, his huge mouth biting at anything that moved. He didn't seem to care which side he mauled – it looked like he was doing both equally.

The colossal wolf slashed his way towards our camp.

A group of Odin's fighters attacked Fenrir, and the rest clashed with the jötnar. The Aesir and shades of Vikings past were no match for the enormous wolf. He cut through them easily, shaking the ground as he ran towards us.

Fenrir bounded through the snow, an overgrown and horrifying puppy, his enormous jaws opening as he ran. He snatched Nick around the waist and shook his massive head from side to side, like a terrier worrying a rat. Nick's arms and legs flailed like a broken rag doll. The monster's huge maw opened, and Nick's body tumbled out, staining the snow red even before he hit the ground.

"Nick!" I screamed, running to him, even though he lay directly underneath Fenrir's dripping tongue.

I started frantically packing his body in snow, hoping the cold would slow the blood loss. Intellectually, I knew that he was going to bleed out, probably in less than a minute, and there was nothing I could do about it. Even a Level I trauma center wouldn't be able to save him – the damage was catastrophic and irreversible. But I couldn't just sit and watch him die.

Then Odin's warriors surrounded Fenrir, attacking him from all sides at once. A man who looked like a younger version of Odin grabbed Fenrir by the chain around his neck. This must be Vidar. He was wearing one shoe made of iron, and when Fenrir tried to bite him, he stuck the shoe in the wolf's mouth. He couldn't close his massive jaws, and Vidar grabbed Fenrir's top jaw and yanked upwards. Now he was wedged in Fenrir's mouth. The wolf couldn't close his jaws, but Vidar couldn't do anything to harm him.

Halle, spattered with blood, swooped down on Rädsla, leaping off the mare before her hooves touched the ground.

"This is for my father, you monster!" she yelled.

Her long bright sword plunged into Fenrir's heart. He yelped, then started making choking, gasping sounds, and the electric blue glow of his eyes dimmed. Blood poured from his mouth, covering Vidar. As the wolf's strength ebbed away, the young god was able to free himself. Halle pulled her sword out of Fenrir's chest, and used it to slice open his belly.

At the fall of Fenrir, the jötnar lost heart and retreated, leaving a swath of dropped weapons and helms behind them.

"You will not have your prize!" Halle growled.

Bloody parts of a dozen or more men poured out of the wolf's stomach onto the snow. There was one body, battered, but whole. Odin. Halle wiped the gore from his face.

She nearly fell over when he coughed and opened his eye.

Odin was alive, after all. But Nick was not. I could not keep any sort of control over myself as his sightless eyes stared up at my face. I sobbed, and I shook him by his lifeless shoulders.

"Nick! Come back! We need you here with us. Emily and McKenzi and Aiden and Kyle need you. I need you. Please stay with us. This is all my fault. If I hadn't grabbed your hand and dragged you into this mess, you'd still be alive and with your family. It should be me laying there dead, not you. I would give anything to trade places with you," I begged his corpse.

I felt the pressure of Quinn's hand on my back, but I ignored it. I didn't deserve to be comforted. I'd just killed my brother-in-law.

I could see the armored toes of Halle's boots as she moved in and stood near Nick's body.

"At least you're happy, huh, Halle? You got what you wanted," I snarled at her. When I raised my head and looked up, I expected her to be smiling, but her face was stony and drawn. Next to her, looking around in confusion, stood Nick's ghost.

"Did you mean that?" Odin asked, sitting up.

My gaze shifted to him. "What? That I'd trade places with him? Yes."

"Marti, no," Quinn's voice sounded behind me. His grip tightened around my shoulder

Odin stroked his beard, considering, then flicked slime and blood off his fingers. "As you wish."

He stretched out his hand towards me, and immediately I felt light headed.

What had I just done?

I did not want to leave Cassie an orphan. But I knew that between Nick, Emily, and my parents, she'd have a pretty good life. In fact, she probably wouldn't even remember me. Sad for me, but probably better for her. She'd be so much safer without dangerous fae creatures hanging around all the time. Creatures I couldn't seem to leave alone. Quinn would outlive me by hundreds of years anyway, so this just a tiny blip in the timeline, hardly noticeable on his scale.

"Stop this! Please, Odin," Quinn begged.

"It is not your choice," Odin replied.

I wasn't entirely sure it was mine, either, but there didn't seem to be any going back now. Funny the things that a person will agree to when they think those things can't possibly happen.

I closed my eyes. Euphoria started to seep in to my consciousness. I'd died before, and recognized the feeling.

Suddenly, it stopped, and I was jolted back into my body. I opened my eyes to see Halle's face just above mine.

"Halle! What are you doing?" I was angry, thinking she was still trying to take Nick for herself.

But she didn't move, and the light in her eyes was fading, taking my rage with it. The strength left her arms, and she collapsed on top of me.

"Halle, my daughter! What have you done?" Odin's voice cracked.

He crawled over and scooped her up in his arms, cradling her like a small child.

"I promised," she wheezed.

And then she was terribly, awfully still.

Nick groaned, and sat up. He coughed and vomited up water and little chunks of ice – the snow I'd packed his body in earlier. His eyes opened, and glowed green.

"Nick? How do you feel?" I asked, still trying to process what had just happened.

"I had the weirdest dream…Why are *you* here?" He blinked, his eyes returning to normal, and looked around, first at Quinn, then Odin, holding Halle. "Maybe it wasn't a dream."

He pulled up his maille coat and shirt. Jagged, bloodstained holes remained in his clothing, but his skin was unmarked, as if Fenrir's wicked jaws had never crushed the life out of him.

"I don't…understand," Nick said.

Quinn spoke, his voice was raw and soft, barely audible above the wind. "When I asked Halle to help me protect Marti, she promised that she would. A Valkyrie's word is her bond, Nick, and she will not break it. Halle couldn't allow Marti's life to be traded for yours."

Nick jerked his face toward me. His mouth opened, but no words came out.

"You told me that Valkyries couldn't be killed," I said, practically accusing Quinn, tears streaming down my face. I felt searing guilt for every negative thought I'd ever had about Halle.

"They can not be," Odin broke in, his eye glistening with extra moisture. "Halle was not killed. She willingly sacrificed herself. There is a difference." He regarded Nick for a few moments before he spoke again. "Your soul is your own, but your body now contains the life force of a Valkyrie. Since the beginning of time, such a thing has never happened. Even I cannot see how this will affect you. There is no prophecy for this event." Odin brushed some snow of off of Halle's face. "And sometimes, even the prophecies are wrong."

He whistled loudly for Sleipnir. Then he removed some of the quantum leaves from a leather pouch at his waist.

"Treasure this gift," Odin said to Nick.

"I will."

"I'm sorry, Odin. If I'd known…" Quinn said.

I took Halle's cold hand in mine. If she had a ghost, I couldn't see it. But I felt sure that somewhere, somehow, she could hear me. "Thank you, Halle. I know we didn't always get along, and I'm sorry for that. But what you did…I owe you more than I could ever possibly repay."

I stood up and moved to Quinn and Nick.

"Thor is not dead. He needs serious medical help, but he is still alive. Or at least he was a few minutes ago."

"Thank you," Odin nodded, and a single tear slid down his craggy cheek, freezing into a glittering crystal just before it reached his beard. He took it and folded it into my hand. "Never forget."

He threw the leaves around us, and the scenery blurred, shifting into the steamy green heat of my backyard. And we were up to our knees in water.

Chapter 26
World of Difference

After all that we'd just been through, had we still failed to stop Ragnarök? Was this the beginning of the flood?

I wasn't sure what time it was, but it was dark. Night or storm clouds, it was hard to tell. I think it was some of both. The wind whipped the trees around and drove the rain nearly horizontally. Fat raindrops pummeled my skin like dull needles. I shielded my eyes with my hand. My coat was waterproof, but that didn't matter. My head was soaked in a matter of seconds, and cold water ran down the back of my neck and into my clothes.

I put the crystal tear in my pocket and started slogging toward the back door. The water was nearly up to the top step.

"Wait!" Delilah appeared in front of me. "You can *not* go in there."

"Yes, I can. It's my house. I'm not going to stand out here in the middle of a storm. Besides, I have to find Cassie."

Nick looked at me, to the seemingly empty space in front of me, then back at my face.

"No, girlfriend. Cassie is fine. You and Nick have been gone a week. Emily and your parents are beside themselves. You can't just show up together like you never been gone. What you gonna tell your sister about running off with her husband?"

"I don't know, but we can't just stand out here in the rain." I had to shout to be heard above the weather. *Gone a week?* I shuddered to think about the condition of Alpha and Betty, with no one to feed or water them for seven days.

"Let's go to Kai's. We can get it sorted there," Quinn said.

"No," Nick said. "I'm going home to my family."

"Nick, we've been gone a whole week. What are you
going to tell Emily when she asks where you and I have been for
that time?"

He sulked.

I turned and noticed that Quinn was missing. Oddly
enough, he was by the birdbath, and appeared to be smelling the
only plumeria flower that hadn't been torn off the bush by the
strong wind.

He waded back to where Nick and I were standing.

"You couldn't wait for better weather to stop and smell
the flowers?" I asked.

"I'm getting us a ride," he said.

"From a flower?"

"You'll see. Come on."

Nick grudgingly followed Quinn and I out of my
backyard and onto the sidewalk. It was treacherous going – the
sidewalk was underwater and limbs were down everywhere. The
storm drains were blocked with debris – that's what was causing
the flooding. One of the street light poles had been knocked
down and lay across the road. It was a good thing the power was
off. Fighting wind, water, and debris, it took about three times as
long as usual to get to the Tenth Sphere. I think I've probably
had drier showers.

The only car anywhere in sight, a black SUV, idled in
the parking lot.

"That's our ride," Quinn said.

Nick looked skeptical. I reached for the door.

"Wait," Quinn said, covering my hand.

"The driver's name is Frey. He's been burned, so he can
be a bit hard to look at. But he's worth his weight in gold."

Nick nodded, and opened the front passenger door.
Quinn opened the rear passenger side door for me, and we all
climbed in out of the storm.

Quinn was right. Frey was hard to look at. His face was
scarred and ropey, and one eye was an opaque white. I redirected
my focus to the car. The seats were covered with plastic tarps. A
good idea, given that we were wringing wet.

"*Ta*, Frey. You're a lifesaver. This is Nick and Marti. We're in need of a portal."

The driver simply nodded and put the vehicle in gear.

I started shivering in the air conditioning. Frey turned on the heat before I could even say anything. Maybe he found the noise from my chattering teeth obnoxious. Nick sat glowering in the front seat, arms crossed over his seatbelt.

"Alright, Quinn. How were you able to get Frey to come get us by talking to a flower?" I asked.

"Each flower had an attendant faery. These flower fae are messengers, if you know how to ask. And since they exist in multiple dimensions at once, messages are as close as you'll likely get to instantaneous."

I would have liked to have snuggled up against Quinn to get warm, but the middle seatbelt was covered by both tarps. He was half a mile away, against the opposite window.

At least it didn't take long to get to our destination, and Frey drove us into a lovely dry garage. I was still dripping wet when I got out of the SUV. Frey opened a clothes dryer by the door to the house and pulled out three warm bath sheets, one for each of us.

Quinn herded the recalcitrant Nick upstairs, and I followed. He took us to a room with two large portraits. One of them was of a green-eyed woman, the same woman who had come to my house and tried to heal Quinn when he'd been attacked by a werewolf, a month ago, and he'd spent several days at my house, fighting for his life. The other, I recognized as Mr. Underhill. I'd met him a few weeks ago, when I'd first encountered Quinn.

"Walk through the picture," Quinn said.

Nick looked at him quizzically.

"Did you just say 'walk through the picture'?" I asked.

"Yes."

"Which one?" I responded.

"Doesn't matter. They go to the same place."

"Which is?" asked Nick.

"Faery. Now go."

Nick balked. So I took the lead. When I stepped through the woman's picture, I found myself in a very long, dim corridor, lined on both sides with portraits. Nick stepped out of the man's picture, then stood dumbstruck. Quinn had to maneuver around him when he came through.

First, he led us to through a maze of corridors until we got to a brighter hallway. He knocked on one of the doors, but there was no answer. His shoulders slumped just a little, but he straightened up and we continued down the hall. At the corner, there was a receptionist's desk. It seemed out of place in a castle, but nobody had asked me when they'd done the design layout. The receptionist wasn't there, but an astoundingly large bouquet of white roses and ferns sat on the desk.

Quinn scowled at the flowers. "I wonder who died."

"That's a funeral arrangement?" I asked.

"Yes. From the size of it, I would think it would be an MIT leader. I know most of them, but I don't know a lot of the team members. Let's go into town and see what we can find out."

We followed Quinn to the exit. There were some children playing in the bailey, but otherwise, the castle seemed deserted. It was warm and bright outside, and I upgraded the condition of my clothing from waterlogged to wet.

"Come on, Nick. You like mysteries, don't you?" I asked.

"Not this kind."

On the edge of the town square was a water mill. I doubted it still ground wheat because there was a sign out front that read *The Waterhorse Inn*, with a black ribbon wrapped around it. Quinn tried the door, but it was locked.

"I don't have my key with me."

He looked pale and I noticed his breathing had gotten shallower.

"Are you okay?" I asked him.

"Maybe. The *Waterhorse* has been in my family for generations. For them to put a mourning band around the sign and lock up, it must mean that a family member has died. They're probably at the funeral."

"I'm sorry." I reached out for his hand. He squeezed my fingers, but let go. I guess he was too agitated to be comforted.

Quinn hurried down the cobblestone street, which narrowed into a smaller road that quickly turned to gravel, then dirt. As he'd predicted, there was a large gathering of dour looking people dressed in black and grey. There were no chairs left, so we stood at the back.

A man that looked very similar to Quinn, but maybe a little younger, was just taking the podium.

"That's Graham," he whispered.

"My brother was taken from us far too soon," he said.

Quinn frowned, then scanned the front row. Then he looked puzzled. Then he smiled.

"Why are you smiling?" Nick whispered to him, looking somewhat revolted.

"I have four brothers. Graham is the one talking. Those two on the aisle of the front row are Robbie and Laurie. The one on the other side of the tall woman with grey hair, my mum, is Kade. It's not often you get the chance to attend your own funeral."

"Why do they think you're dead?" I asked.

"Excellent question," he replied.

"You have to say something," Nick said. "You can't just sit here and let them think you're dead. That's cruel."

"You're right, of course," Quinn said. He still had an impish grin. "But wouldn't you be interested to know what people said at your funeral?"

Nick looked away. "Maybe," he mumbled.

Quinn took a few steps over to a tall man with waist-length blond hair. "Excuse me," he said. "I was traveling when I heard the news, but I don't have much information. How did he die?"

"He was on an MIT mission. Frost Giants got him."

Quinn nodded. "How terrible. Thank you," he said.

He looked at Nick and put his finger to his lips, as if he needed shushing. Graham had put his hand over his face to compose himself. Quinn stepped quietly down the aisle, until he was about halfway to the podium.

Graham started to speak again. "…and he can never be replaced. The memories that we have are all that's left-"

"Excuse me," Quinn said. "I hate to interrupt, but I think there's been a terrible misunderstanding."

"Quinn!" Graham shouted.

Nick and I waited at the edge of the crowd while all of his friends and relatives hugged him, kissed him, or shook his hands.

The woman that Quinn had pointed out as his mother stared malevolently at Nick and I most of the time.

"I hope she doesn't think we had anything to do with this," I said.

Nick shrugged. "If I thought one of my boys was dead, I'd be pretty pissed at the person who seemed responsible, even if it turned out that he was fine."

"Fair enough," I said.

After the initial furor of Quinn's sudden and unexpected return, I noticed that he'd moved away from the crowd and was standing alone by a gravestone, a white rose in his hands. I didn't see any rose bushes around, so he must have plucked it from one of his own funeral sprays. He knelt down and placed the flower on the grave, then rose, trailing his fingers along the top of the headstone as he returned to the swarm of former mourners.

A short time later, Nick and I sat in the posh office behind the door that Quinn had knocked on earlier. An older woman, introduced to us as Dame Rowan, sat at the heavy desk, and Quinn, Malik, Aleksei and Eoin sat in front of it.

"I think that explains why I wasn't able to contact you," Quinn said to Malik. "You and the others had been recalled because you thought I was dead. It was very clever of Balcones to make a show of having my coat and my cell phone. He knew we were watching him. I guess he got it off me when I went to the old lady's – I mean Loki's – hut."

"Old lady? Loki?" Rowan asked.

Quinn gave her a summary of recent events. He needed to debrief Rowan and his team, anyway, and now seemed a good time.

"Is shame Balcones got away," Aleksei said.

Rowan studied Nick. "This one is a puzzle," she said. "We shall have to monitor him."

Nick scowled.

"For his own good," Rowan continued. "A Valkyrie's life force has never been transferred to a human before, much less to a male. It is hard to know what the side effects might be."

"I'm going to need a little help with the time dilation," Quinn said. "I think we'll leave in the morning, but we need to arrive Sunday a week ago, Mundane time. The best I can do is get them back on Thursday. As it stands, Nick and Marti have been missing for a week. That's going to raise a lot of questions when they show up, especially from Nick's wife."

I gave Malik a sidelong glance. He'd sent me off on a completely different timeline not too long ago. That should be no problem for him.

"Time is easy," he said, with a quick, apologetic smile.

It was settled. Nick and I would return to Mundane time very early Sunday morning, the day after Boris' gala. Quinn would attend Halle's funeral and spend some time with his family, then be back in time for Cassie's birthday, which had happened yesterday. I had enough trouble managing things when time flowed in only one direction.

After the meeting with Dame Rowan, we adjourned to the *Waterhorse Inn*. A celebration of Quinn's return from the dead was in full swing by the time we arrived. His brothers were all very nice to me. I attempted to introduce myself to his mother.

"I'm Marti," I said, extending my hand. "It's nice to meet you."

She looked at me coldly, her eyes solid black. I knew from my experience with Quinn that was a bad thing. "I detest humans."

Then she turned on her heel and stalked away.

Alrighty, then.

Nick and I each got our own room at the inn. I didn't have the stamina to stay up all night, partying with the fae, and I fell asleep not long after midnight. It seemed far too early when Quinn came and knocked on my door.

"Time to go," he said.

Robbie fixed breakfast for Quinn, Nick, and me. I wondered if Quinn was as good a cook. After stuffing ourselves with fluffy pancakes, beans on toast, scones and clotted cream, and fresh fruit, we headed back to the castle, which Quinn told us was formally known as *Titania's School for Girls*. It also housed the local MAMIC offices.

"MAMIC?" I asked.

"Mundane Activity Monitoring and Intervention Center."

Nick almost smiled. "Can't get away from alphabet soup anywhere, huh?"

Malik was waiting for us in Rowan's office.

"This is it, Nick," I said. "We're going home."

He nodded.

I was sure he missed his family as much as I missed Cassie. I couldn't wait to hold my baby in my arms again.

Malik said a few words I didn't understand and waved his hand. Everything started to spin. I thought I was going to be sick. Lights flashed, and suddenly Nick and I were standing in front of Boris Cherngelanov's mansion. Lulu and Belinda were loading up the car.

"There you are," she said. "It's after two. We've been looking all over for you."

"I was looking for my cell phone. I seemed to have dropped it somewhere."

"I told you the one on the kitchen counter looked like hers," Belinda said.

Nick and I went to retrieve it.

Chapter 27
Reunion

News of Boris Cherngelanov's death made the front page of the paper. Irina reported that he had been out ice climbing and fallen to his death. His body, sadly, wasn't recoverable. She would, however continue the good work of the Cherngelanov Foundation.

Sveklá knew that there was a secret door in the wine cellar, but he didn't know where it went. He'd looked through it once or twice, seen a prisoner detention area, knew it was unusually cold, but he knew nothing of Bright Falcon or Fenrir. The door had never had anything to do with him, and he didn't see why he should be concerned with it now. It was enough that Irina knew about it.

She knew that Sveklá would be suspicious of Boris' disappearance, but he would not ask many questions. She had won his loyalty. As long as she allowed him to be her lover, he would forgive her anything.

It was a lavish memorial service, and it took place as soon as was possible after the cleanup from the tropical storm and flooding. Armloads of wreaths and a roomful of white lilies and roses surrounded a portrait of Boris. Irina had worn a long, plain black dress and a black veil. She wanted people to assume she had been crying over her husband's unexpected death. Sveklá stood by her side at the funeral, as she knew he would do in front of the Odessa Group.

After the service, a buffet lunch would be served, so that the mourners could spend time reminiscing about the dearly departed. She'd wanted to call it a wake, and bring in musicians, but dancing at one's spouse's funeral is generally considered bad form in the United States.

Hadrian and Sara attended Boris' funeral, she as a representative of the Greene-Childe Foundation, and he, publicly, as her companion. But he was also there in a professional capacity. None of his surveillance targets put in an appearance. However, both Marti Keller and Lulu Miranda had worked at a party held by Cherngelanov right before his untimely death. Hadrian's supervisor decided that his surveillance of the neighborhood would continue until further notice. Hadrian did call the DA on the way to the funeral and ask that the charges against Benjamin Fayllor be dropped. Hadrian knew he was innocent, and his chance to flush out the real killer had probably ended with Boris' death. Win some, lose some. It may turn into a cold case, but it would always be open until the killer slipped up. It might take a while, but they usually did.

It was Friday, and Hadrain met Sara for lunch at Baba Yega's. They sat on the deck, in the shade, under the big fan, and it was much more pleasant than anyone had a right to expect on a July day in Houston. He was just returning from the restroom when, through the open door, he was stunned to see Marti and Cassie sitting at the table, talking to Sara.

Crap. That was a complication he really didn't need. Should he go say something, or just wait it out? Now that he'd decided to put some effort into winning Sara back, he didn't want to be evasive about their relationship. On the other hand, part of his surveillance operation depended on the appearance of him being available. That he genuinely liked Marti and found her attractive was a different can of worms that would be disastrous to open. He supposed he could fake food poisoning if he needed a diversion.

He got closer to the door, but continued to lurk. They didn't see him – it was bright outside and much less so inside. Cassie started struggling and wiggling.

"I have to go," Marti said. "There's no reasoning with her now that she's learned how to walk. It was so good to run into you, Gracie. I will definitely call you next week to set up lunch."

Sara stood up and they hugged each other, squirmy baby notwithstanding. "I'm looking forward to catching up."

"Bye, Gracie."

Hadrian waited for Marti to go around the corner and out of sight before he went back to the table. "Who was that?" he asked casually.

"Her name's Marti. She was Schmidt when I knew her, but she's Keller, now. We were best friends in school, until she moved away in senior year. She practically lived at my house. After her dad had that bad truck accident, things got a little tough for her, and we lost touch. I haven't seen her in years."

"And she called you Gracie."

Sara laughed. "Sara Grace, remember? When I was a kid, everyone I knew called me "Gracie." Well, except for my grandmother. She always called me "Sara Grace." In college, I decided that "Sara" sounded more grown up."

"Makes sense."

With more than six million people in the Greater Houston Metro Area, how could it be that his girlfriend was an old friend of one of his surveillance targets? Life was weird, sometimes.

"Is your power back on yet?" Hadrian asked.

"No." Sara shook her head. "The shopping center across the street has power, though."

"Stay at my apartment? I have hot water." He tilted his head.

"You really know how to tempt a girl."

"That's my specialty."

Sara laughed and leaned over to kiss him. "I'll see you after work, Blackbird."

Chapter 28
Make a Wish

I hugged Cassie to within an inch of her life. She fussed and struggled every time I picked her up, it seemed. But maybe because I was picking her up all the time. As far as she was concerned, I'd only been gone one night. She didn't know I'd missed her for an entire week.

On Sunday afternoon, Nick showed up at my door with a chef's knife in his hand.

"I have to show you something," he said.

Whatever it was, he did not look happy about it. Cassie was busy alternately whacking Mr. Buns against the coffee table and gnawing on his ears. She could keep herself entertained for a few more minutes. I stepped over the baby gate and into the kitchen.

"What is it, Nick?"

I was a little ashamed that I kept the table between us. I didn't like to think that my brother-in-law would hurt Cassie or me, but he did have a big knife, and he was agitated.

"Watch," he said.

He put his left hand palm-down on the table, then drew the knife across the back of it. I gasped as blood started running down his hand.

But then a green fire sparked at the starting edge of the wound and crackled and shimmered down its length. As it passed, the wound healed without leaving the faintest scar. It was like it never happened. Even the blood on his skin vanished when the green fire touched it.

"This is not possible," he said, slapping the knife down on the table and scooping his hand through his hair.

"I think," I said, hoping I was right, "that is Halle's gift."

He exhaled forcefully. "How far does this go? How big a wound can it heal?"

"I don't know, but go experiment somewhere else. You are not allowed to commit hari-kari in my kitchen. Even if it doesn't really kill you."

Nick laughed softly. "Yeah, I guess that could be a problem, if it doesn't work."

I looked at the back of his hand closely, ran my finger along it where there should have been a cut, trying to find any traces of the wound. Nothing. "Well, on the plus side, it seems like a handy fringe benefit for a police officer."

"Maybe. Hadn't thought of it that way. All I know is that now I'm some kind of freak and I can't tell anyone, not even my wife, about it. You're dating a sea monster, so it's not like you're going to tell anybody."

"Wow, Nick. Thanks for that incredible vote of confidence," I said. "I'm sorry you got dragged into this, but how was I supposed to know that this famous philanthropist was really a crime boss with an inter-dimensional portal to a Russian gulag in his wine cellar? He was supposed to be one of the good guys, remember?"

He frowned.

Delilah appeared, partially. I could see her, but she was transparent.

"Girl, you need to tell that man that sometimes what you want and what you need are two different things."

I thought of a proverb my husband used to like. "'The bamboo that bends is stronger than the oak that resists.'"

"You sound just like Ryan," Nick said.

Delilah winked at me.

"Yeah, how about that?" I replied. I had seen Nick's corpse and I'd seen his ghost, but I wondered what, if anything, he recalled about his death. "So, just out of curiosity, what do you remember about our little adventure?"

"Falling through a door painted on a wall, being in a freezing cell, getting turned into a seal and being hunted by orcas, riding a flying horse, talking to Thor, being killed by a gigantic wolf. Suddenly waking up, and finding out it wasn't a dream."

"I saw you, standing next to Halle, before…"

"Before she died? I remember that." His brow furrowed. "It was hard to go back. My body just seemed so cold. And difficult."

I knew how hard it was for him to admit that. "I know."

Now that he knew I wasn't crazy, I wondered if I should tell him about how I first met Quinn. But I decided against it. He already has as much as his brain could deal with at the moment. Perhaps another time.

On Thursday evening, I sat with about half of the regulars while Lulu began smudging the room for Circle. Hunter didn't show. Marilyn was disappointed enough that she made sure she was on the opposite side of the room from me. It wasn't my fault he wasn't interested in her, and I wasn't sure how to feel about his seeming interest in me. Maybe he was just a friendly neighbor – he hadn't made any real overtures. But maybe there was more to it. He always seemed to be around at just the right time. Either way, I was glad I didn't have to think about it tonight. Hunter was certainly appealing. But I was looking forward to Quinn's return.

I wasn't sure how that was going to work out. It wasn't fair for him to remain in dog form during the day for propriety's sake. But I wasn't willing to invite a man I'd only known for a month and a half to move in with Cassie and me, either. If he could pop in and out of dimensions so easily, I don't suppose dating would be such an issue. Phone calls and texts might be a little hard, though.

"Let's get started," Lulu said. "Tonight, we're going to explore telekinesis." She handed each of us a piece of paper, a pencil, and a small plastic cube.

I dutifully placed the cube in the center of my paper, and outlined it so I would be able to see if it moved. I tried imagining it moving, being the cube, matching my vibrations to the cube, and not making it obvious that I was just blowing on it for an hour. Nothing. Nada. Zip.

Lulu finally broke the Circle, and walked around collecting all the pencils and cubes before we went downstairs for refreshments.

"Honey, look at that! You really did well on this exercise," she said.

There must be some mistake. I looked at my paper and found my little cube sitting in the upper left corner.

"Yeah. How about that?"

Delilah?

I heard a disembodied giggle.

Not funny.

"But you were trying so hard, girlfriend. I just wanted to give you a little win."

I gathered my things to go home, glad that I had all my supplies laid in. Tropical storm Elvira was supposed to make landfall tomorrow afternoon, and I was delighted to not have to go to the store and face long lines and empty shelves tonight.

I spent Friday morning putting masking tape on all the windows and securing any loose objects outdoors. Cassie was my special little "helper." Mom thought we should start Cassie's birthday early and have a hurricane party, but I wanted to be home when Quinn showed up. I told her that it wasn't fair for us to all be partying while Nick was pulling a double shift.

It was dark thirty on Saturday morning when I heard Quinn's knock. The wind had died down from Category 1 to breezy, but the outermost rain bands were still dumping buckets of moisture on us. The power had been off for nearly twelve hours. Water was everywhere, and I was a little concerned about it coming in the house when I went to let Quinn in. Outside, I heard a high-pitched, whining bark and a snort.

I turned the deadbolt and opened the door.

"Is that a puppy?" I asked, looking at the wriggling thing in his arms.

He looked down at it as if he wasn't sure what it was. The dog stretched up and licked his face. "Seems to be."

He came into the kitchen and set the damp pup on the floor. The black dog looked up hopefully, his tail wagging his entire body. Judging by the size of his feet, at least one of his parents was a Great Dane.

"His name is Cu, but you can change it, if you want. I know how fond Cassie is of Bruce, so I thought a puppy would be a good birthday present."

"Does that mean she won't be seeing Bruce anymore?" My heart sank.

"It means that she also likes Quinn, so now she can have her cake and eat it too."

I couldn't help but laugh. Cu apparently thought it was funny, too, because he danced and capered about on the tile as if he thought the idea of eating cake was an excellent one.

"This is an actual dog? He doesn't turn into anything else?"

Quinn was smiling as he shook his head. "Nope. Always the form of a dog."

I couldn't help but think there was more to it.

A warbling came from down the hall. "Sounds like the birthday girl is up."

I went to get her. After she was changed, I brought her into see the puppy. If he was too rambunctious, he would, unfortunately, have to go back with Quinn.

Cassie squealed with delight when she saw Cu. The puppy was better than perfect with her. It was almost like he'd heard my thoughts about sending him back if he wasn't.

It was close to 7:00. If dark clouds hadn't been drenching us with rain, it would have been nearly full daylight. I looked through the tape on the window until I saw Quinn, Nick, and myself appear in the back yard, argue for a few minutes, then leave. I'm glad that Delilah had talked me out of coming into the house. It would have been too weird to have run into my future self in the past. Or was it my past self in the future? Anyway, the me out in the rain right now would have been shocked to find the me who got back a week ago in the house.

That's when it hit me. "The storm drains. Remember how blocked up they were? Are? If we could open up that big one across the street, we could probably stop all the houses from flooding."

Quinn nodded.

While I fed Cassie her breakfast, he waded outside to remove the fallen tree branch that had lodged in the storm sewer entrance, trapping debris and causing all the flooding. The water level gradually started going down.

My father would not be up yet, but I'm sure Mom was already in the kitchen, baking Cassie's cake. I thought maybe we'd wander over around 10-ish. Or whenever there was a break in the rain, whichever came first. The party was supposed to start at 11:00.

Cassie and Cu played together in the living room like they'd known each other all their lives. When I picked Cassie up to give her a bath and put on her party clothes, Cu fell asleep, sprawled on the floor like a dog-skin rug. I didn't want to leave him home without supervision, so Quinn carried him like a little hairy baby. His half hour nap was enough to refresh him, because when he saw Cassie again, he nearly turned himself inside out with joy. Kyle and Aiden could hardly get a look in. It was just as well. They couldn't go out in the backyard in the deluge, anyway.

"Where's Bruce?" Kyle asked grumpily.

I glanced at Quinn. "You remember that I found Bruce, and I thought he might belong to someone else? He found his home."

"Who is your friend, Marti?" my mother asked.

"This is Quinn," I said. I wasn't sure whether to introduce my mother as "Adele" or "Mrs. Schmidt," so I did both, and let Quinn decide what to call her.

"It's nice to meet you, Mrs. Schmidt," Quinn said.

"Likewise," Mom answered.

After a while, lunch was served, then cake. Cassie was too young for a piñata, but we played Velcro the Tail on the Donkey and had a rousing chorus of "Head, Shoulders, Knees and Toes."

"Where did you find Mr. Hottie?" Emily asked when she and I were cleaning up the kitchen.

"You wouldn't believe me if I told you." *Oddly enough, I was on a date with another guy. Nick's friend, Ian Chambers, to be precise.*

She waited for me to dish on the details, but I didn't. "He's cuter than your neighbor. What kind of work does he do?"

He goes undercover to hunt demons. "Law enforcement," I said out loud.

"Figures."

By the time all of Cassie's presents were opened, she was falling asleep sitting up.

"I think the birthday girl needs a nap," I said.

"Put her in the crib in our room," Mom said.

We stayed around until the rain let up, around dinner time. Dad was amazed by the wide array of card games that Quinn knew. He was even good at card tricks that baffled the boys, and he kept everybody entertained until we ate supper.

When we ran next door to my house, both Cassie and Cu were drowsy, so I put her straight in her crib and folded up a blanket for the puppy.

"You know Balcones may still be after you?" Quinn asked.

"I can't believe he got away."

"You know that means I'll have to be here for a while longer, to keep an eye on you, and make sure you're safe."

"I see."

Quinn took my hand and led me to my bedroom. He closed the door and then he kissed me, a long, deep kiss that made my knees turn to water.

"My brother taught me a secret to make it safe for me to make love to you. Do you want me to show you?"

"Please."

"Sit on the bed. You can lean against the headboard, if you want."

I moved the pillows and sat cross-legged on the bed, leaning against the headboard. My skin tingled with anticipation. I had tried to convince myself that I didn't want him. But I had failed. There was nothing I wanted more just now.

Quinn sat in front of me so we were knee to knee. "Take a deep breath. Try to breathe into your solar plexus. Now, think about pushing energy out of you abdomen, just above your belly button. Imagine a white ball of it forming just outside of you."

It took a few tries, but finally, he said, "I see it. Good. Now come with me."

His physical body still sat on the bed, but there was now a glowing, transparent double of him, standing on the floor beside us. He carefully picked up the ball of white energy that I'd extruded and carried it with him. I was able to see everything that happened, in 360°. It was a little hard to understand, and I thought it was peculiar that each of us had a silver cord that attached our physical bodies to our non-physical ones.

Almost immediately, we were at a gazebo on the beach. The water was topaz blue and the sand was golden. He began to caress me. I couldn't tell where he ended and I began. My form began to stretch out, and our energy merged and twined together.

It was amazing. We did things that just couldn't be done with physical bodies. Gender, gravity and physical form were all irrelevant. Ecstasy didn't seem to be a strong enough word to describe it, as our energies melded, separated, and combined again. It was exhausting, though. When I couldn't take anymore, my consciousness snapped back into my body as if it had been attached by a bungee cord.

Still, my body buzzed from the combining of energy that I'd just experienced. It was so different from physical contact, much more intense. But there was also a distance, and unreality about it that made it slightly unsatisfying, and I wondered if this was love, or enthrallment. It felt pretty damned good either way.

Quinn stretched out on the bed. I put my head on his shoulder, and shivered with pleasure.

"Did you like that?" he asked.

"That was incredible. Can we do it again?"

"Any time you like."

Bonus Material

Virginia

"This mission should be simple. I don't believe we need to wait for Eoin to finish his secondment. Retrieving the ring will be nothing for the four of us. It's winter in the Mundane world. Queen Elizabeth's not got her money back from this investment. This foray into the New World hasn't been good to the colonists. They're half starved, so even if they did know what it was they'd found, they haven't the strength to put up much of a fight." Halle's waist-length golden braids bobbed slightly as she shook her head.

"Why does MIT look for ring? Is not problem for Aesir?" Aleksei asked.

"It's cursed," replied Halle.

"Is the curse demonic?" Siobhan asked.

"No."

Siobhan shrugged. "Then we aren't duty bound to stop it, are we?"

"Just because the curse isn't demonic, doesn't mean that demons cannot employ it to their full advantage. If they were to take it from the humans, they could use it to wreak a lot of havoc. We can save ourselves a great deal of work by getting it first. Besides, Andvari has offered a handsome reward for its return. MAMIC could use the gold."

Siobhan sighed. "How are we meant to find this ring - what is it called again - Andvaranaut?" she asked.

She sat between Aleksei and Quinn at a heavy oaken table in a conference
room in the Mundane Activity Monitoring and Intervention Center (MAMIC). Halle leaned over the opposite side of the table.

"With this." Halle pulled a silver dagger from her belt. "When it is near Andvaranaut, the blade will glow. The brighter the glow, the closer the ring."

"How does it know?" Siobhan asked. "What if there's another gold ring?"

"It isn't sensitive to rings. It's sensitive to cursed objects."

Halle's answer appeared to satisfy Siobhan, but Aleksei scowled.

"How came magic Viking ring to New World? Has only been known hundred years by humans," he said.

"Not true. The red-skinned Skraelings were there when the sons of Erik the Red arrived. When Erik was banished from Iceland, one of his sailing crew gave him the ring as a gift. Probably, he was just trying to get rid of it. Anyway, because of the ring, the Newfoundland colonies were cursed, and they failed. As the Vikings explored further down the coastline, whoever had the ring either died there with it or deliberately left it behind. It was lost for a millennium. Then a dryad saw English colonists with an extraordinary gold ring and reported it to MAMIC. And here we are."

"You say is cursed. What is curse?" Aleksei asked.

"Standard misfortune curse, plus added destruction."

"If they did know what they'd found, they'd be happy to be rid of the bleedin' thing," Siobhan said.

"Is gold, *da*?" Aleksei said. "Humans and gold, is bad mix." His blue skin looked glossy under the flickering lamp.

Quinn was leaning back in his chair, rocking it back and forth on two legs, drumming his fingers softly on the table and staring out the tiny window.

Halle shot him an unhappy glance, then continued. "We'll set up the portal entrance in the woods on the far side of the island. Aleksei will get close to the encampment and signal us when the humans have gone to sleep. Then we'll move in and collect the ring, and if our luck holds, they'll never even know we were there." She looked from Aleksei to Siobhan, but her gaze settled on Quinn. "Does that sound like a good plan? Quinn?"

The finger drumming continued.

Aleksei cleared his throat.

Quinn looked up. "What?"

"I asked your opinion on the operation," Halle said crisply.

"They're humans. Vermin. Instead of sneaking around, why don't we just eliminate them and take the ring?" Quinn asked.

"That's a great idea. Except for the half-dozen treaties it violates. MAMIC would banish us for sure. But you know that."

"Then I'm sure your plan is fine."

Aleksei and Siobhan exchanged uncomfortable looks.

"I've just remembered that Aleksei and I have a training course we need to be off to. We're already late as it is."

Siobhan grabbed his wrist and guided the Lesovik out of his chair. Confusion shaped his expression. "Huh?"

"You know," she replied, cutting her eyes towards Quinn for an instant, "that course we signed up for. The one about alchemy, remember?"

"Oh. That one. *Da*, is time to go."

After the door closed behind Siobhan and Aleksei, Halle straightened herself up to her full six foot height. "What is this about?"

"I've packed my things," Quinn said.

Halle frowned. "Because?"

Quinn ran his hand through his dark hair. "This arrangement we have is just not working for me anymore. I would never try to keep you from being who you are, what you are, but…I want something different."

Halle shook her head. "Something different?"

"I have been able to overlook your…appetites when it was just once or twice a decade, but now, it seems to be once or twice a month."

The Valkyrie sat down with a thud. "I don't know what to say." Halle's eyes blinked rapidly, as if she were feverishly searching her brain for the right words. "I had no idea you felt that way."

Quinn closed his eyes, breathed in deeply, and let the air out. "I also think," he swallowed, "that it's undermining your authority as team leader. After this mission, I'm going to request a transfer to another team."

Halle cocked her head to one side. "What do you mean you think it undermines my authority?"

Quinn put his elbow on the table and rested his forehead on his fingertips. "There's not a delicate way to put this. When you screw anything that holds still long enough, it makes people question your judgment."

Halle slapped her palms loudly on the table as she stood up. "Get out," she said, her words falling like pebbles from her perfect red lips.

Quinn got up and left. The conversation, such as it was, went better than he expected. She hadn't tried to kill him. But it was still early.

He'd get his things from the small house they'd been sharing for the past eighty years or so and take them back to the Waterhorse Inn. As he made his way down the main staircase into the great hall, he pondered his situation.

His mother always kept rooms available for her five sons, even though she didn't often stay there herself. He hoped she was in her country place for the week, because he couldn't stand the thought of receiving the inevitable the I-told-you-so-now-when-are-you-going-to-find-a-nice-kelpie-girl-and-settle-down lecture. He was only one hundred thirty two, far too young to start a family. Perhaps in another three or four of hundred years. He and Halle had gotten together not long after they graduated from Mundane Intervention Team (MIT) training, just over a hundred years ago, but it hardly seemed like any time had passed.

"Quinn? You okay?" Siobhan asked. She was sitting by the enormous empty fireplace with a mug of hot coffee in her hands, waiting for him.

He gave her a half smile. "I will be. I just broke things off with Halle." He couldn't bring himself to tell her he was planning to leave the team, as well.

"I'm sorry."

Quinn shrugged. "I knew it would be a challenge. Should have known she would be more than I could handle. I've got to go do a few wee errands. I'll see you when the team meets back here tonight. Cheers."

The default time for a mission to start was midnight. They don't call it the witching hour for nothing.

Siobhan, Aleksei, Quinn, and Halle stood in a dim corridor of the MAMIC building, in front of a portrait of Halle.

"Are we ready?" Halle asked. She avoided looking at Quinn.

She went through the portal first, stepping through the painting of herself, and out onto a wooded island off of the coast of what would be known as North Carolina in about another hundred and fifty years. The other fae followed her out of the portrait.

The quartet slipped through the trees, crunching through the frozen snow, until they were within sight of the palisades surrounding the settlement. Halle's dagger was faintly lit. But their plans for a stealthy approach proved unnecessary.

Angry shouting exploded through the air.

Most of the words were unclear, but "Gold," "Traitors," and "Die" were unmistakable.

The MIT crept towards the settlement. Currently, all they could see was part of the circle of sharp-pointed palisades, grey in the moonlight, that surrounded the dwellings. Firelight, probably torches, occasionally flickered through the gaps between the rough-hewn logs.

The crack of arquebus fire shattered the night, first one, then a dozen or more. A cloud of acrid gunpowder smoke drifted towards them. A group of humans, English by their dress, spilled out of the gates. Quinn estimated there were more than fifty, but fewer than one hundred men and a handful of women.

"Ease up, Bill!" said one of the men, who was wearing an especially floppy hat.

"I said we're goin'. You can stay wif 'em, if you like," another man, presumably Bill, answered.

"I just want the cap'n to know where to look for us, when he come back with supplies, that's all. Please, gov'nor."

Bill considered for a moment. "Alright ven. Be quick about it."

Someone held a torch over him while the man with the floppy hat scratched letters into the gatepost. Even Quinn's sharp eyes had trouble reading it, but he thought it said, "Croatoan."

As soon as he was done, the mob stampeded in the opposite direction of the MIT.

"That was unexpected," Halle said.

"The curse?" Siobhan asked.

"Humans need no help of curse to slaughter one another," Aleksei said.

Quinn nodded. "That should make our job easier."

"Unless the group that just left has the ring. Aleksei, you follow and see where they're going. The rest of us will search the houses," Halle said.

Aleksei trotted silently into the trees and melted into the deep shadows.

Halle led the way to the settlement, stopping often to listen and observe. Quinn heard high-pitched crying, but the team saw no further movement as they approached the open stockade gates.

When the MIT first entered the fortified village, nothing seemed to be amiss.

A wagon, laden with barrels, stood near the village center. A bare foot stuck out from behind one of the wheels. The fae fanned out and approached the cart. This was the source of the wailing.

On the other side of the dray, one male lay on his back, his shirt soaked in blood, empty eyes staring at the glistening stars. An arquebus rifle lay near him in the dirt.

A woman, her clothes also stained crimson, sat with her back against the wagon wheel. She, too, held a rifle, but was too weak to lift the heavy weapon. A thin baby in a grubby white gown clung to her neck, bawling. Blood ran in a thin streak from the woman's nose and mouth.

"Please," she said, panting. "Take care of Virginia."

Her breathing was rapid and shallow, and the blood gurgled loudly in her chest as she struggled for air.

"Of course," Halle said, her voice saccharin sweet. She took the baby and handed her to Quinn. The child was so weak from hunger that she didn't have the strength to cry any more. She just made mewling sounds as she huddled against Quinn for warmth. She was shivering, so Quinn opened his heavy cloak and tucked her inside, being careful to keep her away from the brass buttons on his doublet.

Halle frowned as she knelt by the dying woman. If there was a cursed ring anywhere nearby, her dagger wasn't picking it up. The parts of it that showed through her scabbard remained dim. "Can you tell us where the ring is?"

"Ring?" The trickle of blood from her mouth had stopped flowing. She was almost out of time.

"Yes," Halle said, "a gold ring, perhaps that somebody here found recently?"

"Husband…Anaias." Her head lurched toward the dead man on the ground.

She went into a terrible fit of coughing, then her body went rigid and she made an eerie, choking gasp. Her head slumped onto her chest. The baby was now an orphan.

Halle pulled out the enchanted dagger and waved it over the man's corpse, just in case. The blade's faint glow remained unchanged.

"Let's check the houses. I'll look for the ring, and you two look for survivors — we don't want any surprises." She looked at the bulge under Quinn's cloak. "If you want that thing to live, you probably ought to feed it."

Siobhan and Quinn found no survivors, but they did find a bony cow with a little bit of milk in her udder.

Siobhan located a wooden pail and milked what she could from the cow, then turned her loose. There wasn't much forage for her in the compound. Siobhan would make sure she left the gate open, but the animal would be on her own in the forest. She wished her well.

Inside one of the rough houses, they spotted a pewter ladle. She used it as a cup while Quinn held the baby, who drank the warm milk greedily, but not skillfully.

"How old do you think she is?" Quinn asked.

"I would guess she's at least one year, but not as many as two."

When the pail was empty, Quinn rewrapped the damp and sticky child in his cloak.

"What are you going to do with her?" Siobhan asked.

"I can't take care of a baby, especially not a human baby."

"Will you just leave her here, then?"

Quinn looked down at the small child who was drowsing against his chest and sighing softly, comforted both by the milk and the sound of his heartbeat.

"I can't do that, either."

Siobhan smiled at him, almost laughing. She started to say something, but Halle shouted for them.

"Quinn! Siobhan! I think I've found it," Halle called from the largest of the ramshackle buildings.

Parchment pages, sealing wax and metal stamps were scattered on the table where Halle had emptied out the contents of a tall cupboard.

One, perhaps because of its ornate calligraphy, caught Quinn's eye. The document granted the governorship of Roanoke Colony to John White, in the Year of our Lord 1587. Almost two years ago.

Halle had used brute force to break into the false bottom of the cupboard, and a shattered board also lay on the table. She held a locked wooden box in one hand and scanned it with the dagger, which glowed blue-white. She grinned as she used the blade to pry open the lock.

A primitive flint arrowhead lay inside on a little cotton pillow.

Halle swore in old Norse.

"Two cursed objects?" Siobhan asked.

"So it would seem," Quinn said.

Halle ran from house to house, looking for a surge of light from her dagger, but got nothing.

"The mob that left here earlier must have it. We've got to find Aleksei," she said.

They started off in the direction the mob had been heading when the MIT arrived. Virginia was so light that Quinn almost forgot he was carrying her. The colonists' tracks were difficult to miss in the snow. In its sheath at Halle's side, the little dagger glinted with a pale blue glow.

It did not take long to find the colonists. In the fifty yards or so they'd travelled into the woods, the group had splintered into factions, which were now arguing about what to do with a cask that sat in the middle of the clearing where they were gathered.

"They will kill each other," Halle remarked.

"That's a problem?" Quinn asked.

Baby Virginia moaned softly from under Quinn's cloak as a snowflake fell on her exposed cheek.

All eyes looked at her. Even with the heat of Quinn's body and his thick cloak, the child was still visibly shivering. And the weather was getting worse.

"I'll go," Quinn said. "Siobhan, would you take the bairn?"

"No. Let me. None of you is invulnerable," Halle said. "But I am."

Never one for subtlety, the Valkyrie put her hand on the haft of her axe, left the cover of the stand of mountain laurel, and strode into the middle of the group of colonists. A ripple of silence preceded her, as the settlers noticed her approach. The man with the floppy hat stopped carving letters on a tree at the edge of the clearing.

"What have we 'ere?" said Bill. Up close, Halle noticed that he had bad skin and missing teeth. He was lean, but still appeared strong. But not as strong as her. No human would ever be as strong as her.

"I would ask you the same question," Halle smiled.

Some of the men laughed nervously, apparently wondering if she was utterly mad or seriously dangerous. "That's none of your concern," the wiry man said. "Shove off, Miss, while you still can."

"What's in the box?" Halle asked, unfazed.

The man took a large step forward, invading Halle's personal space. "It's a ring, Miss. You wanna be me bride?"

Then the man made the last mistake of his life.

With his right hand, he drew a small blade from his belt. With his left, he grabbed Halle's breast.

Her eyes glowed green. A wind swirled around her, faster and faster, picking up loose snow and forest debris. The man began to howl in pain as green fire flowed down the hand he used to grasp Halle and up his arm, taking clothing and flesh with it. In moments, he lay screaming and bleeding in the snow, every inch of his skin gone.

"Witch!" yelled a panicked voice behind her.

An arquebus was pointed at Halle. She raised her arms and more green fire danced around her fingers. Her face became distorted and beastlike. With a yell, she brought her arms down to shoulder level. The fire leaped from her fingers onto the men, vaporizing each as it touched them.

When it was over, Halle stood inside a messy circle of brown slush where there had been pristine snow only moments before. She went to the box, opened it, and discovered that it contained nine rings. That is what made Andvaranaut so desirable. Every ninth day, it produced eight exact duplicates of itself. It wouldn't take long to become rich that way. Too bad about the misfortune curse. Halle wondered if the duplicates, too, were cursed. She snapped the box closed and turned to face her team.

"What have you done?" Aleksei asked.

The Valkyrie smiled bitterly. "Did I not tell you there was a destruction curse on this ring?"

The lone survivor still lay in the snow, moaning in agony. Taking pity on him, Siobhan pulled her bright rapier from its scabbard to strike the coup de grâce. She assessed her target and plunged the sword into his heart to end his suffering.

In silence, the fae made their way towards the portal, passing the village on the way. Halle stopped.

She looked at Aleksei and Siobhan, then nodded towards the two bodies behind the wagon.

"Bring them."

"Whatever for?" Siobhan asked.

"They stood up to a thieving mob. They must have been very brave. They deserve to be laid to rest properly."

Three small boats had been dragged up on the beach just behind the palisaded wall. Halle pushed one out into the water just deep enough for it to float.

"Put them both in here."

Aleksei and Siobhan did as they were instructed. Halle took a tinderbox from the leather pouch that was slung around her hips and set a fire in the boat. She gave it a hard shove and let the receding tide pull it away from the shore as the flames got higher.

"Let's go," she said.

As soon as they made it back through the portal, Quinn made a bee line to Dame Rowan's office with Virginia. Rowan admired the child and stroked her cheek. "I'm sorry, but there's no one available just now to care for a baby. And Titania's School for Girls doesn't take them that young."

"What am I supposed to do with her? I can't very well take her to the Waterhorse, now can I?"

Rowan gave Quinn a warning look, but let the outburst slide. "I'm sure you'll come up with something. Perhaps she has some relatives you can track down. Right now, I have more pressing issues. I must speak with Halle about what happened on this last mission."

Quinn nodded and left. Virginia was beginning to stir, and she'd probably need feeding.

"My ma could never resist a babby," Siobhan said to Quinn when he came downstairs into the great hall.

He spent the next three days with Siobhan's family, watching Virginia begin to fill out and become a contented, happy toddler. Her goofy, mostly toothless smile melted his heart, and he found it extremely difficult to leave her behind when he and Siobhan were called back to MAMIC.

Quinn, Siobhan, and Aleksei sat in the armchairs in Dame Rowan's office, waiting for her. When at last she swept in, she paced the room near the windows instead of sitting at her desk.

"I regret to inform you that Halle is gone. She has been sent to personally return the ring to Andravari. Perhaps he'll lift the curse. She is not banished – she's free to come and go as she chooses. There were, after all, mitigating circumstances. The ring was beshrewn to cause misfortune and destruction. She could not entirely help acting under its influence. Still, she cannot retain her position as team leader. She has a new assignment – monitoring the Frost Giants in the northlands. They get some peculiar ideas from time to time, and it's best if someone keeps an eye on what they're up to."

Quinn examined the rug. He hoped that his breakup with Halle had not contributed to her downfall. He cared about her, much more than he wanted to, but he had also come to realize that their romance had been doomed from the start.

"I have given this a great deal of consideration," Dame Rowan continued. "Your team is now short one member. I'm going to add a new team lead. His name is Beckett, and he will be arriving with Eoin in a fortnight. Until then, consider yourselves on holiday."

Quinn spent every moment he could at Siobhan's family home with Virginia. As far as she knew, he was her father, and no one ever told her anything different. Even though she was not his blood, he loved her as if she were. Still, he kept any news of her from his mother. Humans had killed his father so long ago that he barely remembered him. But his mother vowed revenge on any and all humans she encountered, and she'd raised her sons to loathe the creatures as well. Until Virginia became his foundling, he believed that humans were just pathetic demons without any magick.

When she was five, Virginia began boarding at Titania's School for Girls. As time passed, Virginia grew from a timid child into a strong and self-possessed young woman. Quinn taught her everything he knew when she entered the MIT training program, and she easily found a spot on the team of her choice. When she fell in love with Niall, one of Siobhan's sidhe cousins, and married him, Quinn gave her away at the handfasting. He was proud grandpa to their son and two daughters, and great-grandpa to their happy broods.

But the lifespan of even a long-lived human is brief, compared to fae. All too quickly, Virginia grew old and died. Quinn openly wept at her funeral, and fell into a terrible sadness. Siobhan was the only one who was able to pull him out of it, and they soon became inseparable.

Whenever Quinn returned to Blackthorne from a mission, he never failed to leave a white rose on Virginia's grave.

If you've enjoyed reading this book, I would really appreciate it if you would take a moment to leave a review. Thank you!

About the Author

Artemis Greenleaf has devoured fairy tales, folk tales and ghost stories since before she could read. Artemis did, in fact, marry an alien and she lives in the suburban wilds of Houston, Texas with her husband, two children and assorted pets. She writes both fiction and non-fiction and her work has appeared in magazines and as novels. For more information, please visit artemisgreenleaf.com.

Made in the USA
Charleston, SC
15 February 2014